"Cayna, you act as backup! Q
             wn the b

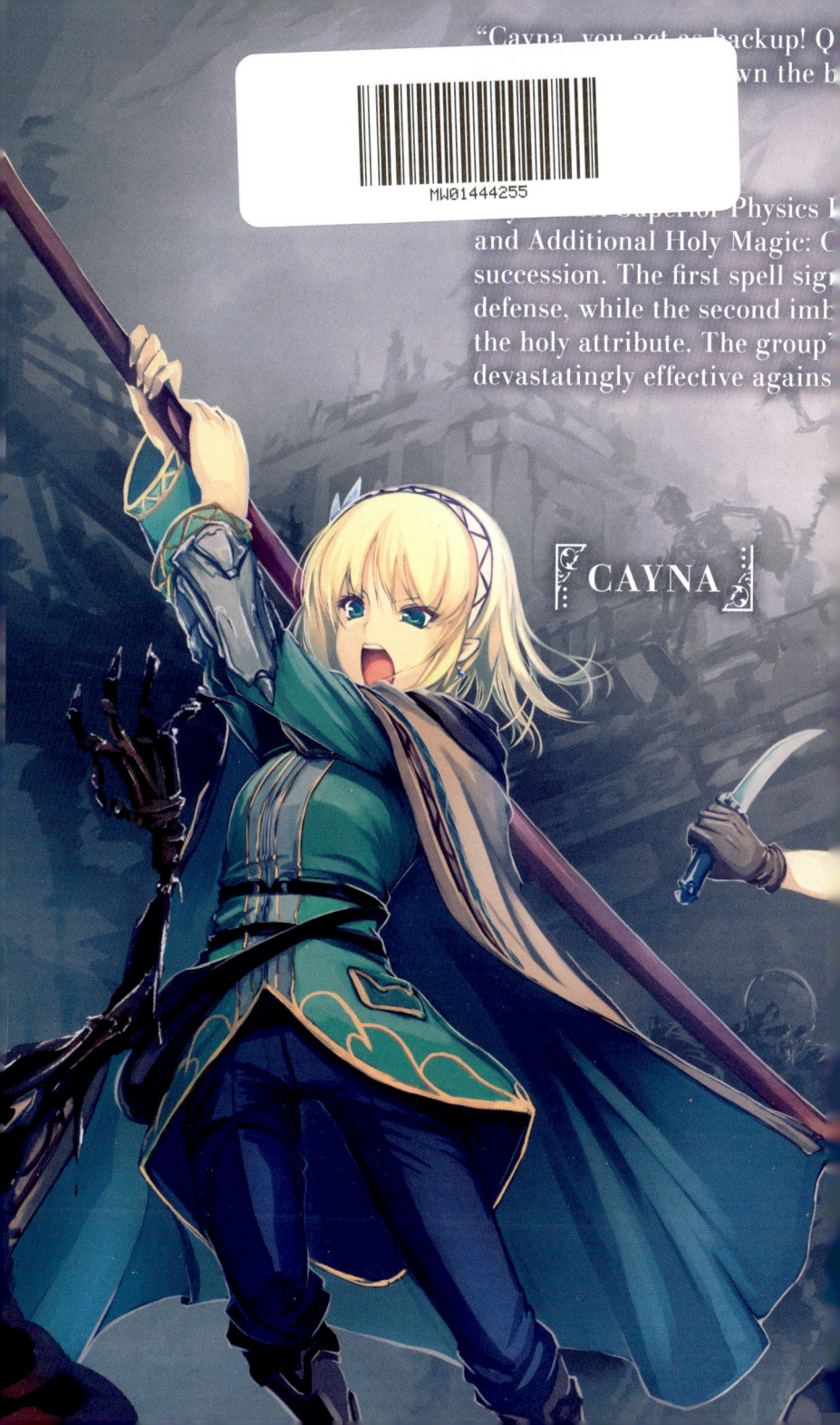

              xperior Physics
and Additional Holy Magic: C
succession. The first spell sig
defense, while the second im
the holy attribute. The group
devastatingly effective agains

CAYNA

"A-are you the Guardian of this tower?"

uolkeh, you squash the
oss."

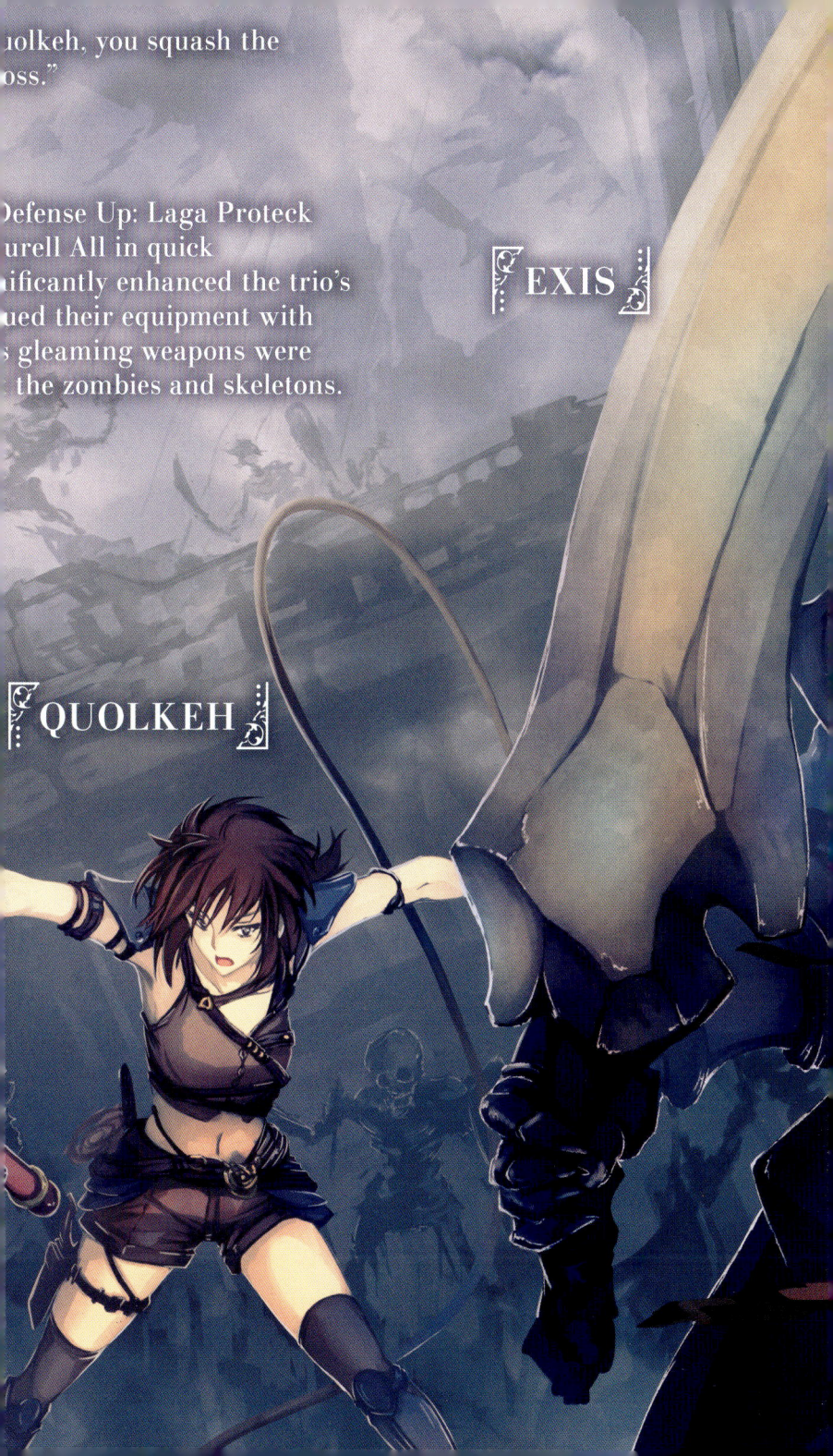

Defense Up: Laga Proteck
urell All in quick
ificantly enhanced the trio's
ued their equipment with
gleaming weapons were
the zombies and skeletons.

「EXIS」

「QUOLKEH」

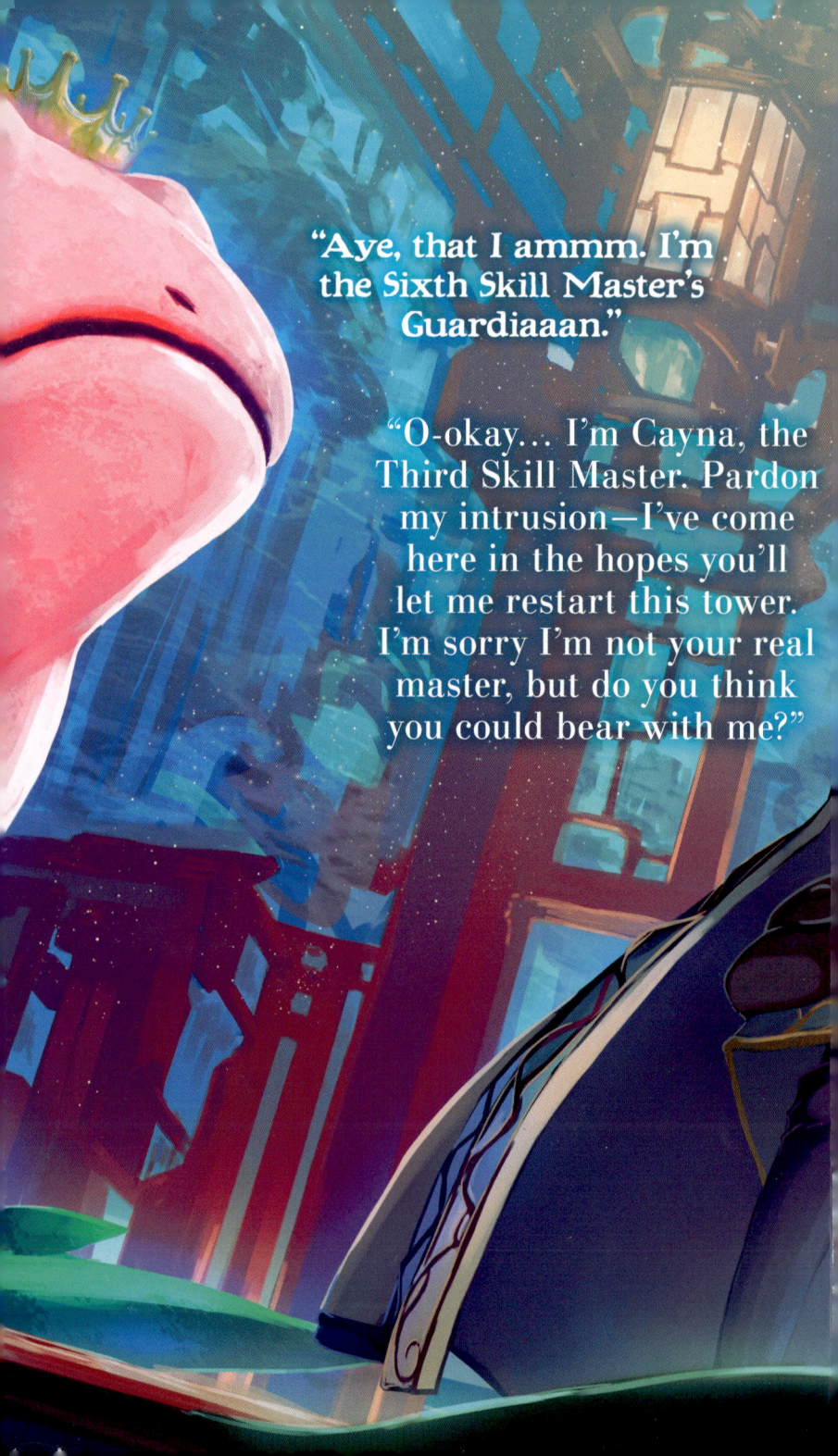

"Aye, that I ammm. I'm the Sixth Skill Master's Guardiaaan."

"O-okay… I'm Cayna, the Third Skill Master. Pardon my intrusion—I've come here in the hopes you'll let me restart this tower. I'm sorry I'm not your real master, but do you think you could bear with me?"

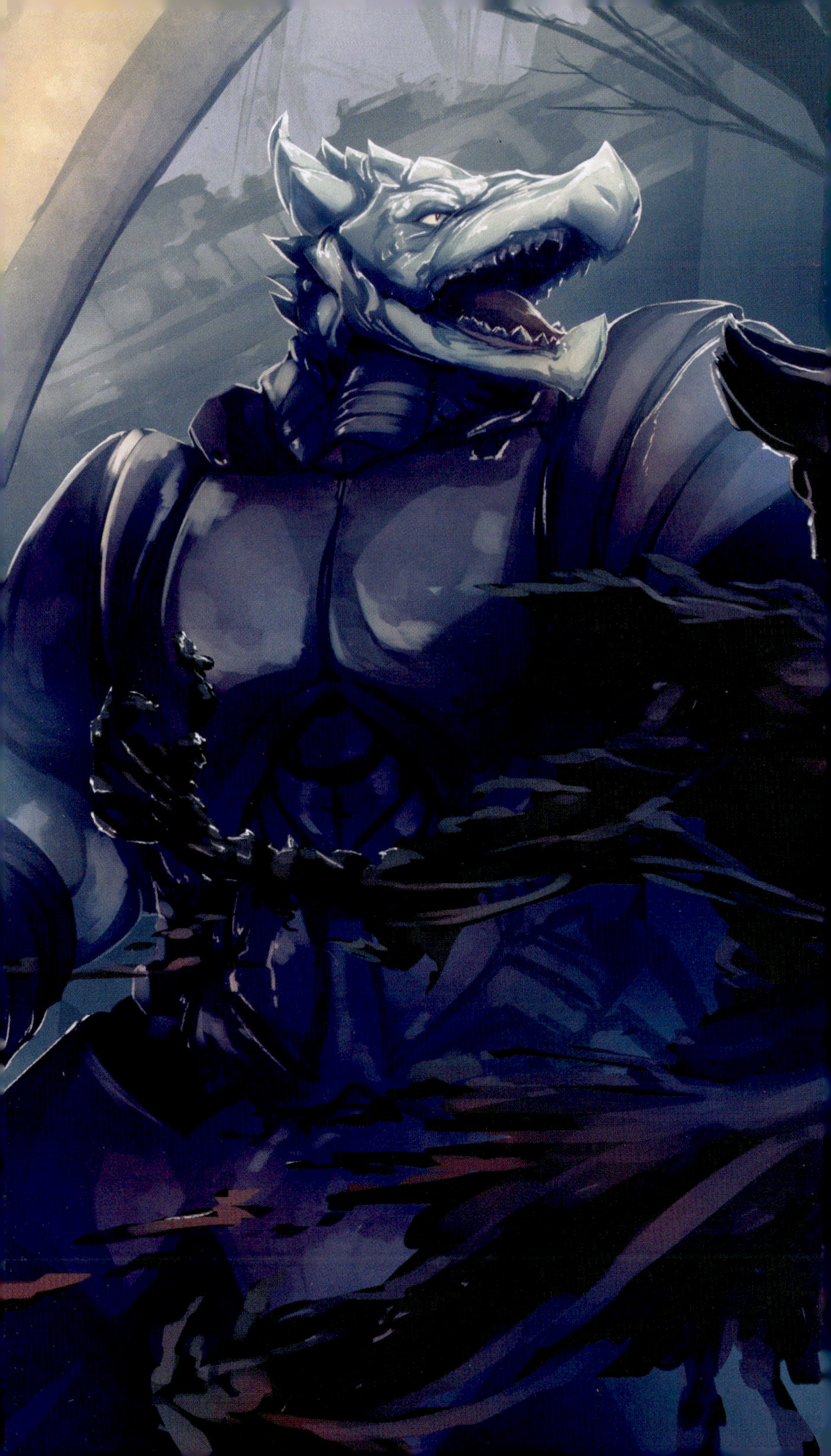

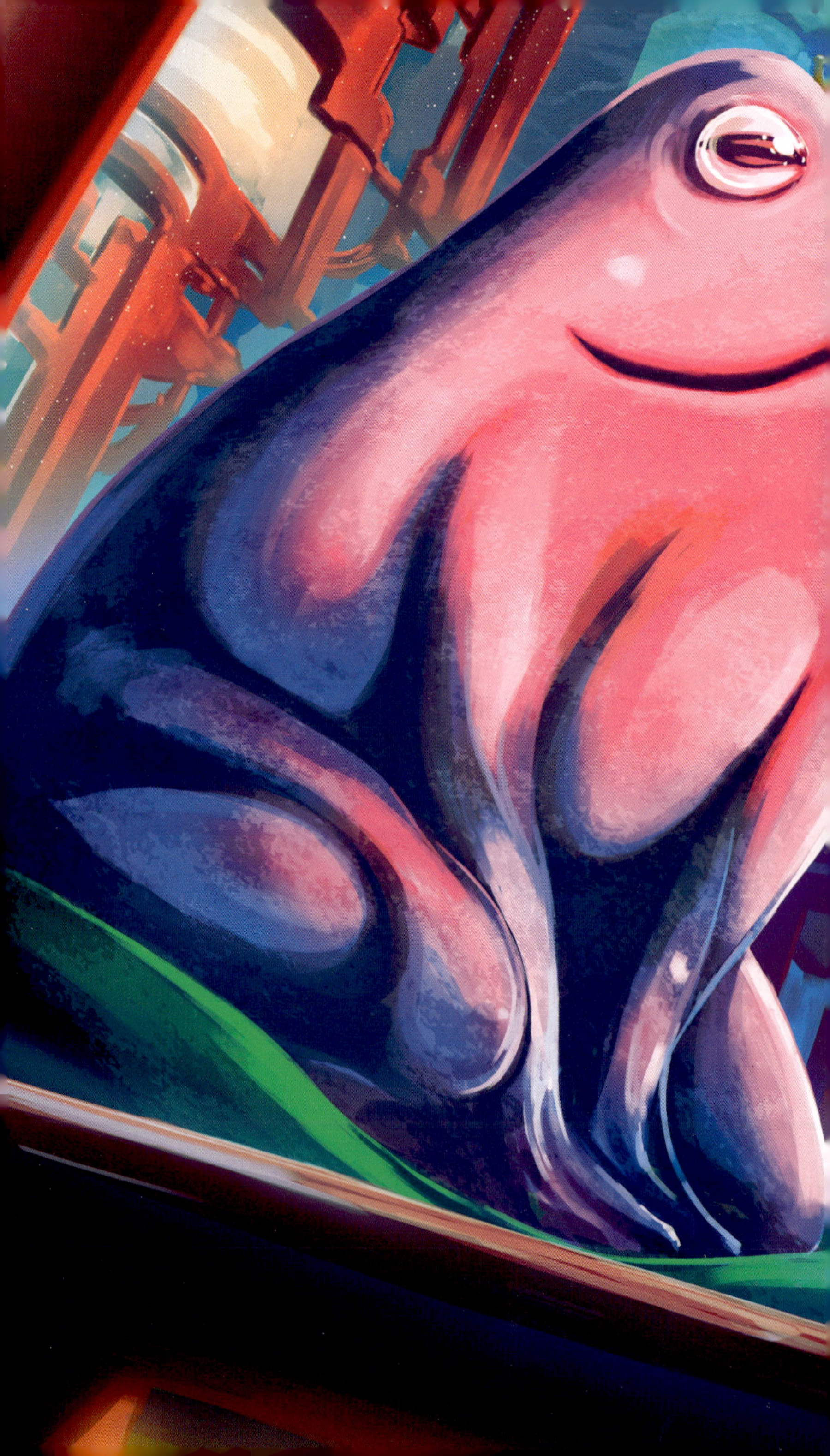

IN THE LAND OF LEADALE

3

Ceez

[ILLUSTRATION BY]
Tenmaso

Yen On
New York

In the Land of Leadale 3 Ceez

Translation by Jessica Lange
Cover art by Tenmaso

This book is a work of fiction. Names, characters, places, and incidents are the product of the author's imagination or are used fictitiously. Any resemblance to actual events, locales, or persons, living or dead, is coincidental.

RIADEIRU NO DAICHI NITE Vol. 3
© Ceez 2019
First published in Japan in 2019 by KADOKAWA CORPORATION, Tokyo.
English translation rights arranged with KADOKAWA CORPORATION, Tokyo through TUTTLE-MORI AGENCY, INC., Tokyo.

English translation © 2021 by Yen Press, LLC

Yen Press, LLC supports the right to free expression and the value of copyright. The purpose of copyright is to encourage writers and artists to produce the creative works that enrich our culture.

The scanning, uploading, and distribution of this book without permission is a theft of the author's intellectual property. If you would like permission to use material from the book (other than for review purposes), please contact the publisher. Thank you for your support of the author's rights.

Yen On
150 West 30th Street, 19th floor
New York, NY 10001

Visit us at yenpress.com
facebook.com/yenpress
twitter.com/yenpress
yenpress.tumblr.com
instagram.com/yenpress

First Yen On Edition: July 2021

Yen On is an imprint of Yen Press, LLC.
The Yen On name and logo are trademarks of Yen Press, LLC.

The publisher is not responsible for websites (or their content) that are not owned by the publisher.

Library of Congress Cataloging-in-Publication Data
Names: Ceez, author. | Tenmaso, illustrator. | Lange, Jessica (Translator), translator.
Title: In the land of Leadale / Ceez ; illustration by Tenmaso ; translation by Jessica Lange
Other titles: Riadeiru no daichi nite. English
Description: First Yen On edition. | New York, NY : Yen On, 2020.
Identifiers: LCCN 2020032160 | ISBN 9781975308681 (v. 1 ; trade paperback) |
    ISBN 9781975308704 (v. 2 ; trade paperback) | ISBN 9781975322168 (v. 3 ; trade paperback)
Subjects: CYAC: Fantasy. | Virtual reality—Fiction.
Classification: LCC PZ7.1.C4646 In 2020 | DDC [Fic]—dc23
LC record available at https://lccn.loc.gov/2020032160

ISBNs: 978-1-9753-2216-8 (paperback)
       978-1-9753-2217-5 (ebook)

10 9 8 7 6 5 4 3 2 1

LSC-C

Printed in the United States of America

IN THE LAND OF LEADALE

3

IN THE LAND OF LEADALE CONTENTS

THE STORY THUS FAR	001
PROLOGUE	007
CHAPTER 1 The System, Knights, a Misunderstanding, and a Fog	013
CHAPTER 2 A Butler, a Ghost Ship, an Adopted Daughter, and the Palace of the Dragon King	047
CHAPTER 3 The Abandoned Capital, a Maid, Relocation, and an Enterprise	091

ILLUSTRATION BY Tenmaso

CHAPTER 4
Sightseeing, a Rescue, a Voice from the
Heavens, and a Predicament　　　　155

CHAPTER 5
An Assault, a Lamentation, a Doting
Parent, and a Request　　　　215

EPILOGUE　　　　255

BONUS SHORT STORY
The Day He Became a Knight　　　　261

CHARACTER DATA　　　　275

AFTERWORD　　　　279

The Story Thus Far

Keina Kagami perished while playing the VRMMORPG *Leadale* after a power outage shut down her life support. The next instant, however, she awoke in an unfamiliar inn and realized she was in the body of her game avatar. Keina was further shocked when Marelle, the inn's proprietress, informed her that Leadale's seven nations had been destroyed and since replaced by three new nations currently ruling the continent.

From this information, Keina concluded that two hundred years had passed since she had last played the game. She decided her best option was to live on as her avatar, Cayna, and she began contributing to the prosperity of the local village and finding her way forward.

Then in a nearby forest, she discovered her Guardian Tower, where her Guardian informed her that the rest of the towers were currently low on magic and thereby inoperable, prompting Cayna to boldly set out on a journey to gather information on the players who seem to have abandoned their towers.

After running into the head of a merchant caravan—a kobold named Elineh—and the mercenary leader (Arbiter) assigned to protect him and his group, Cayna accompanied them to the Felskeilo capital, all the while learning basic knowledge about this new world.

Cayna then registered as an adventurer and accepted a request to capture a runaway prince. In the process, she got to know Prime Minister Agaido and his granddaughter, Lonti. She also reunited with her children—that is, the sub-characters she had submitted to the Foster System during the Game Era: a handsome elf named Skargo, who had inexplicably ascended to the position of High Priest, the third most influential person in the nation; a gorgeous elf named Mai-Mai, the headmistress of the Royal Academy, who is now married; and Kartatz, a sensible dwarf craftsman and the boss of a large shipyard. For Cayna, who has never dated, let alone been married, having three full-grown children is a source of much confusion.

Soon after, she confirmed that the Ninth Skill Master's tower was in the royal capital's Battle Arena and successfully activated it. After many twists and turns, she at last learned from this tower's Guardian that *Leadale*'s service had ended. Despondent that she could never hope to meet any other players, Cayna holed herself up in a barrier of her own making and refused to come out. However, with the encouragement of her children, she once again set out for more adventures.

She then took a job escorting Elineh and his caravan to the northern nation of Helshper. On the way, she stopped by the remote village and solved a mystery surrounding an odd wail coming from a well. The culprit turned out to be a mermaid named Mimily, who had been swept away from the depths of the sea for unknown reasons. Cayna modified the public bathhouse she had previously built so it better suited Mimily and used the money she earned from solving the mystery to pay for the mermaid's daily necessities.

Later on, the caravan crossed the Ejidd River thanks to Cayna's skills and was ambushed along the nation's border by bandits from the west. With the help of a beast Cayna had summoned earlier for an unrelated purpose, the group overpowered this threat. Cayna's magic turned the bandit leader into ice flowers and shattered him to bits and pieces.

Upon arriving in Helshper, Cayna delivered a letter from her daughter to Caerick, the founder of a large company with branches dotted across the continent. There, she learned another shocking truth: Caerick is Mai-Mai and her first husband's son—in other words, he is Cayna's grandson. She further discovered that Caerick has a son of his own, making her a great-grandmother despite having done nothing at all.

A rift formed between grandmother and grandchild over a slight misunderstanding, leading Caerick's older twin sister, the knight Caerina, to offer her apologies in his stead. This only bewildered Cayna even more.

However, upon learning there might be a Guardian Tower in the heart of the bandits' den in the western continent, Cayna accepted Caerick's help and prepared an attack. She forced her way into enemy territory and even got Caerina involved, and before long, it came to light that the den leader was a player of the demon race. Enraged by his selfish motives and outrageous actions, Cayna challenged him to a battle.

Unable to compete against a Skill Master who was going all out, the demon player nearly lost his life, but the Helshper knights arrived just in time to apprehend him. Cayna then used her Game Master privileges to reduce the demon player's power to a tenth of its former strength, and he wailed with fury as the knights took him into custody.

Upon arriving at the Guardian Tower and reactivating it, Cayna learned it once belonged to her terrible friend and former fellow guild member Opuskettenshultheimer Crosstettbomber, aka Opus. A small fairy appeared from a book Opus's Guardian gave Cayna and has yet to leave her side.

Cayna then decided to invest the reward money she received for expelling the bandits along with her share of the profits from the wildly popular Buddha statues Elineh sold into Mimily's well-being. When she stopped by the remote village later, she found that Mimily had started a laundry business at Lytt's suggestion.

Upon returning to Felskeilo, Cayna took on a request from the Adventurers Guild to obtain meat for a fancy restaurant. Incidentally, she soon ran into Lonti and Lonti's friend Princess Mye in town and ended up agreeing to be their guard while they accompanied her on her quest.

Meanwhile, also in Felskeilo, Mai-Mai's husband, Lopus, attempted to re-create one of Cayna's ancient arts. However, when he tossed his illicit failure into a Collection Point that had been used in times of war during the Game Era, a giant dolphin-like penguin monster appeared from within. This threat was then dealt with by a captain of the knights known as Shining Saber and an adventurer named Cohral, two former guild members who are evenly matched in skill.

With the help of the players, the knights, and a team of mages, Cayna successfully contained the penguin monster and used her incredible magic to deal the final blow.

Running into the two players Shining Saber and Cohral gave Cayna some hope that her partner in crime, Opus, is still out there. Happily killing two birds with one stone, she also obtained information about the next tower.

She soon returned to the remote village and learned that a group from Otaloquess had arrived as well. However, their quest for knowledge was a mere front; an Otaloquess spy within the group solicited Cayna for information.

It so happens that Otaloquess's Queen Sahalashade is a Foster Child who was created during the Game Era by Sahana, a fellow high elf and a little-sister figure to Cayna. Suddenly learning she's an aunt to the queen brings Cayna further consternation, and she complains that it must be some sort of curse that everyone she knows is an influential figure.

Exhausted, Cayna promised to take Lytt through the skies as soon as her tower search came to a good stopping point.

Prologue

The continent of Leadale was surrounded by water on three sides.

The land to the east had a steep mountain range that protected the continent from invasions. No one had ever seen what lay beyond those mountains, and there were no records of anyone having reached there. According to one theory, a region larger than all of Leadale itself was nestled on the other side, and some scholars insisted that Leadale was merely a peninsula extending from this massive, unknown continent.

Without any solid proof, such theories were mocked and written off as mere delusions. According to records, some attempted to cross the eastern mountains in the past. However, after they all failed to return home, it was only natural that fewer and fewer people were willing to journey to such a murky destination. The monsters that inhabited the mountains were all incredibly powerful, and many people insisted it was best to give up on the missing, since they'd most likely been eaten.

A lucky few had likely made it through to the other side. It was possible they never returned because either the trip had been too perilous or life past the mountains was too wonderful to go back. Unable to discern the truth, a hopeless fear of the mountains spread among the inhabitants of Leadale.

The Ejidd River, which flowed down the mountain range and through the continent, supported the livelihood of the people. It was particularly beneficial to the citizens of Felskeilo and Otaloquess, but its vital contribution to the traffic and trade of fishing resources was immeasurable. One of the river's tributaries connected to a lake that served as a water source for Helshper's highlands; the tributary itself provided a means of transportation.

However, development was rather slow in the region when it came to marine resources. The nation of Helshper looked out on an ocean to the north, but most of its coast was made up of steep cliffs that kept the land safe from invasions and were impossible to traverse unless you had a goat. Fearless adventurers would occasionally stop and collect eggs from magic birds for work, but that was about the scope of things. Even then, only half or so managed to accomplish their task safely.

Unlike Helshper, Otaloquess was surrounded by wide, shallow beaches to the southwest. The nation was so heavily forested that even the shoreline was lined with mangrove-like vegetation. But although mangrove forests in the real world grow in seawater, Leadale's mangroves thrived in both fresh and salt water. Their roots provided excellent homes and hiding places for small fish, which in turn attracted natural predators. Eventually, the monsters that fed on those predators gathered in the area, rendering it too dangerous for the average person to traverse.

Although fields were no longer rife with outrageous monsters that appeared the moment you stepped out of town like they had in the game, several areas still posed a real and credible threat to the people of Leadale.

PROLOGUE

Because of the rough terrain along the northern and southern nations' coasts, fishing was restricted to Felskeilo's entire western shoreline and Helshper's southern beaches.

Then a peculiar disaster struck the two nations' fishing villages.

First, a fog enveloped just one village. It was early morning. The villagers who had awoken before the crack of dawn couldn't hide their surprise. Neither their knowledge of the wind, the seasons, and the temperature nor their many years spent by the ocean could explain the strange fog.

Just as the dubious villagers were gathering together to talk things over, the thin wisps of drifting fog suddenly grew dense. Unable to see even the faces of their friends next to them, the fishermen panicked at this unforeseen turn of events. They shouted and fled into their respective homes. Some pushed their fellows aside and hid in other people's homes amid the chaos, but one man made it back to his own house.

His wife and child saw the odd look on his face and greeted him with concerned expressions of their own. As he quickly stumbled in and shut the door and windows with a tense countenance, the rest of the family finally noticed the strange phenomenon occurring in the village.

◆

The situation came to light several days after the appearance of this thick fog. A peddler traveling between the fishing village and the capital had come to the village to stock up on dried fish.

As soon as he arrived, he sensed an eeriness to the silence. Every door in the village had been left open, and he could tell something strange had happened. The man very cautiously searched the area but couldn't find a single villager.

It was then that he discovered a multitude of footprints leading from each house to the shoreline. But although he followed them to the water's edge, no trace of anyone could be found.

It took several more days for the rest of the country to learn of this event, and by the time any adventurers got moving, they learned that the same fate had befallen another fishing village to the south.

CHAPTER 1
The System, Knights, a Misunderstanding, and a Fog

After freshening up at Marelle's inn, Cayna left the remote village for Felskeilo early the next morning.

She entered the capital through the eastern gate and, humming a little tune to herself, made her way toward the western one. Cayna was bursting with excitement, already imagining her new home in the village and what life would be like there. Figuring she would require daily necessities, she perused the market for furniture and cutlery. Li'l Fairy was drawn to the various knickknacks, and she left Cayna's shoulder to gaze at a wooden cup.

Just as Cayna nearly got caught up in browsing and forgot her main mission, she received a stern warning from Kee.

"Cayna! There are more important tasks at hand."

"Whoops. Wow, that was a close one. At any rate, we better find the Palace of the Dragon King first..."

As Cayna left the market and headed for the western gate, she passed by the Adventurers Guild. At that very moment, she incidentally ran into the members of the Armor of Victory as they were leaving the building.

"Hey there, Cayna."

"Morning!"

Cohral raised his hand, and Cayna gave a slight bow. She greeted the other four members, and he asked them to go on ahead.

"We'll be waiting by the gate."

"Don't take forever, Cohral."

"Yeah, no worries. I'll be right there."

The four adventurers left Cohral with Cayna and headed toward the eastern gate.

Insisting the foot traffic around them would only get in the way, he pulled her off to the corner of the street.

"Need something?" she asked.

"Yeah, I was hoping you'd hear me out for a second. It's about the system."

"You mean the game system?"

"That's right. Something's been bothering me."

Cayna realized she'd checked only her stats and skills after first awakening in the remote village.

"...Oh."

"'Oh'? That's all you have to say? You obviously haven't been paying attention."

"Um, well, y'know. Ha-ha-ha."

She gave a dry laugh in an attempt to play dumb, but Cohral shot her a reproachful glare. Cayna apologetically admitted, "Sorry, it slipped my mind."

The game system Cohral mentioned had several other useful features outside of stats, skills, and the Item Box. However, a number of those functions weren't responding in the slightest.

For example, the Log Out option was no longer on the menu screen. The Guild Chat option was similarly unresponsive; back in the game, it allowed you to contact your fellow guild members from anywhere. That said, none of her guild members were still around;

CHAPTER 1

neither were there even any guild houses to serve as relay points, so the function was useless.

"It was the Friend Display that tipped me off."

"The Friend Display?"

Cayna opened her stats screen and checked her registered friends. She saw Cohral's and Shining Saber's names in white at the very top, but the rest were grayed out. When *Leadale* was just a game, gray indicated the person was unavailable, while names in white were logged in.

Cayna examined her own friend list and wondered if Opus or her other former guild members were still around, but Opus's name was grayed out. She heaved a lifeless sigh.

"I get why you're all emotional, but I happened to realize something," said Cohral.

"Yeah?"

"Shining Saber's always been on my friend list, but his name was grayed out until I reunited with him the other day. Seems to me that names show up again if you meet the person."

"If we meet, huh...?"

Cayna didn't have many registered friends. Aside from her guild members, there were only the thirteen Skill Masters and her friends from the high-elf community. One of the Skill Masters had permanently left the game, so their name would definitely stay grayed out.

"And the names of any friends you've run into but don't remember meeting will turn white, too."

"Huh? That doesn't make any sense."

"Mm, I was surprised, too, but I realized what was going on after I tried sending a message. My friend was pretty surprised himself."

A large group like a guild could use a group chat, but it was possible for individuals to communicate through a system similar to private messaging. This had apparently remained unchanged from the Game Era."

"To tell the truth, he and I had met once before, but it'd been so long that neither of us recognized each other."

"Oh? You said you came here ten years ago, so does that mean your friend's even older than you?"

"That's right. I mean, he's this, like, dignified-looking middle-aged guy now. No way I would've been able to recognize him!"

Cohral made a fist of indignation, and Cayna could only smile awkwardly in response. He must have once seen the man as a little brother, yet now that same person was his senior.

At this rate, there was no question a high elf like her would sooner or later be tending to Cohral's and Shining Saber's deathbeds. Such a thought didn't strike her at the time.

"The problem is that even though we ran into each other about two years ago, he only showed up on my friend list recently—come to think of it, not much longer after I met you."

"…What?! Are you saying it has something to do with me?"

"You're a Limit Breaker and a Skill Master with Game Master privileges, yeah?"

"That doesn't mean I can mess with the system itself! Game Master privileges are useless if there aren't rules in place."

Her uncle's company had actually been responsible for managing *Leadale* back when it was a game, but Cayna was a regular user who had no special benefits. Even if she'd been offered such perks, she would have firmly refused.

"Huh? …Wait. Hmm?"

Cayna couldn't think of a single product her uncle's company had created with its pooled resources.

"Any ideas, Kee?"

"No, none whatsoever."

CHAPTER 1

Even said product apparently didn't have a clue.

In that case, Cohral was just doubting her. No real harm done. Otherwise, the only other change that occurred before Cayna met Cohral and Shining Saber was the addition of Li'l Fairy. However, seeing how the fairy was hiding in her hair and trying to avoid Cohral's gaze, Cayna decided not to mention it.

"Anyway, I have no idea what's going on with that!"

"Reaaaaally now? 'Cause you sure seem suspect to me."

Cohral continued to eye her warily, and she tried shooing him off with a wave of her hand.

"Hey, more important: Your friends are waiting, right? Off you go!"

If the two dawdled too long, the knights she planned to accompany (unbeknownst to them) would likely leave without her. Cayna gave Cohral a push from behind, but he wasn't so quick to give up. As he made his way toward his friends, he told her, "Tell me if you find out anything else!"

"Is something like that really worth obsessing over?"

"His fixations are beyond your comprehension, Cayna."

"Can't argue with that. There's no way someone like me, who forgot there even *was* a friend list, could understand his dedication."

Cayna gave a self-deprecating smile and headed toward the western gate.

Cayna soon realized why the western gate was noisier than usual. A large group of people had gathered around the walls.

A multitude of carriages were stopped outside. People ran around caring for the horses, and several merchants who appeared to own said horses chatted animatedly with one another.

A large group of children watched these people with hopeful eyes. There were a number of adults as well, of course, but the average citizen didn't have so much free time in the early morning. People stared across the main road as they eagerly waited for the knights to pass.

"What's everyone doing?" she asked a nearby woman.

"It isn't every day we can watch the knights leave in such huge numbers! It's one of the few joys we have."

Cayna tilted her head curiously and wondered whether such an event was really a big deal. The woman smiled, amused.

Incidentally, the group of carriages outside the gate included a few caravans as well. According to a soldier posted at the gate:

"I don't wanna say this too loud, but they're a nasty bunch. They try to leech off the knights for protection along trade routes. They've probably got some scheme where they'll spread gossip if they get attacked by thieves or monsters and the knights fail to rescue them. What a bunch of lowlifes—too stingy to pay for their own convoy."

Given the vitriol with which he spoke, Cayna concluded that this must have happened multiple times. Even in the game, the weak had often swarmed around the strong, so she actually found herself impressed by how prevalent freeloaders were, even in other worlds.

Although Cayna wasn't a freeloader strictly speaking, there was no question that she planned to hitch a ride with the knight corps without their permission. She felt a bit guilty.

It was around nine AM when she overheard the soldier while she waited outside the western gate, keeping her distance from the caravans so that no one thought she was involved with them. There were no proper clocks in this world, so she depended on the time displayed on her stats screen to keep her informed.

"Sheesh, *finally* they're here."

Cayna closed the stats screen she had been staring at to kill time and peeled herself away from the wall she'd been leaning against.

When she peered beyond the gate, she saw a group of knights on horseback—including Shining Saber in his white armor—waving to people along the roadside as they headed her way. Shining Saber was at the forefront. Cayna had heard he was the captain of the knights

CHAPTER 1

but never imagined they'd run into each other here. Feeling awkward, she quickly hid in the shadow of a gate column.

This had the opposite effect and made her appear even more suspicious. The eyes of Shining Saber and several other knights fell on the shady figure.

Naturally, the encouragement and cheers the townspeople lavished on the group were not for the knights alone. There were soldiers carrying the flag of Felskeilo Knight Corps at the front, twenty knights on horseback, and a procession behind them that included eight carriages and another eighty marching soldiers. Finally, at the tail end, ten canopied carriages held the march's food supply and equipment. At a glance, there appeared to be a total of around one hundred people.

It was an iffy number when the goal was to get rid of the bandits, but since the knights were entering a neighboring nation, they had taken into account that they mustn't appear too threatening.

That was what the western gatekeeper had told her anyway. He also said a small number of elites had been chosen in order to complete the mission as quickly as possible.

Cayna had considered waiting for the knights' group to pass so she could follow the tail end of the procession, but she jolted as Shining Saber's suspicious eyes bored into hers. He, of course, gave a similar reaction but was shocked to find the strange character to be Cayna. Suspecting a person of being up to no good was an occupational hazard common to Shining Saber's line of work.

The knights departed first, followed by the soldiers, carriages, and supply wagons. The collection of caravans maintained their distance but followed soon after. Cayna then moved to take up the rear. The knights on horseback progressed swiftly, but she figured their speed wouldn't be too unreasonable, since the foot soldiers were coming along as well. Plus, she could summon a beast of some sort to ride so she wouldn't fall too far behind.

* * *

Once they were a considerable distance from the capital, a knight on horseback approached her from the front of the line. It was Shining Saber. He walked alongside her and called from his horse.

"What do you think you're doing? Were you plannin' on trailing us and blowing everyone away from behind if we weren't worth your time?"

"Why're you acting like some kind of inquisitor?! I just figured I'd follow you to that fishing village so I can search for the Palace of the Dragon King!"

"Ah, Cohral mentioned something about that… At any rate, are you really going on foot? The demonstration for the citizens is over, so things are gonna speed up a bit with the soldiers now in the carriages."

"Oh, so that's what all the carriages are for."

She'd been wondering why the knights were bringing carriages along, but Shining Saber's statement made everything clear. The march picked up speed as they were talking; even the distance between their group and the caravans was growing little by little.

She knew she had various ways of keeping up even if the gap between her and the knights widened, but Shining Saber nodded with a "Hmph." He suddenly took her hand and pulled her onto his horse—and, of course, held her in his arms like a princess as he gripped the reins.

"Kyah?!"

"I'll even give you a special seat. Look, don't worry about it—this is thanks for all your help with the Event Monster. Hey, quit movin' around; otherwise, you're gonna fall… Huh?"

The only members of the opposite sex who had ever held Cayna in their arms were her doctor and her father. Her face reddened in an instant, and her mouth set in a straight line as she sat frozen. Shining Saber may have looked like a dragoid, but he was a human player inside.

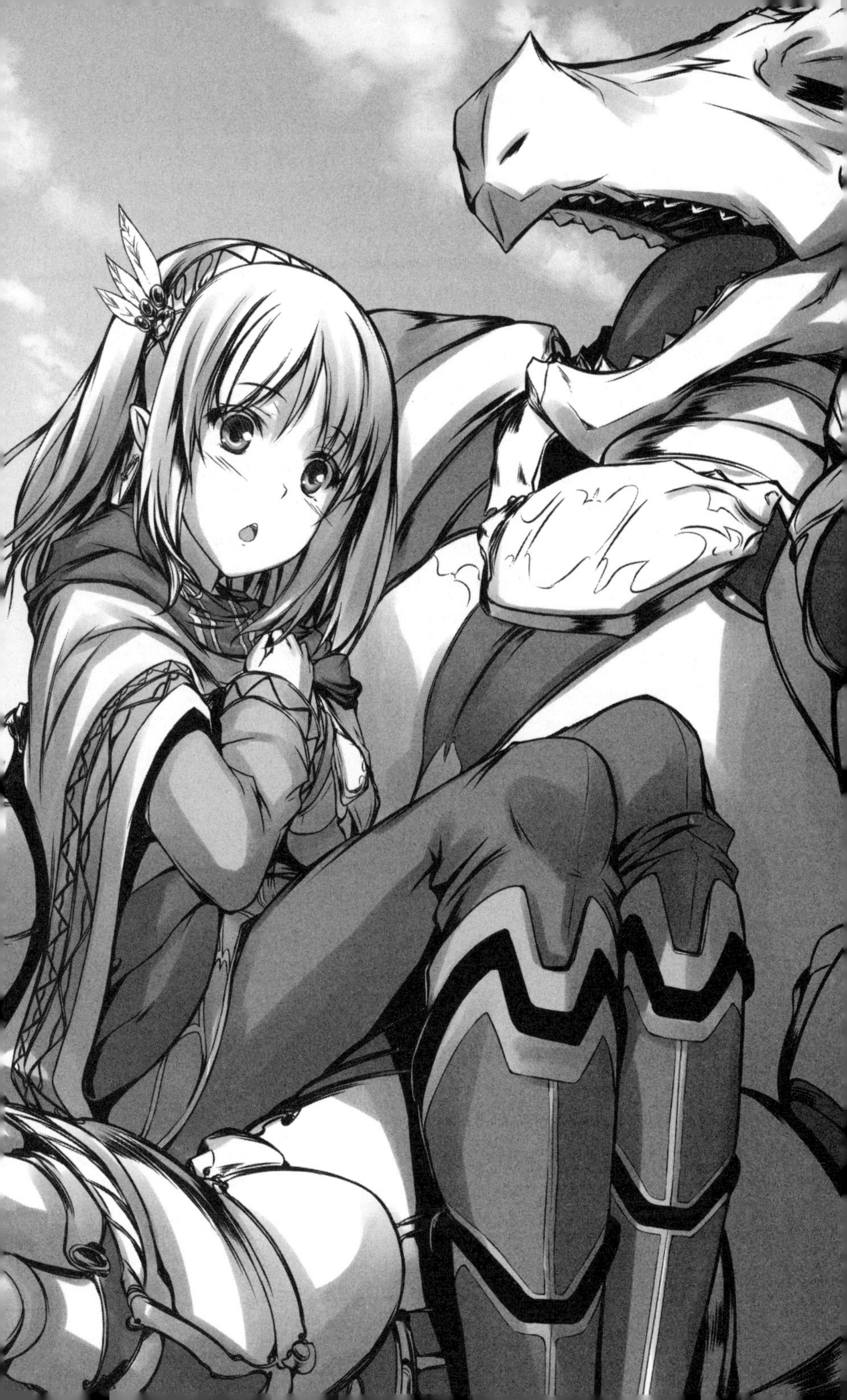

Immediately taking note of Cayna's Good Looks (which included a light Charm effect), Shining Saber reflected on his own actions and gasped. He was behaving just like some fairy tale prince. Flustered and embarrassed, he swiftly admonished himself: *There were so many other ways she could ride with me, so why'd I choose the princess hoooooooold?!*

The two sat together in silence and avoided each other's gaze.

Finally, Shining Saber offered his apologies in dribs and drabs.

"Uh, sorry. I wasn't thinkin'..."

"...No, it's okay. You were being nice. I get it..."

However, Cayna was clearly not her usual easygoing self, and her voice was extremely small. Shining Saber held her like she might break at any moment and didn't seem to even consider putting her down. In a way, he was at his wits' end as well.

However, the procession's current pace had sped up and was threatening to leave them behind. As his horse trotted faster, heading to the front, both the knights assigned to the rear guard and the co-captain gazed with wide eyes at their returning leader's eccentricity.

Feeling the inquisitive stares surrounding her more than any gaze she'd ever felt before, Cayna curled in on herself. Her face turned so bright red that she thought she might die at any second.

"Uwagh... Shining Saber, you idiot..."

"Uh, sorry. I didn't plan for any of this to happen, but all I can say for now is sorry."

As their captain repeatedly bowed his head to the beautiful elf in apology, it wasn't long before his subordinates began looking at him with lukewarm expressions. Shining Saber was so busy apologizing that he noticed all too late.

"So you had a girlfriend, Captain."

"...Huh? What're you guys talkin' about?"

"To think he's been getting all lovey-dovey on military campaigns. Our captain's a man among men."

CHAPTER 1

"Damn, I'm so jealous!"

"Hold on—you got the wrong idea!"

"Captain, it's not nice to deny it right in front of her. Why not just admit it?"

"Yup, you have our blessing. Right, everyone?"

"""""""YEAAAAAAAH!!!"""""""

The knights' fervor hit max levels over something that wasn't true in the slightest, and the soldiers within the carriages peeked out their heads to see what was going on. Shining Saber lost control of the conversation, and the red-faced Cayna stewed with complicated feelings over becoming a couple officially recognized by the knights. Rather than complain, she gave his arm a stiff pinch.

"GYAGH! OW, OW, OW, OW, OW, OW, OW! How hard do you plan on squeezin'?!"

"Don't underestimate a Skill Master! I've even got a Double Pain skill!"

Now that she'd gotten past feeling so embarrassed she might die, Cayna returned to her usual self and started launching a counterattack. However, even this scene looked like nothing more than a lover's quarrel, and the stares around them only grew warmer.

The journey was expected to last two days, and the knights and their entourage began setting up camp by the side of the main road after completing the first day's distance. The people in the caravans that had been tailing the knights were huddled around their bonfires a short distance away.

"Guess they're not gonna come and say hi," Cayna noted.

"Those folks tend to keep to themselves. They won't ask for help unless something happens. And when they do come over, it's usually to make some weird, false accusation."

It was here that Shining Saber and Cayna were finally blessed with the opportunity to clear up their misunderstanding, though it was more a matter of him believing what she had to say. After loosely explaining the events that led to her ending up on his horse, she said, "I'm sorry for the confusion," and bowed her head. Finally recovered from her embarrassment, she also gave a short self-introduction to the knights and another bow.

"It's nice to meet you. My name is Cayna, and I'm an adventurer. Please pardon me for earlier. It might be easier just to tell you that I'm Skargo's mother."

"""""WHAAAAAAAAAAAAAT?!"""""

"You're into that sort of thing, Captain?!"

"Never thought you'd be into widows!"

"I'm completely disillusioned."

The knights immediately cried out in shock, but for some reason, they also fixed Shining Saber with pitiful gazes and offered their condolences. Several made strange statements: "So I guess the High Priest will call you Stepdad, huh?" "I'm so jealous you'll get to hear Lady Mai-Mai call you Stepdad!"

"Are these knights okay…?" Cayna wondered aloud.

"Sorry, I should've trained my subordinates better."

Nevertheless, she spent more time with the knights, and before she could have any say in the matter, it was decided that Cayna would sleep with the female knights.

"It's kind of like… How do I put this…? Birds of a feather flock together," said Cayna.

"Is that a compliment or an insult?"

"…A compliment, I guess?"

"Why was that in the form of a question?!"

Back in the Game Era, knights would only talk about quests and the like. In simple terms, they were stern and inherently formal.

However, Shining Saber's subordinates were a chill group that

CHAPTER 1

didn't act the least bit stuffy. Even if you took their different races and circumstances into account, each was shockingly swayed by personal feelings.

"Hold on! What if you get too friendly with the knights, and this turns into some sort of buddy-buddy guild?!"

"Don't worry; I'm still tough on 'em when I need to be. They ain't so bad."

His dear subordinates all had full faith in this situation they believed was going on between Shining Saber and Cayna. Whispers of "He's got a shot, right?" and "They're pretty cute together" quietly swirled.

She heard the comments all too clearly, but since objecting would mostly likely be seen as an attempt to hide her embarrassment, she feigned ignorance.

Shining Saber, on the other hand, chased them around while yelling "DAMN YOUUUU!" so her efforts bore very little fruit.

"Do they love him, or are they just messing with him...? Is this country going to be okay?"

As someone going by the knights' set schedule, Cayna expected she would arrive near the fishing village around the following afternoon.

"Huh?! Aren't you going to join us the entire way, Lady Cayna?"

"No, no. I have somewhere to be, so I only planned to join you until we came close."

"You can freeload off us all you want, Lady Cayna, so stick with us till the end!"

"By the way, why do you keep calling me Lady?"

""""Oh yeah, about that. We'll happily flatter you if it means getting delicious food!""""

A frown formed on Cayna's face, and she looked behind her at

Shining Saber. He made a chagrined expression and raised a single hand in apology. After all, Cayna just found out their main motive was to escape stale bread, dried meat, and water. Even so, it looked like there were some knights with flasks of diluted alcohol.

Seeing she didn't have much choice, Cayna visited the group of caravans a short distance away, bought some meat and vegetables, and put her Cooking Skills to work. The result was a dumpling-and-vegetable soup reminiscent of the famous *suiton* dish from Gunma Prefecture.

Hot meals were apparently a rare occurrence during marches such as this, so the soldiers were eternally grateful. Some even cried as they ate.

"What do these people normally eat…?"

The chef herself was completely flabbergasted by this scene, which brought to mind the image of schoolchildren without lunch. After Cayna cooked them both dinner and breakfast, the knights and soldiers all tried various ways to stop her when they found out she would be leaving.

Fed up with their *Gimme! Gimme!* attitude, Cayna created a Cooking Skill scroll and passed it to Shining Saber. A knight captain who doubled as a cook was pretty unheard of, but since Shining Saber was the only one in his group who could use scrolls, there weren't any alternatives.

"The knights remind me of all those players who used to beg for freebies. It kind of made me laugh," said Cayna.

"Back in the game, I used to wonder what the point of Cooking Skills was, but now I see they come in pretty handy," said Shining Saber.

"Didn't you know? There was a special quest that activated if you gave certain NPCs their favorite food and raised your Friendship Level with them. You'd get this skill that boosted your vanguard."

"Seriously…?"

Shining Saber started groaning and shooting Cayna sidelong

CHAPTER 1

glances. He was clearly dying to ask her for this skill. When Cayna crossed her arms to form a large X in front of her, his shoulders instantly dropped, and he hung his head.

She only meant to tease him a bit, but the onlookers interpreted their exchange as something else entirely. The female knights firmly grabbed Shining Saber's arms and shoulders.

"H-hey?! What's with you guys?"

"Captain, we've misjudged you."

"Could we speak with you over there for a moment?"

"Harassing her right in front of everyone like this—have you no shame, sir?!"

"Huh?"

Both Shining Saber and Cayna were dumbfounded. They were the only ones who had no clue what was going on, and before they realized it, the entire knight corps had the two surrounded.

"Heeeey now. Just hold up! What did I even do?!"

Several people pinned Shining Saber down and dragged him into the shadow of a carriage.

"Ummm...?"

Cayna ignored the captain's cries as he pleaded innocent from afar; it seemed the knights had begun lecturing him on how to treat a lady. At least, that was the impression she got from what she overheard.

Unable to let this slide without comment, Kee issued a warning to the clueless Cayna.

"He glanced at your chest, and you made a no signal. Perhaps they think he's trying to mate with you?"

"Mate?!"

Cayna's face instantly turned crimson, and the middle-aged co-captain bowed his head.

"I am terribly sorry, miss. I assure you we will give the captain a *thorough* talking-to, so I hope you will pardon this incident."

"Huh? Er, uh—r-right! D-don'tworryaboutit!"

She grew so incoherent that she stumbled over her words, which only served to stoke the knights' fury. They raised cries of "That damn captain. What's he doin' treatin' widows like that?" "Co-captain! Let's tie him to a tree for the night!" and "I say we give him a taste of his own medicine!"

The comments against their own leader were harsh indeed, but perhaps it was the knights' way of expressing their affection. Cayna had often heard at the Adventurers Guild that knights were "disgusting," but that didn't seem to be the case at all.

The knights likely did more than lecture Shining Saber, because he came back looking slightly the worse for wear. Cayna let loose a smile.

"What the heck? I was innocent, too… You know something I don't?"

"Hee-hee-hee, it's a secret."

"What's that supposed to mean…?"

Shining Saber once again drooped his head, but upon realizing he was still under the watchful eye of his subordinates, he hurriedly straightened his posture. Cayna couldn't help but burst into laughter at the sight. The laughter spread around her, and it wasn't long before all the knights were in stitches.

In the midst of this merriment, Cayna had a thought.

In a world relatively safe thanks to the abundance of level-300 players, when would that vanguard-boosting skill he wanted ever have been useful?

She pondered this casually but never imagined the events it would set off.

Determined to prevent any more misunderstandings during the day's travels, Cayna did not ride with Shining Saber on his horse but instead used Summoning Magic to call upon the centaur Heigl.

CHAPTER 1

"Ah! My lady! I, Heigl, have arrived!"

"Watch where you're swinging that spear! It's dangerous!"

Cayna broke into a cold sweat as the tip of a spear passed right in front of her. Kee had put up a protective wall, so she knew it couldn't harm her. Even so, that didn't mean she wanted to see a pointy weapon slice the air next to her face.

Centaurs were generally well-liked by the knights because of their warrior-esque dispositions and good manners. That said, the lady knights took issue with them given how some of the male knights responded to their hot-blooded tendencies.

"There's another one of these guys?"

"He was pretty much like that when I called him. Real-life summonings are nuts, right?"

Shining Saber rubbed his temples and sighed in consternation. Apparently, a knight of similar disposition was currently stationed at the castle.

"Just the thought of two of him makes my head hurt."

"I can lend you two or three steeds to guard the castle if you want," Cayna offered.

"Is it just me, or is there something spiteful about the word *steed*?" asked Heigl.

"Guess it's not just you," Cayna replied.

Incidentally, Shining Saber was riding atop his horse, while Cayna was sitting sidesaddle on Heigl's back. The centaur refused to be treated as a packhorse, but when asked how he felt about riding with the knights, he very willingly agreed and replied, "If my back may so suit you." Nevertheless, seeing as Cayna was his master, this was a special exception.

Shining Saber and Cayna chatted casually as the knights continued their advance, but both looked up at the sky dejectedly and grimaced as gray clouds gathered in the direction of their march.

"Hmm. Looks like we're in for a shower," he said.

"Guess we've got no Rain-Shielding Magic."

"Rain-Shielding Magic? The heck…?"

Just as Shining Saber halted their forces to get a grasp on the situation…

…a mist blew in from somewhere and blocked his vision.

"What is this?"

"Wait! Where did this mist come from?!"

"Uwagh, the horses!"

"The horses are suddenly going berserk?!"

"Everyone, calm down! Calm the horses!"

Before they knew it, the mist covered everyone's footsteps. It reached up to the horses' bellies and invaded the floors of the carriages. Moreover, the horses had no idea what was going on and quickly grew agitated. Several reared up and sent their riders falling before any had a chance to react. Since Heigl was still calm, he went around putting them at ease.

The soldiers farther behind were also bound up in the net of mist. Since Cayna's Beast Master skill could calm only one animal per cast, there was no way she could take care of them all.

As this was going on, Kee reported that the mist *"has a hostile air,"* and Cayna soon switched gears.

"This looks like mist, but it's something else!" she shouted.

"Cayna! Can't you do something?!"

The mist seemed to twist around her with a will of its own, and Cayna released as much magic upon it as she would any malicious presence.

`Magic Skill: Purification Barrier Level 2: Landia: Ready Set`

"Release!"

The moment she cast the spell, a thin undulation of light centering around Cayna spread across the surrounding area. The spell

CHAPTER 1

drilled a cylindrical hole into the milky-white mist covering the land, dispersing the mist and revealing the original grasslands below in the blink of an eye. Every bit of mist that the wave of light touched was vaporized without a trace.

Even the mist that bound the soldiers like thick ivy released them one after the other. They stumbled and fell on their bottoms, but no one's life appeared to be at risk. A level-1 spell would have merely purified the area, but since her level-2 magic cured any abnormalities in people and animals, even the horses touched by the wave returned to their senses.

A minute after Cayna cast her magic, not a single fragment of the mist was to be seen. The weather was still a bit touch and go, but the strange presence from earlier was nonexistent.

As everyone helped the fallen to their feet, the co-captain gathered the injured and entrusted the magic users with healing. Shining Saber went around checking the entire group and confirming with each commanding officer that no other trouble was going on.

Cayna was absolutely certain the mist had risen up from the ground like a trap and felt it was the work of human hands.

"What do you think, Kee?"

"Yes. One can assume this was a malicious plot of some kind."

Strangely enough, Li'l Fairy didn't seem afraid for once. If anything, she looked angry as she lightly struck the back of Cayna's neck. Despite the tension in the air, the strikes tickled her and made Cayna smile.

"Thanks for letting me travel with you this far."

"Sure thing. We did have that incident earlier, though. Be careful out there."

Cayna said good-bye to Shining Saber and the others in front of the road that led to the fishing village where eyewitnesses claimed to have seen the undersea palace.

"*Sniff.* All that delicious comfort food…"

"Just thinking about going back to dried meat and stale bread is… Ngh."

Behind Shining Saber, the knights who had been completely brainwashed by Cayna's cooking peered from the shadows of the carriages, visibly distraught.

"Ummm, what about *them*?"

"Ah, ignore 'em. They'll be in for a walloping later."

Shining Saber grumbled something about how they were "an insult to knights." The co-captain and others smiled uncomfortably.

"Safe travels," the co-captain said to Cayna.

"Same to you."

"Do stop by the castle when you return to Felskeilo. We'll inform the gatekeeper."

She had gained a lot of fans in the past two days, and a smile rose to Cayna's lips. It was almost entirely thanks to the Cooking Skills that had helped her win the knights over with food. There were even people hoping to invite her to the castle so she could prepare tastier dishes made from proper ingredients.

She would refuse, of course. If Cayna went to the castle, Skargo would probably hang around her day and night, and it would only add to her stress.

"I'll walk on my own from here."

"I see. Aye, 'tis for the best."

Spear in hand, Heigl looked tense as he beheld the strange sight down below. He and Cayna had left the knights and on their smooth journey instead took a small path that led to an open field with a view of the ocean. The fishing village in question appeared to be farther down. Things had grown quieter now that the knights were gone, but that brought other abnormalities to light.

Aside from the centaur's hooves and the faint sound of rippling water, they couldn't hear anything at all. The air was temperate and vaguely familiar as it drifted by.

"My lady! I sense a most disturbing presence."

"It *is* strange that we don't even hear any birds…"

In the Game Era, seabirds would start squawking by default as you approached the coast, and you'd also be able to hear the distant chatter of villagers. The lack of both was enough to tell her this silence was clearly unnatural.

The strong scent of seawater made Cayna grimace. Since most smells in the game aside from food were indistinct, this was the first time she'd ever experienced it.

The gently sloping, barefaced rock was covered in sand, and among the shrubs and weeds that dotted the terrain was a small road that carriages could somehow pass through.

It halted midway and disappeared into a congestion of thick, cream-colored fog.

"Well, fog is the next step up from mist."

"The village is not visible in the slightest. Remain on your guard, my lady."

"I think there was a horror movie like this. What was it called again?"

She suspected the village was located in an area a distance away that was buried in thick fog and looked like a clump of low-pressure clouds. Although the wind was blowing enough to rustle her hair, the fog remained immobile. Refusing to move the slightest inch, it swirled around lazily.

"Uwagh, what's going on…?"

"It certainly appears dangerous here."

Heigl's stern face grew even more severe as he prepared for battle.

Cayna, predicting this fog would be the enemy of the drainage system, took out the Eternal Flame from her Item Box, unsheathed it, and prepared a wall of both physical and magical defense.

As they drew closer, the fog seemed to swirl into a semicircular dome in an attempt to preserve its bizarreness and create a wall to keep out intruders. The inside was completely hidden, and even Cayna's Probe Magic couldn't seem to tell her if something was approaching.

"*I will bolster your defensive wall.*"

As soon as Kee said this, an indistinct phosphorescence wrapped around Cayna. There was about a twenty-centimeter gap between this and her clothes, so she could clearly make out the shining human-shaped armor surrounding her. Heigl glanced over at Cayna, but she showed no surprise.

Probe Magic extended a person's eyesight by displaying a radar cross section in the corner of their vision. The user was always at the center, allies were green dots, and enemies were red. One's usual visual radius of about ten meters became one hundred meters. It was an essential skill for solo players like Cayna, who preferred to go it alone.

However, when it came to observing the fog from outside, the screen displayed a red error message, even though she was within range.

"The fog is keeping us out… Why does this feel like a quest I've seen somewhere before?"

"My lady, requesting permission to carry out a raid."

"We aren't the forty-seven ronin, so just hold on a second. We could always just blow all the fog away, but if it turns out the villagers were totally fine to begin with, we'll only be causing more trouble."

"Yes, as you command."

First, Cayna stuck her magic staff halfway into the fog. She took it out several seconds later, but it didn't seem to be burnt or dissolved in any way.

"My lady, we cannot discern the fog's effects using such a high-ranked weapon."

CHAPTER 1

"...Yeah, you have a point."

Cayna offered Heigl's exasperated comment a sheepish reply.

Regardless, none of the weapons in her possession would damage easily. Since Heigl's spear was high-grade as well, she was left with no choice but to take out a kirina grass leaf from her Item Box and casually stick it in the fog.

"Cayna!"

"My lady?!"

Flustered voices both inside her head and next to her rang out.

"Don't worry—it's fine. It doesn't sting or anything... Huh?"

Her hand wasn't red when she pulled it out. However, the kirina grass leaf she was gripping wilted in a matter of seconds.

"Oh?! How very odd!" cried Heigl.

"I guess it's not absorbing any water, huh?"

The wilted leaf fell apart at the merest touch.

"It is really safe to keep going?"

"Fear not, my lady! Entrust everything to me!"

Heigl thumped his chest and walked into the fog. Cayna hurriedly followed suit.

Inside, their vision stretched no more than about five meters. Heigl remained ever-vigilant, and he held his spear at the ready as he looked around them and slowly made his way forward. Cayna's defensive wall was in full effect, so a membrane of light visibly enveloped her in their dim surroundings.

Weak light shone only from the top of the fog dome, so they couldn't even confirm where the shadows of the houses were until the two were within the village.

As Cayna casually checked her status, she jolted when she saw the status of Heigl, who was displayed as a party member.

This was because his HP, which had just been displayed as *"Current value: Max,"* was dropping before her very eyes. He should have been equipped with techniques that reduced physical and magical effects, but her guess was that the damage caused by the fog exceeded this.

"What the—?! The fog inflicts damage?!"

Cayna let out a frantic cry and quickly tried to cast Simple Substance Recovery on Heigl. However, at that very same moment, human-sized shadows appeared from deeper within the fog. They came from behind as well.

"My lady!"

The attack came faster than her radar could pick up. Heigl put himself in front of Cayna, and she saw him go flying as he took the hit.

She used that moment to put distance between herself and the quintessential zombies now swaying, transfixed, in front of her. They had ashen skin; clouded, directionless eyes; and clothes so shredded and tattered, they barely clung to the zombies' bodies. Not only that, their skin was torn off in places, revealing glimpses of reddish-brown flesh. The horrid stench of rotting meat hovered in the air and forced Cayna to grimace.

One might say that zombies, whose repulsiveness in 3D games differed from that of real-life corpses, were popular small-fry characters. Even so, however much the zombies of other games were resigned to this fate, the ones in *Leadale* weren't all simply low-level.

Occasionally, among their brethren were several high-level zombies that appeared deceptively unassuming.

"*Gwaaaaaaghhhh…*"

They let out garbled moans and mobbed the living. Heigl, who had been blasted away, left her with a "M-may you be ever victorious…" as his image faded and disappeared. The centaur was level 250, so he shouldn't have been toppled with such incredible ease. These zombies were the same level as him at the very least.

CHAPTER 1

Concluding that only players had the ability to create zombies of this level in modern Leadale, Cayna faced the monsters and cast Magic Skill: Simple Substance Recovery Dewl Level 9.

Casting healing magic on the undead was the same as inflicting Attack Magic on the living. The zombies were completely dyed in white light, and every inch of their bodies crumbled to dust. It wasn't long before not a single trace was left. If some level-400 player had cast a spell on them meant to fill HP when on the verge of death, the zombies wouldn't have stood a chance.

"Where'd these guys even come from?!"

Cayna had only just entered the dome moments before, so she'd assumed any area behind her was "outside." Perhaps there was a trick to it that spirited people away to someplace within the dome the moment they stepped inside, just at the forest maze did.

She cast Holy Light on the short sword she'd bought in Felskeilo and illuminated the area around her. The shining white light extended only about three meters, but it pierced through the cream-colored fog. Even with its narrow range, this type of Holy Magic would purify the area as long as the light persisted.

The fog seemed to be releasing a poison via some sort of technique. Catching her breath as the film of light around her dissipated, Cayna began walking toward the large shadows vaguely visible on the other side of the fog.

She immediately made her way toward the residences.

They were as worn-out as the ones back in the remote village, but this didn't seem problematic, despite people still living in them. Cayna could smell the tide, but the earlier stench of zombie wafted by as well. She stopped and pondered.

"Well, now what?"

She had initially come looking for the Palace of the Dragon King;

this bizarre situation was not part of the plan. Maybe she ought to deem the inside of the dome as "all zombie" and burn down both the village and the fog dome with her greatest firepower. Or perhaps she should determine the cause of this accident and, if possible, eliminate the threat.

As she leaned against a house and thought this over, a red dot popped up in the corner of her radar. Two—no, three of them seemed to be heading toward her from the radar's periphery. From the groans and swaying shadows, she determined them to be zombies and tossed her Eternal Flame in their direction.

The flaming long sword transformed in midair and landed on four feet. It was only about the size of a knee-high dog, but it was actually a metal lizard cloaked in flame and as powerful as a level-400 monster.

All at once, she heard *"Uwagh"* and *"Skreeek"* coming from the monster showdown. On the other side of the fog, crimson hues danced like flames in every direction. After a short while, the fighting came to a halt, and the fiery lizard casually sauntered back. It jumped toward Cayna, transformed back into a long sword in midair, and returned to her hand.

After confirming the sword wasn't chipped or broken in any way, Cayna jumped up on a roof where she might gather her thoughts in the midst of enemy territory. She returned the Eternal Flame to its sheath and moved from house to house while masking her footsteps. Luckily, the buildings were fairly close together, and there was no need to touch the ground as she made her way past each neighboring roof.

As Cayna moved along, she spied squirming figures below and decided to conduct a few experiments.

First, she used Wind Magic to release a voice behind the zombies. As soon as Cayna cast Magic Skill: Transmission and took a slow look in the needed direction, a *"Waghhh!"* rang out. The zombies turned and pursued the sound deeper into the fog.

CHAPTER 1

"Looks like these guys don't have the same perception of 'life' as normal zombies and don't race toward it the same way, either. They'll even respond to magic and sound...," she murmured nonchalantly.

Kee said nothing. He was usually retrieving data about something she'd said at times like this, so Cayna didn't pay his silence much mind.

Tired of carrying her short sword, Cayna was about to leave it on the roof when she turned around and thrust it behind her.

A small clang of metal against metal rang out, and there stood a lightly armored woman defending against Cayna's sword with her hand guard. The white dot on the radar indicated she was either an ally or another player, but Cayna attacked, since she didn't believe anyone approaching from a blind spot was likely to be either.

However, the target of Cayna's attack gave a look of surprise and backed away with a flustered expression. She soon disappeared into the fog, but Cayna knew what direction she'd gone and constructed a small Flame Lance in her hand.

An instant later, a sound came flying from the other side of the fog as a whip struck, but its aim was sorely off. The weapon returned to the fog; Cayna now had a rough location and tossed her Flame Lance. A very unladylike "*Dwaaaagh!*" immediately rang out.

"I'll send two hundred more next time..."

"I give up! You win! Don't send two hundred!"

Responding to Cayna's absentminded murmurings, the offender appeared while waving a white cloth.

The timidly approaching figure was a female human warrior in leather armor. She had whips wrapped around both arms. According to Cayna's Search, she was level 430. She could also see the woman was definitely a player.

Still, no matter how much of a warrior one might be, her appearance was extremely slovenly. Cayna looked at the mass of unruly hair loosely gathered at the woman's neck and tilted her head. She felt as if she'd seen her somewhere before.

The woman noticed Cayna placing her hand on the long sword at her side and waved both hands in a panic.

"H-hold on! These guys around here respond to magic! Don't draw your sword!"

"How do you know that? Don't tell me you're the reason for this mess?!"

"You got it all wrong! We've been stuck here, too, and freakin' out over what to do. Please, you gotta believe me…"

"The probability that she is lying is low. However, it seems she has not yet told the whole truth yet, either. What will you do?"

Kee analyzed and reported every detail of their opponent. The warrior tearfully pleaded with Cayna, and Cayna sensed no dishonesty. She remained vigilant but eased up on the woman. For the time being, however, the Eternal Flame would remain in Cayna's hand.

Giving a sigh of relief, the woman searched the shadows of the houses while gesturing for Cayna to follow.

"If you try anything funny, I'll blow this place sky-high!" Cayna warned.

"What kind of coercion is that?! Anyway, blowin' the place up *would* be a problem. There's a survivor."

"Huh?!"

They crossed the roofs for some time and finally arrived at a small storehouse at what appeared to be the edge of the village. Inside, a casting net was hanging on the wall, poles were gathered in a corner, and small boats were piled upside down on top of each other. It looked like the storehouse held the village's fishing equipment.

The woman lifted a floorboard in the very center of the room and nodded toward the stairs that appeared, indicating for Cayna to proceed down them. About ten or so steps later, they arrived at a door. The woman knocked on it in a three-four-two pattern.

After a short while, a low voice responded "Come in," and Cayna slowly opened the door.

Her radar informed her that there was another player inside, so she entered with caution.

This room was half as wide as the one above. It had to be a bunker of some sort. The stench of fish hit her nose, and she saw a number of jars and earthenware pots along the wall. There were also two open barrels that contained dried fish and vegetables pickled in salt.

Curled in a tight ball was a gray dragoid; he seemed to be the player. The other person was a petite human crouching in the corner with a blanket over them. This one appeared to be a child. Faintly shining stones were placed on the floor, and both people looked slightly luminescent.

"See, Exis, I knew somebody'd come," said the woman. "My, what a surprise. She seems way freakin'… She seems quite a bit stronger than me. Bet she's a player…uh, I daresay."

"You sound kinda different all of a sudden," Cayna noted.

"Shut it—er, please be quiet. I got— I have my reasons!"

The dragoid named Exis didn't respond to their conversation and instead stared at Cayna with his mouth agape. The strange woman slapped him across the face to snap him out of his stupor, and he went to grab Cayna.

The next instant, Cayna sensed a threat to her feminine virtue, so she drew her long sword. She pointed the flaming blade at the dragoid's throat…

"…Uh, I just wanted to check."

"You must be a pretty starving lizard to attack other races."

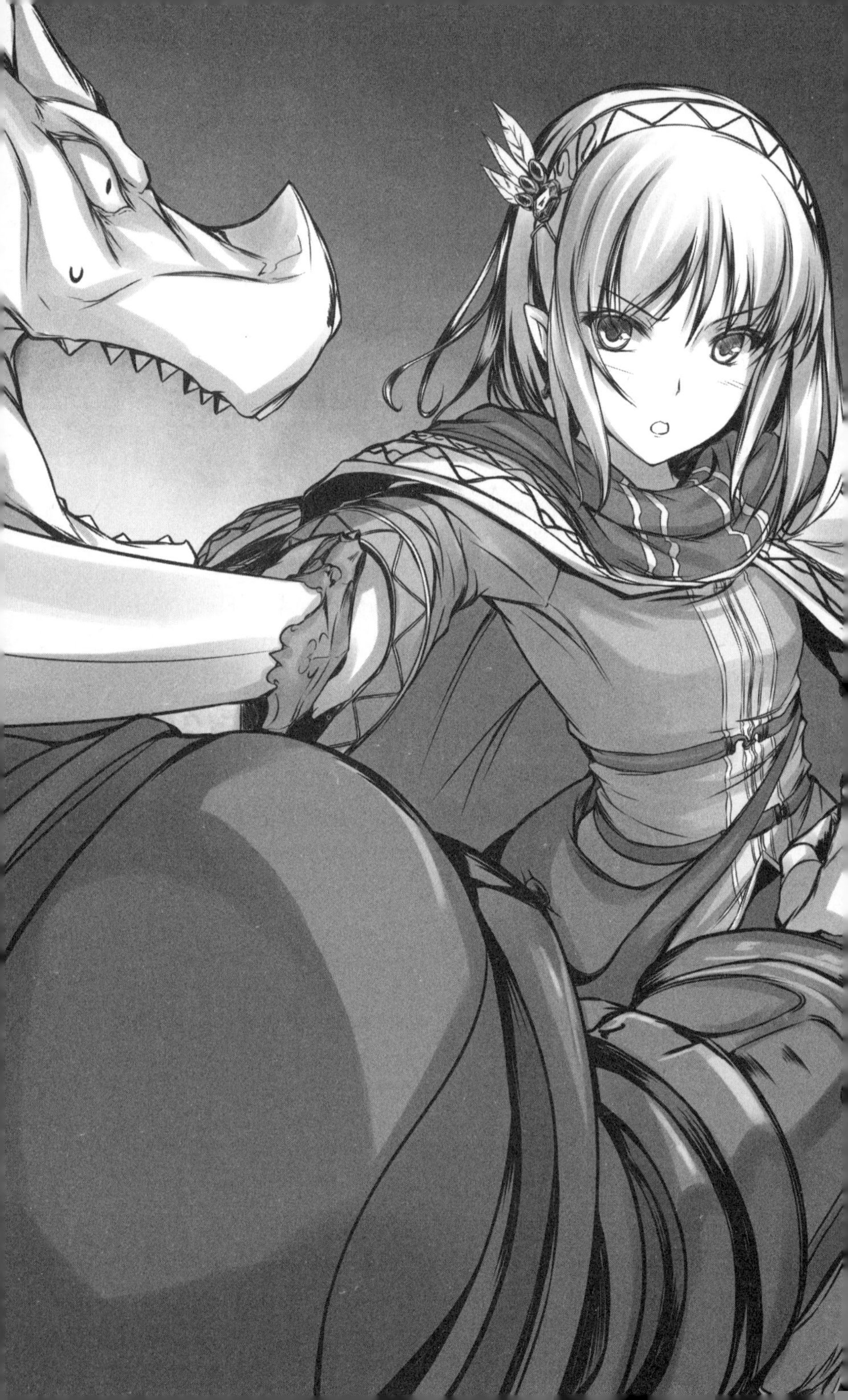

CHAPTER 1

Both halted in the center of the room. Cayna's long sword gave her the advantage in terms of reach, and the dragoid, unable to close the distance, stood stock still with his arms outstretched. Her sword stopped just short of cutting off a scale from his neck.

"Y-you're Cayna, right?! You're the only one who would have a sword like that as a default weapon."

"Unfortunately, I don't know anyone with a name as pleasant as yours," she mumbled as she checked the dragoid's status.

In the field where his name should have been, there was a haphazard line of letters that read *Xxxxxxxxxxxx*. There had been plenty of names made up of single letters in the game, but it was hard to know what to call such a person when you came across them. That was probably why this dragoid went by Exis.

The woman told Cayna she was frightening the child, so she put away the sword in her Item Box.

Cayna faced the pair once again, and they all introduced themselves.

"I'm Cayna. I came to this village to talk to people."

"'Sup—I mean, hello, I'm Quolkeh. I came here on a job for the Adventurers Guild. The big guy here is Exis."

"Don't call me big! You can't tell right now, but I used to be a different character. My main was Tartarus."

"...Tar... Tarta... Tart... Ah, Tartar Sauce!"

"I knew you'd call me that! You really are Cayna! You're alive, you fool!"

Tartarus was a player in her guild, Cream Cheese, and one of the few who used elven magic as his go-to. Rather than rely on sheer firepower, he used techniques that pinpointed his opponent's weakness. However, this dragoid dressed in full armor and wielding a giant sword couldn't be more different from Cayna's recollection of Tartarus. He used to be pale, skinny, and hidden in robes from head to toe, so it didn't match her image of him in her mind at all. As a matter of fact, weirdo players had made up a majority of their guild, and he'd been one of the few voices of reason who provided a much-needed cutting remark. This dragoid warrior was the polar opposite. At level 630, he was by far the strongest player she'd met so far.

Cayna finally remembered where she'd seen the gray dragoid and the lightly armored, whip-wielding woman before.

"Now that I'm getting a closer look at the two of you, I think I asked you for directions back in Helshper."

"Oh yeah, now that you mention it, you're that chick—er, lady who asked about the Crescent Moon Castle."

At the time, Cayna had been under the impression that the woman was more of a big-sister type. However, ever since she went up against Cayna, her masculine mannerisms were growing more noticeable. When Cayna pointed this out, Exis gave a heavy sigh.

"I told you to watch your phrasing, Quolkeh! We're the same gender, so talking like that will only make people more suspicious of him."

"I couldn't help it! I thought she was gonna kill me. How could I *not* give myself away?!"

"Well, yeah. Cayna's a member of the Cream Cheese guild."

"Say what?!"

Their brief exchange switched on a light bulb in Cayna's mind. She had asked Opus about such players before. After confirming that Quolkeh's status said *"Human: ♀; Name: Quolkeh,"* she got to the heart of the matter.

"Quolkeh, are you a guy IRL?"

"Gah..."

Bull's-eye. Quolkeh clutched her chest as she avoided Cayna's gaze. She looked like she'd just been slapped across the face.

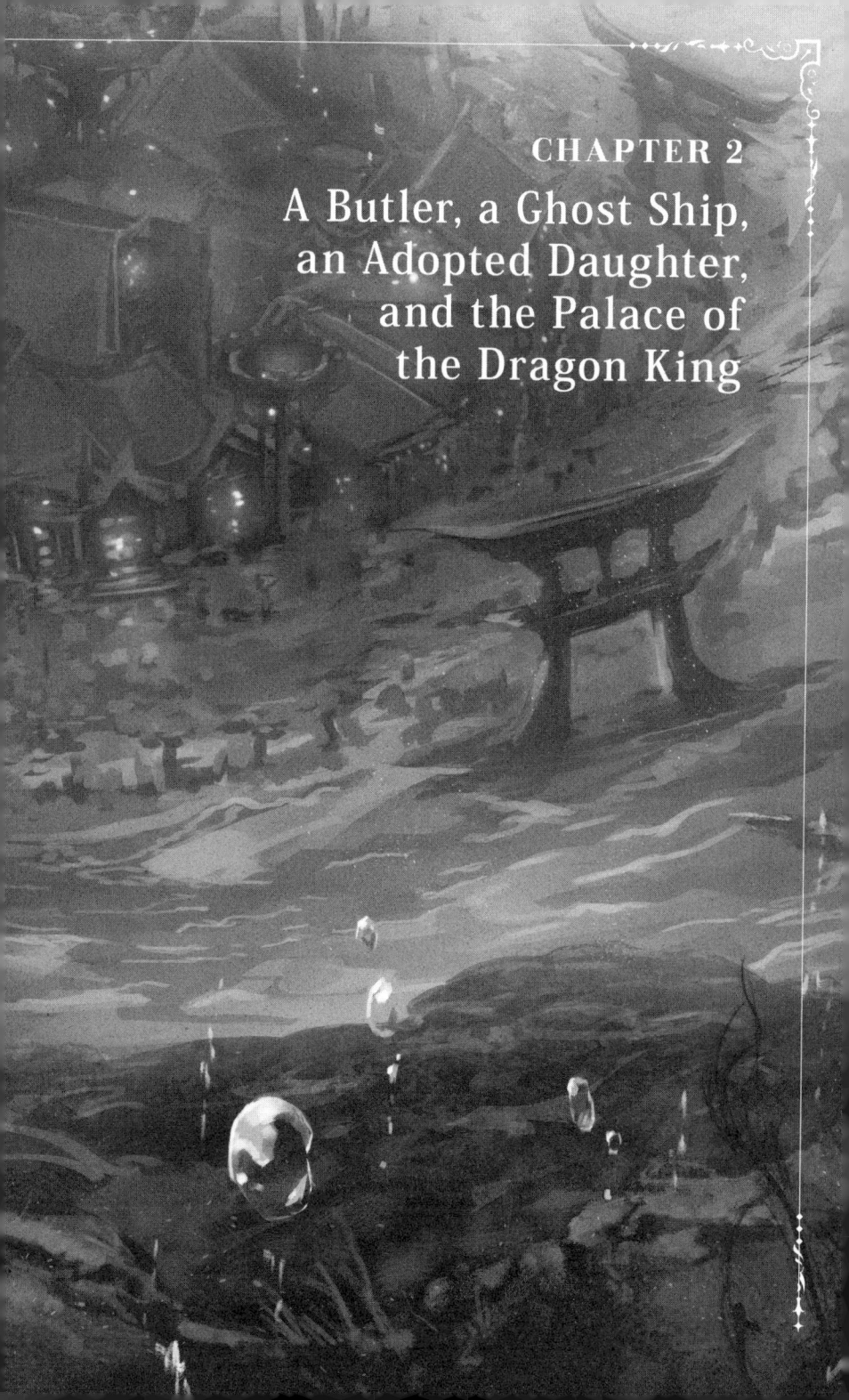

CHAPTER 2
A Butler, a Ghost Ship, an Adopted Daughter, and the Palace of the Dragon King

Setting aside personal player circumstances for the time being, Cayna and the others went around explaining their current situations.

"I came here about a month ago. A bunch of stuff happened, and now I'm looking for some towers."

"Geez, vague much?!" said Quolkeh.

"We'd be here all day if I explained everything! I've met three other players so far, and one of them is in jail."

"A lot of things aren't adding up here. Jail?" asked Exis.

"Yeah, remember those bandits who were causing trouble when we met in Helshper? Their leader was a player. I beat him down, but those knights came over and swiped him right out from under me."

Cayna gave a cute wink and stuck out her tongue with a "Tee-hee." Exis paled and took a step back.

"Y-you're creepin' me out!"

"What's with that reaction?! I'll give *you* a beatdown!"

"At least that'd be more like you!"

Quolkeh and the blanketed child stared in shock at the duo's sudden comedy act.

Li'l Fairy floated over to them from Cayna's shoulder, but

apparently, the child couldn't see her. She circled around them a few times but realized as much when she got no reaction. Li'l Fairy then dejectedly returned to Cayna's shoulder.

""Wh-What's that?""

Quolkeh and Exis were shocked instead. They stared at Li'l Fairy in sheer disbelief, their mouths agape.

Realizing she was visible, the fairy rushed back into Cayna's hair.

"This is Li'l Fairy," Cayna said blankly.

Exis slumped his shoulders, while Quolkeh stood frozen, mouth still open.

"I sort of got her from Opus. Or, actually, I guess it's more like he entrusted her to me."

"*That* son of a bitch is here, too?!"

The shock must have been pretty great, because Exis was shouting.

Cayna smiled awkwardly and gave a wave of her hand. "Nah, I haven't seen him. I feel like he's still around, though."

"You gotta be kidding me…"

As Exis held his head in his hands and looked up at the ceiling, Quolkeh gave a questioning look. "Who's Opus?"

"A moron I can't get rid of."

"The worst kind of bastard to get mixed up with."

Cayna's and Exis's respective opinions were on completely opposite ends of the spectrum, but Quolkeh seemed to understand the impact this person had on them. She simply murmured a disappointed "Oh, I see…"

Cayna summoned a Flame Spirit before the stunned child, who hadn't yet come to terms with the situation. The small, flaming monkey was about thirty centimeters tall and filled the small room with an orange glow as it playfully jumped around in front of them. The child gave a small smile as they watched the baby monkey repeatedly hop, fly, run around, and tumble about. Upon finally

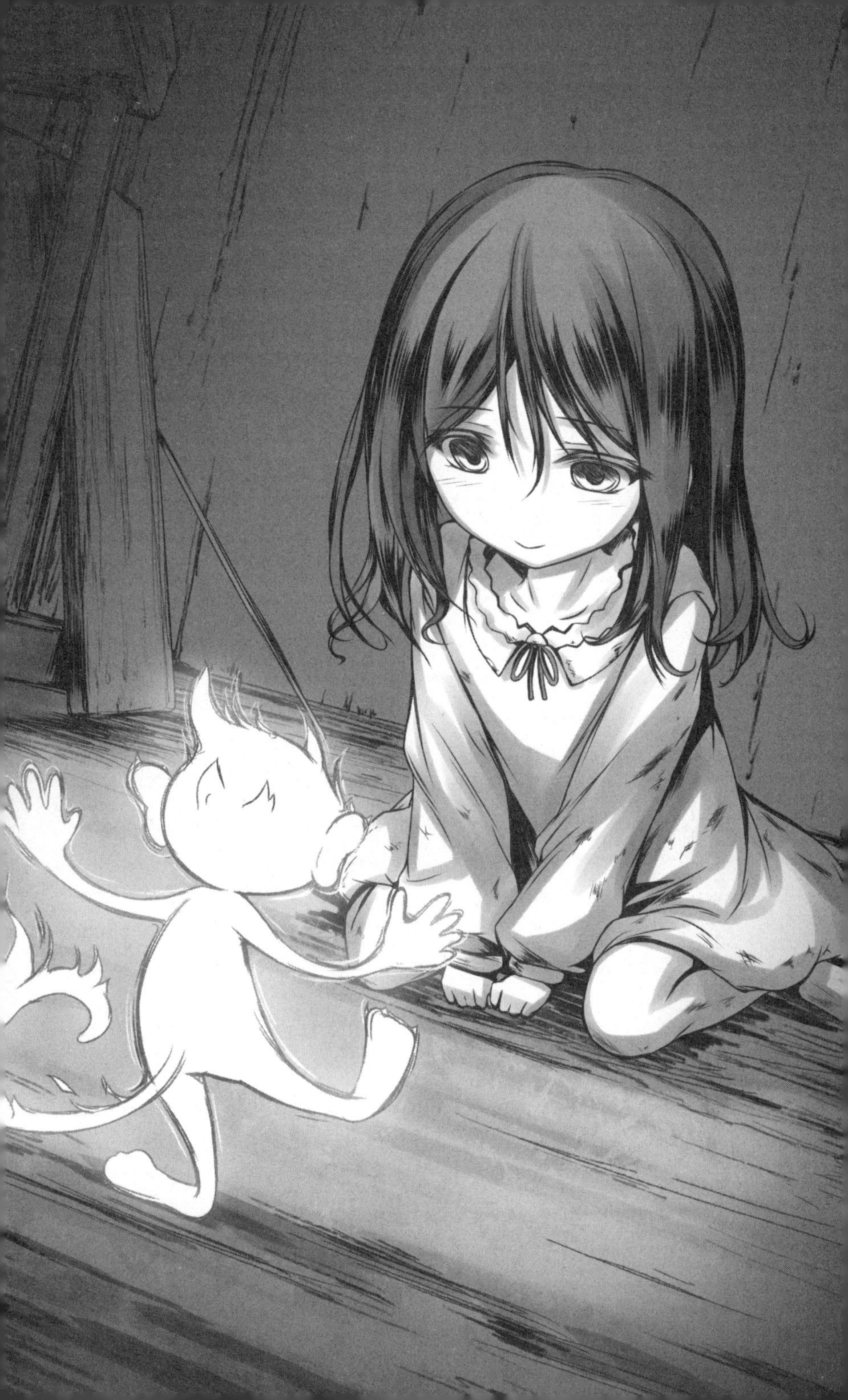

dropping their blanket for the first time, Cayna realized the child was a young girl.

The three looked on with bated breath and heaved small, quiet sighs.

""*"Phew…"*""

Perhaps feeling a slight weight lifted off his shoulders now that the monkey was taking care of the girl, Exis began talking about their own situation.

"For us, it all started when we took on a request from the Merchants Guild in Helshper. The fish were disappearing from the ocean, so we set off to a fishing village about three days away on foot. When we got there, though, there were no signs of a struggle, but everyone was gone. All the doors were left open, there were no bodies, and we found footprints that led into the sea. The investigation came to a dead end."

"Sounds pretty crazy to me…"

"We then decided to head south to check on the other fishing villages," said Quolkeh. "Everything was fine here until two days ago. Sometime around that evening, though, the villagers started kicking up a fuss. They were asking stuff like 'How are the boats?' and before anyone knew it, the entire village was suddenly engulfed in a fog. Goodness, everyone collapsed and turned into zombies. Why, they even began attacking at random, if you can believe it. Some dreadfully strong skeletons were even mixed into the group. There was no chance of escaping to the outside, so at a loss, we fled here and met this dear child."

"Can you stop trying to sound girlie? You're failing at it, and it's super-weird."

"Gweh…"

Quolkeh resigned herself to Cayna's pointed comment and hung her head.

The little girl's name was Luka, and she was apparently this village's sole survivor. Of course, Cayna continued to speak kindly to the little girl even when she asked for her name.

There were no other children her age in the village, and this storehouse had become Luka's playground. Since the fog had never infiltrated the cellar and a charm of protection was put in place to protect the food stores, she had escaped the disaster.

If they hoped to leave this place, it seemed like the group would have no choice but to pass through the foggy village. And if they hoped to find freedom, the others would have to take Luka with them.

There was a high chance a child would turn into a zombie the moment they touched the fog. Having said that, though, it wasn't like everyone else could just go out to find the cause of the fog while they left her behind. It was truly a tricky situation.

"Still, I had a rough time killin' the zombies. They used to be villagers…," Quolkeh said.

Exis, being equipped in metal armor and not suited to clandestine missions, had been entrusted with looking after Luka while Quolkeh occasionally went outside and reduced the zombie population to a manageable size.

"I thought you were a high-level zombie at first, Cayna. That's my bad."

"No, now I get where you were coming from. I went overboard back there, too."

"You goin' overboard is worse than any massacre. I don't trust you for a second."

"What're you agreeing with me for, Exis?!"

"Gah! Enough! Quit fightin' every time you open your mouths!"

Sensing the two getting ready for another comedy showdown, Quolkeh stopped them just in time. Having returned to himself, Exis drew a simple map of the village on the floor and devised an escape.

Although the shared storehouse was on a higher elevation than the village, it was closer to the sea. They considered escaping by water, but no one knew how to operate a boat. On top of that, even if Exis took off his armor, his weight would still overload the small boat. Thus, it was decided that they'd quickly find the source of the fog and destroy it.

"We have plenty of battle options now that you're here, Cayna. Luka will be safest with you, so we'll go crush the source in the meantime," said Exis.

"I'm pretty sure no one will be able to touch her if I put a barrier around the storehouse, though."

Cayna often listened patiently while talking with the other children in the hospital, so Luka quickly grew attached and clung to her clothes.

The girl appeared to be barely ten but seemed to have developed a quiet demeanor from growing up in this village of scarce children.

Since leaving the poor girl on her own wasn't an option, Exis and Quolkeh offered to destroy the source of the fog themselves. However, Cayna proposed it was better that she join them as a rear guard. Based on what his main character was like, Exis acknowledged that his range of techniques in battle depended on whether he had backup support.

"You're the same as ever, Mr. Nice Guy Tartar Sauce. You're willing to prioritize children at the cost of our own mobility?"

"Quit callin' me Tartar Sauce. I'd feel bad leaving her here alone in a place like this."

"No one said anything about leaving her alone…"

Cayna took out a blue handbell and a red handbell from her Item Box and carefully looked over each as she deliberated.

Quolkeh wasn't familiar with the items and was thus uncertain of their effects. However, Cayna and Opus had used them back in the game and gotten Exis (formerly known as Tartarus) mixed up in the ensuing mess. Because of this, Exis gave a look of obvious displeasure.

"So why the heck do you have two…?"

"'Cause that's how much I played."

CHAPTER 2

"You damn addict."

"I'll take that as a compliment."

"Sorry, but I have no idea what you two are talking about."

Since Quolkeh hadn't had the chance to play the game for very long, she had trouble following the conversations of these overpowered former guild members. Cayna apologized to Quolkeh for leaving her out of the loop and proceeded to explain the handbells she'd brought out.

"Right, sorry about that. You earn one of these whenever you play the game for ten thousand hours."

"And havin' two marks you as someone who has nowhere else to be," Exis commented.

"I'd expect no less of a Cream Cheese member… You guys just don't know when to quit," said Quolkeh.

"These allow you to summon either a butler or a maid, and for a thousand gil, they'll serve the summoner for up to ten days. Their level is half the user's."

"I see. So you're planning to have them accompany me and Exis?"

"*Bzzz.* That is incorrect. I'll be coming with you. One of these two will stay here to protect Luka. I wonder who I should call, Cie or Rox?"

"Not the maid if you can help it," said Exis. "I might drop dead from rage if she shows up here in the flesh."

Quolkeh didn't know if something had happened, but by Exis's expression, she could tell that just hearing the name alone had worn him out. She was itching to learn more about this problematic maid but exercised self-restraint when she realized there was no time for that in their current situation.

"It costs money, though, right? A thousand gil might be a bit of a stretch," Exis remarked.

"Yeah, but when you convert a thousand bronze coins to Leadale's modern going rate, it equals ten gold coins."

""That much?!""

The two cried out in shocked unison and fell backward. Confused by their reaction, Cayna replied with a question of her own.

"Huh? Don't you two have money from the game? One gil equals one silver coin..."

As Cayna gave a brief explanation of the local currency, the two lost their minds in tandem. Exis balled his hands into fists and ground his fangs with a snarl. Quolkeh held her head in her hands and huddled in a corner of the room. The pair's eccentric behavior frightened Luka, and she clung to Cayna's back.

"Ah, I guess neither of you checked your money," Cayna said, looking on them with pity.

Back in the game, you didn't often *see* physical money. Since it was commonplace to view transactions by a displayed numerical value, most players treated their finances like a real-life credit card. After the game world became the real world and both players saw actual bronze and silver coins, they must have concluded that their "credit cards" were useless.

"Don't worry, Luka. This is what they deserve."

"...Mm..."

Both Exis and Quolkeh had a dark, nebulous cloud hanging over their heads. It was an excessively strange scene.

"Dammit. If I'd known that, I could've done something back then..."

"...And I had to swallow my pride working as a waitress at that bar..."

"What the heck have you two been doing this whole time...?"

They had clearly suffered a number of money woes, and such reactions made Cayna pity them from the bottom of her heart.

At any rate, Cayna, thinking of the young girl's safety first and foremost, lightly rang the blue handbell.

Riiiing!

CHAPTER 2

The lingering note trailed off across the storehouse, and a line of light drew across the space directly in front of Cayna.

Vertical lines raced over the wall, hanging objects and all, like a 3D figure. A stately, double-sided door appeared. It was stained with a woodgrain pattern and stuck out in relief from the wall.

Cayna watched Quolkeh's and Luka's eyes widen. The door slowly creaked open of its own accord. A pure-white light from the other side flooded into the space, and just as the sound of clacking shoes seemed to grow closer, a single figure came forth.

Black eyes. Black hair. Black cat ears.

A werecat boy sharply dressed in a semiformal butler suit appeared before them. Behind him, the door soon disappeared without a trace.

He was slightly shorter than Cayna, and after taking a few steps forward, he stopped in front of her and gave a respectful bow.

"It has been some time, Master. I, Roxilius, have arrived. Please command me as you wish."

Cayna smiled at Luka, who had been watching on in bewilderment since the moment the werecat entered. Quolkeh likewise stood there gaping at the outrageous events that had just transpired.

Exis had seen Roxilius countless times, so he karate-chopped Quolkeh and returned her to her senses.

"Don't worry—he's very nice," Cayna assured the nervous Luka while lightly patting her back. "Long time no see, Roxilius. How've you been?"

"I…am not certain I can say everything is entirely well, but there is no question matters have been peaceful overall."

"Gotcha. What about Roxine? Wasn't she with you?"

"That place was like a packed storage closet, so I'm afraid I haven't the slightest idea where that foolish feline might be."

"Your system's basically no different from a store that's closed up shop. All those other players' NPC aides are stuck there, too…"

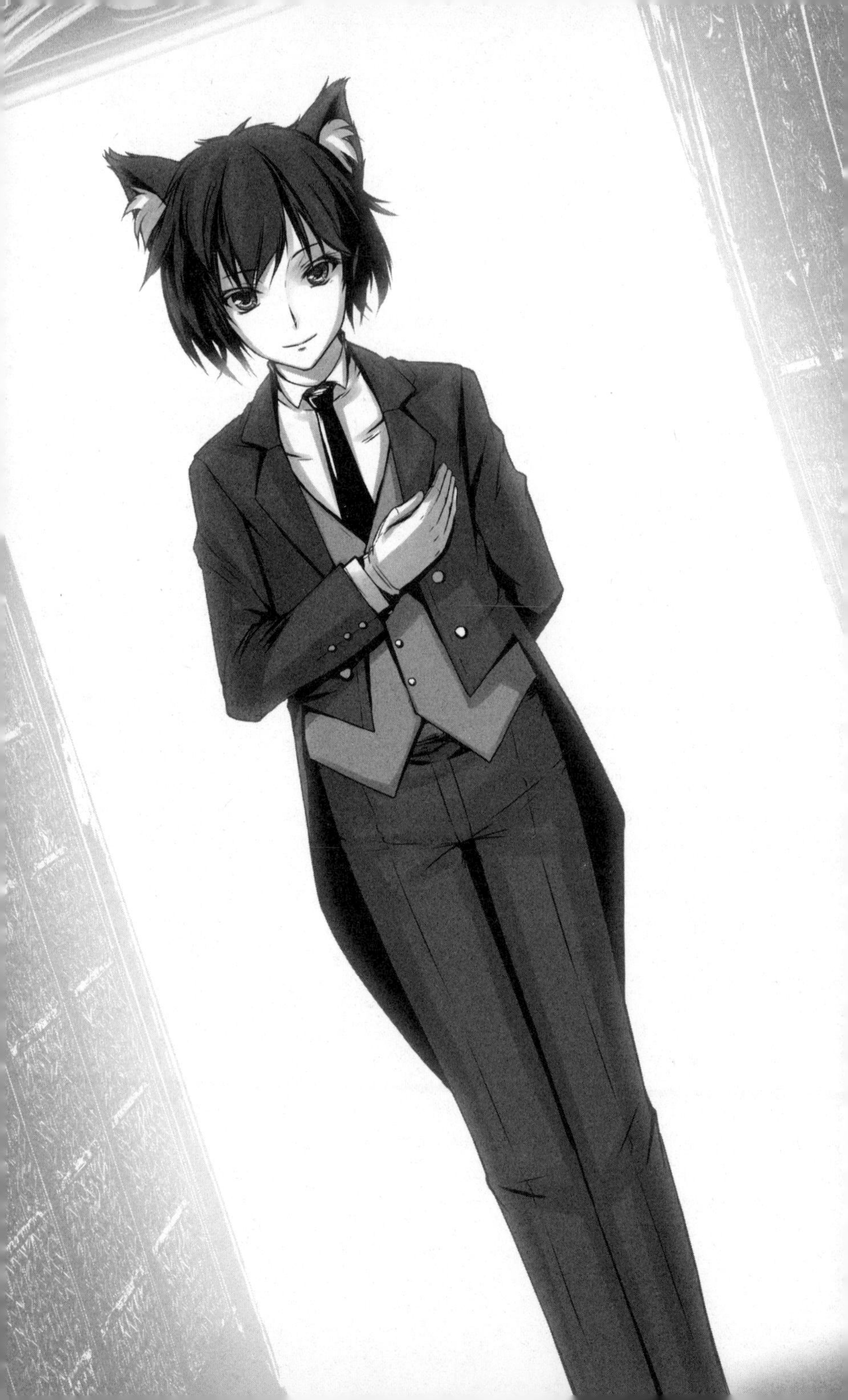

CHAPTER 2

Cayna placed her hand to her mouth as she mulled this over. However, she pushed Roxilius to the forefront when she noticed Quolkeh and Luka staring.

"This is Rox, also known as Roxilius. He's my loyal butler. Oh, and he's level 550. I hope you'll all be friends!"

"Bwagh?!"

Paying no attention to Quolkeh's impressive outburst, Roxilius placed a hand over his heart and bowed.

"I am Roxilius, a werecat butler. Despite my many shortcomings, I hope you will command me as you see fit."

"We'll be heading out to take care of some monsters soon. Could you watch Luka for us?" Cayna asked.

"But of course."

Roxilius dropped to his knees, met Luka's eyes, and gave a deep bow.

"It is a pleasure to make your acquaintance, Miss Luka. My name is Roxilius. I am honored to serve you."

Luka looked back and forth at Cayna and the werecat in confusion.

"It's okay, Luka. If you stay here with this nice man for just a little while, we'll be able to go outside."

Cayna patted the girl's back consolingly, and Luka hesitantly wavered over taking Roxilius's white-gloved hand before finally accepting it.

"I cherish your trust, Miss Luka."

The girl blushed and looked down as he smiled at her gently, but she gave a small nod.

When Cayna patted her head from behind, Luka gazed up in wonder. No longer able to contain herself, Cayna gave her a big squeeze. Luka flailed around in a fluster.

"C'mon, enough of that. Let's get going," Exis urged Cayna as he poked her in the head.

"Okay, Rox. I put up a barrier to keep the hazardous fog outside, but it'll go away once we take care of things. Do me a favor and please watch Luka until then."

"Yes, understood. I, Roxilius, shall protect Miss Luka with my very life."

"Luka, you can stay here with Rox for a little while, right? We'll be back as soon as we can."

Cayna's words brought sadness to Luka's face as the girl gripped Roxilius's pants, but she nodded gently. At her feet, the small fire monkey rooted the three on like a stalwart cheer squad.

As Cayna approached Exis and Quolkeh, she extended the magic staff she'd removed from her earring and gave it a swing.

"Okie doke, it's cleanup time!"

"What are you, a kindergarten teacher or something?" Exis asked.

"Seems to me like she says that kind of stuff all the time."

"Must be 'cause I was bedridden and only hung out with old people and kids in the real world."

"I—I see..."

Cayna's openness about her own circumstances and the casual way she spoke of such gloomy topics made Exis feel awkward. After all, she had always been logged in every time he played, so he'd assumed she was actually some antisocial NEET. He was now undeniably aware that the circumstances in Cayna's life held a shade of nuance.

When the trio got back outside, Cayna cast a barrier around the small storehouse that was surrounded by fog so thick they could hardly see anything at all. The zombies quickly staggered toward them. Their levels were in the two-figure range, so both Exis and Quolkeh dealt with them quickly enough. There wasn't even any need for Cayna to get involved.

"Kee! Search for quests with similar conditions. I feel like I've seen this situation somewhere before."

CHAPTER 2

"Understood."

Getting the sense that a village, fog, zombies, and a boat were all involved somehow, Cayna had Kee look through his vast database to find a quest that matched their current situation. She took this chance to face the zombie groans of "*Ughhh*" and "*Aghhh*" approaching from behind, and she threw the Flame Lance she had produced in her raised hand. Each spot the spears struck instantly carbonized, and Exis broke into a cold sweat as even the heat from the blasts pierced the hordes of zombies swaying behind Cayna's attacks.

"Overpowered as always, I see..."

"You said the same thing back when you were Tartarus."

"I told you—I'm Exis now!"

Exis's weapon of choice was a Dragon Blade about as long as a large dragoid. His equipment was different from the last time she saw him; he'd likely switched things up to better suit his current needs. This weapon, a *Leadale* original, was a type of longsword that had two crescent moonlike protrusions at the tip of the blade. The wielder used its massive heft to hack and chop up enemies in battle. When equipped by a level-630 dragoid, it was powerful enough to decimate a horde of zombies without even using any Weapon Skills.

Quolkeh wielded two weapons at once, and she switched between close and mid-range attacks in battle. The saber in her left hand was ideal for close combat, and she mostly used it to handle zombie attacks as she led them to Exis, who was charged with dealing the final blow. The chain whip in her right hand used Weapon Skill: Slicer to quickly intercept the shadows squirming in the fog. This was a technique that used high-speed whip rotations to shoot wind rings that cut the enemy in midair.

Before Cayna even had time to lend a hand, the zombies surrounding them had been swiftly eliminated and returned to dust.

"You guys are tag-team players, huh?"

"We've been... Er... Why, Exis and I have paired up for over a year now."

Quolkeh had managed this speech pattern somewhat decently at first, but she seemed off her game ever since her battle with Cayna.

The revelation of her true self had thrown her speech into disarray. Even Exis couldn't help but smirk.

"Anyway," Cayna began, "this fog situation matches several conditions from an earlier quest—one that gave you Active Skill: Fortify. The enemy bosses are the Ghost Ship and the pirate captain Terror Skeleton."

"Dang—I mean, goodness, you have quite a good memory..."

"Ah-ha-ha-ha-ha, well, I was waaay too into the game..."

"That's a Limit Breaker for ya," said Exis.

Cayna, of course, smiled and chose not to mention that she'd gotten this information from Kee's ridiculously huge database.

Leaving Quolkeh to keep a close eye on their surroundings, Cayna discussed the plan with Exis.

"...So what next?" he asked.

"We should burn the Ghost Ship and the Terror Skeleton, right?"

"You sure don't mince words."

"It's better than letting them target the next village."

"Can't argue that. Quolkeh! We're heading to the shoreline!"

"Huh? Oh, o-okay."

His sudden booming voice startled her, but she followed after Exis as he broke into a run. Cayna used fire arrows to launch a machine-gun-style attack and clear out any zombies or skeleton sailors that crossed their path.

"What *is* that...?" Quolkeh questioned.

"Just Cayna's normal way of dealing with chumps. Don't sweat it."

"...How is that normal...?"

CHAPTER 2

Cayna's definition of "normal" threw Quolkeh for a loop. The three of them raced through the blurred fog making wrong turns all the while. After a long bit of meandering, the three finally arrived at the shore; they would have reached it much sooner if they'd just continued straight forward.

The dilapidated Ghost Ship had run aground and was surrounded by a fog slightly weaker than other areas. A sour smell wafted in the air, and the visual stagnation was nausea-inducing. The blackish-brown body of the ship was like a well-soaked tree. The sails were dyed black, and they dangled in tatters. The gun turrets on its flanks were antiques whose operational capabilities were in serious doubt. For some reason, only the skull and crossbones on the flag of the lead mast was brand-new.

Just as Quolkeh murmured "Wow, what a dump," a horde of skeletons appeared on the deck and began unanimously rattling their teeth—*clack-clack-clack-clack!* They wore shabby sailor outfits and carried rusted swords.

"They look like they're protesting something...," Cayna observed.

"It's definitely 'cause of Quolkeh's comment."

"What?! It's *my* fault?!"

As Cayna and Exis looked up at the boat, their conversation sent Quolkeh into a panic.

"Wh-what should we do?"

"Just calm down. And Exis, stop trying to freak Quolkeh out!"

"Sorry, sorry, my bad. Anyway, I don't think they'll come down from there, but what's the plan? Punch our way through the hull and storm in?"

Exis swung his Dragon Blade with a low *whoosh* and set his sights on the ship.

"The Terror Skeleton is the core of the Ghost Ship. If we don't beat it first, the ship will use the souls of the zombie victims as fuel to endlessly reincarnate. It'll be a never-ending battle."

"Ah, that kinda quest, huh? Better get to it, then."

"At any rate, let's anchor the boat in place so it can't escape. Then we'll climb aboard."

As Quolkeh, the only clueless one, tilted her head, Cayna cast a spell.

Magic Skill: Underworld Lue Dune: Ready Set

"Drop!"

Directly beneath the Ghost Ship sitting upon the shore, a jagged line that shone with a black light raced across and snapped open without warning. The fissure split the beach and continued along the ocean's surface on the other side as well. The sea didn't surge up, but the Ghost Ship dropped like a rock into the opening. The magic was originally intended to swallow large enemies and seal them off before crushing them to death.

Cayna halted the spell halfway. This raised questions for Exis, who knew what the final result was supposed to be.

"Hey, Cayna! Why'd you stop?"

"An instant kill would be easy enough, but that'd defeat the whole purpose of us coming here. Just thinking about what that little girl went through churns my stomach. Unless the two of you have any reservations about this?"

"R-right. Sorry."

Cayna's glassy stare and low voice caused Exis to take a step back. He sensed her corresponding rage and nodded repeatedly. If he was being honest, those eyes alone looked like they could destroy him and much more. They were terrifying.

Thinking he'd better hurry up and get rid of the source of the fog before he found trouble with those eyes, Exis glared at the skeleton army on the deck, which was now directly adjacent to the land.

""*"Krik-krik-krik-krik...?*"""

Being stared down by a level-600+ dragoid seemed to somehow rattle even the skeleton army.

"Cayna, you act as backup! Quolkeh, you squash the small fry! I'll take down the boss."

"Gotcha."

"Huh? Uh, o-okay!"

Cayna cast Superior Physics Defense Up: Laga Proteck and Additional Holy Magic: Curell All in quick succession. The first spell significantly enhanced the trio's defense, while the second imbued their equipment with the holy attribute. The group's gleaming weapons were devastatingly effective against the zombies and skeletons. Since the magic's impact depended on the caster's power, the way the skeletons vanished at the slightest touch of Quolkeh's whip was highly amusing.

"Everything feels like a cinch now. What's going on?" she asked.

"Don't ever underestimate a Skill Master," Cayna replied.

She swung her magic staff and mowed down any of the close-range skeletons Quolkeh missed. Exis used a single swing of pure firepower to part the sea of skeletons like Moses, and he aimed for the Terror Skeleton arrogantly swaggering behind his minions.

"*Kak-kah-kah-kah!*"

"I don't understand what the hell you're sayin'!"

The Terror Skeleton, which had a saber in its right hand and a hook on the other, resisted Exis's fierce attack to a certain degree. However, it was around level 300. Seeing as it had no hope of winning against a dragoid who specialized in close combat and was over twice the Terror Skeleton's own level, a single stroke sliced it clean in half—head, saber, and all—and it turned to dust.

The moment the Terror Skeleton was defeated, the minion skeletons fell into piles of bones like puppets with cut strings and tumbled across the deck. Not soon after, the Ghost Ship slanted with a *plunk!*, and phosphorescent particles rose up. Together with the scattered light specks floating at random throughout the frame, the ship's image slowly faded.

The three rushed to jump overboard before they got tangled up in it.

"...Well, that sure didn't take long," Exis said.

"That's what happens when you're as powerful as me. Duh!" said Cayna.

Heaving his Dragon Blade onto his shoulder, Exis expressed disappointment while watching the light particles of the Ghost Ship dissipate in midair. As the ship and deck grew increasingly indistinct, the frame suddenly revealed the semitransparent white orbs inside. Countless numbers lifted into the heavens. They were the souls of the villagers who had fallen victim.

"This is gonna be a tough report to make," said Exis.

"What's gonna happen to the fishing village? ...Think it'll be abandoned?" Quolkeh wondered aloud.

"I doubt anyone will want to live in a village that got wiped off the map like it did. Its fate is for the country to decide, right?" Cayna replied.

The souls all escaped before the Ghost Ship finished turning completely to light. The fog then dispersed, and the sky was slowly dyed orange. Twilight reflected off the ocean. Even after the last particle of light disappeared, the three looked up at the orange sky until their melancholy abated. In the meantime, Cayna put her hands together and observed a moment of silence. Exis heard her murmur "Heigl. I've avenged you."

He seemed to think she'd involved helpless villagers in this mess, so he bellowed at her.

"What the hell?! Don't tell me you knew one of those people?!"

"That was my summoning. He got ambushed in the fog and disappeared."

"Oh, okay. I thought you were talking about a villager. Don't be vague like that! It's no wonder you were so resentful. So what'd you summon?"

"...A level-250 centaur."

CHAPTER 2

"Waiting ten days to summon it again must be tough, huh?"

"Yeah."

Having your summoning shot down didn't mean losing it forever. However, you had to wait the same number of hours as your summoning's level before you could call on it again.

It was a good example of how a high level meant more restrictions.

It was then that Exis noticed that Quolkeh had been acting strangely quiet. He soon grew fed up with the way she nervously glanced at Cayna.

"Hey! Quolkeh!"

"...?! Huh? What?"

"What're you zonin' out for? Not feelin' so hot?"

"N-no. I'm just a bit..."

She was trying to show otherwise, but her movements were breaking down and becoming increasingly robotic. Something was definitely up.

"If something's bothering you, I'm open to questions. It'll cost you, though," Cayna stated.

"Um, well, I heard something strange just now. I was wondering if I was mistaken."

"'Something strange'?"

"'Mistaken'?"

Neither Cayna nor Exis had any idea what she was talking about, and they tilted their heads in unison. Seeing that she wasn't getting through to the pair, Quolkeh steeled herself and turned to Cayna.

"You said 'Skill Master' a short while ago, right?"

"Oh, that," Cayna replied with an understanding nod. She did remember saying that to Quolkeh after shocking her with an impressive display of magic.

However, Exis clapped his hands as if in recollection, pointed to Cayna, and added, "She's also the Silver Ring Witch!"

"Wha—?! ...The...the...the Silver Ring Witch?!"

"Huh?"

It was no exaggeration to say that all except a few who encountered the Silver Ring Witch—that is, Cayna in her special equipment with a silver ring floating around her waist—were traumatized in some way.

Seeing as Cayna didn't know the horrified Quolkeh's circumstances, Exis provided further explanation.

"Apparently, she witnessed a horrible tragedy."

"Don't call it that," Quolkeh retorted.

This exchange alone was enough for Cayna, who had been present at the event, to realize what was going on. Her heart didn't want to accept it, but she had no choice.

Three incidents had spread Cayna's alias throughout Leadale: the Monthly Battle of Three Nations, the Monster Raid Outbreak Event in the Blue Kingdom capital, and the Monster Raid Outbreak Event in the Brown Kingdom capital.

The main cause in particular was a version update that went into effect just before the event in the Brown Kingdom. This trial update added a function that allowed range attacks to damage buildings.

Seconds after the event began, the Brown Kingdom capital turned into a massive air raid of burning fields and flying debris. Although NPCs weren't affected, the incident went down as the biggest disaster in MMO gaming history. There was indeed some damage from enemy monsters, but in all honesty, the biggest contributor was the meteorite bombing raids. Any players who happened to be present soon witnessed the town turn to rubble thanks to the hunks of rock falling from the sky.

Not long afterward, footage of the disaster went viral on the Internet. The Admins fixed this trial version and restored the Brown Kingdom capital to its former self. However, seeing as the city had already once been destroyed, many began calling it the Abandoned Capital, and the number of affiliated adventurers severely declined. Of course, whispers of Cayna's infamous alias, the Silver Ring Witch, traveled as well. Needless to say, she didn't show her face in official battles for quite some time after that.

The western sky was growing a deeper orange, so Cayna talked things over with Exis, and they decided to make camp there for the night. Although the threat of the Ghost Ship had finally been taken care of, that wasn't to say nothing else might attack them. Cayna set up a heavy barrier around the area. Since visibility would be poor and there'd be no place to escape, the group also voted against using one of the unoccupied houses. After determining the patrol order, the three went to pick up Roxilius and Luka.

"What's gonna happen to Luka now?" Cayna wondered aloud.

"Maybe she'll stay here if that's what she wants…"

"A kid all on her own? Sounds risky, if you ask me—uh, I daresay."

Exis viewed Cayna's murmurings with long-term insight, while Quolkeh expressed concern.

When Cayna released the barrier on the storehouse and opened the door, she saw Roxilius standing there with Luka. He greeted them with an "Excellent work, everyone" and bowed.

Luka, on the other hand, shook off the cat-eared butler's hand, looked out across the empty village with tear-filled eyes, and ran toward one house in particular.

"…M-Mom…!"

As her reedy voice rang out in desperation, Exis and the others watched in heartbreak. After nodding in reply to the look Roxilius gave her, Cayna followed Luka into the house. The butler gave a respectful bow, then took firewood from a nearby house and used its kitchen to prepare dinner.

* * *

Her vision was murky. There was the smell of burnt, rusted iron mixed with flesh and hair, as well as other charred things she didn't want to imagine. Clouds spread across the blue sky like a haze.

Something that only a short while before had been her parents was lying on top of her, pinning her down. She sobbed and continued to call out her parents' names until her voice grew hoarse, and she eventually fainted from dehydration.

When she awoke, she was in the hospital. Her cousin was looking at her with tears in her eyes.

"Mom… Dad…!"

As Cayna listened to Luka race around the house, the girl's forlorn cries and the sound of every door frantically opening and closing overlapped with Cayna's own memories. The pain, frustration, and sadness that felt like it would crush her very soul came rising up within Cayna all over again, and she gripped her hands tightly. She knew the agony of suddenly losing loved ones who had been happily chatting right next to you only moments before. She understood it so well it hurt.

The sounds within the house suddenly stopped. As soon as she heard sobbing, Cayna stepped inside.

There was the dining table, where the three-person family once discussed their days together.

"UWAAAAAAAAAAAAAAAAGH!!"

The little girl clung to one of the chairs and trembled as large tears poured down her cheeks. She lifted her head with a gasp at the sound of Cayna's footsteps, but upon realizing the newcomer wasn't who she hoped for, her sorrow spilled out all over again.

At this rate, she could see Luka becoming like her own former self. Her old self from only a few years earlier who closed off her hardened heart and failed to recognize the people who were always by her side and cheering her on. Her old, weak self who thought she had nothing more to lose.

Thus, Cayna would try to teach Luka that she would always be there for her.

Cayna wouldn't push her or force the girl to notice her. The time spent quietly with someone simply by Cayna's side had been so precious. She was deeply grateful to her uncle and cousin; now she would pay it forward and offer Luka the same.

Cayna crouched by the girl and rubbed her back slowly and gently. She continued doing so until Luka calmed down and could regain a little peace of mind.

"I'm gonna take care of Luka."

"I see…"

Holding Luka after she cried herself to sleep, Cayna returned to the campsite, where Exis and the others were waiting. Exis and Quolkeh had already finished eating, and Roxilius wordlessly began reheating food for her.

Cayna laid the sleeping girl across her lap, covered her in the blanket provided by Roxilius, and ate quietly. The dinner consisted of a boiled vegetable-and-meat soup and a slightly hard bread packed with preservatives. Apparently, Exis and Quolkeh had given Roxilius whatever ingredients they'd had on hand. Each house had its own store of usable items, but the two had said they didn't use these for safety and sanitation reasons.

The group sat in a circle around what appeared to be the village plaza, and a bright bonfire burned between them. The Flame Spirit that had accompanied Luka was in charge of this. It kept an eye on the perfect flames while adding a log on occasion. Cayna cast a shadow over Luka so the light wouldn't hit her.

After he finished cleaning up, Roxilius stood at attention behind Cayna. She told him multiple times that he ought to sit, but he stubbornly replied, "This is a butler's duty," and refused to move from his position. She eventually gave up.

Exis had apparently suggested the plaza as their campsite since, after a bit of investigation, it turned out that the charm protecting the village from monsters had dissolved. He wanted to be ready in the event large monsters showed up as he anticipated.

Roxilius, who had little experience camping outdoors in this world, openly went along with this line of thinking.

After Cayna finished eating, everyone kept their voices low as they once again began discussing their current situation.

First, there was the matter of Cayna's own circumstances. After Cayna briefly summarized everything that had happened since her time in the hospital, Exis and Quolkeh nodded at the revelation that other players still existed. Cohral was primarily active in Felskeilo and Otaloquess, so the chances he'd run into Helshper-centered players like them were pretty low. Shining Saber was also a member of the knights, so meeting him was out of the question as well. Furthermore, any hope of seeing the bandit leader presently locked away in jail was essentially shot.

Exis's and Quolkeh's own journeys into this world had been very much like Cohral's and the others'. On that final day, they spent hours playing the game to their hearts' content until they passed through a dark space that made them think they'd been booted out, only to end up somewhere in modern Leadale.

They hadn't been fellow guild members like Shining Saber and Cohral, but Exis and Quolkeh were both in parties of their own at that fateful moment. However, their fellow party members were nowhere to be seen, and the two themselves had been tossed elsewhere. After that, each one found a village, learned about this new world, and met by chance at a tavern where they were both working

CHAPTER 2

part-time to pay off a dine-and-dash attempt. After that, they saved money and teamed up to become adventurers.

"And you did all that as a duo instead of a team of six, right?"

"Screw the rules... I mean, uh, forget the rules."

Quolkeh's true identity had already been revealed, but since Cayna wasn't the only newcomer with them this time, she was completely focused on returning to her old speech pattern. Since laughing would have been rude, Cayna stopped herself from pointing out all of Quolkeh's feminine contradictions.

"Well then, why don't we discuss the reward?"

Exis and Quolkeh looked at each other blankly as Cayna once again switched topics. The details of this incident would be primarily reported to the Adventurers Guild, which would in turn pay the reward. Therefore, the pair didn't know what she meant by "discussing the reward."

"Ah, I have no plans to butt in and claim I helped with your request. My goal is to get to the Palace of the Dragon King. What I'm trying to say is that although the whole ordeal left a bad aftertaste, you two cleared the event, so as Skill Master, I'll give you both Active Skill: Fortify. Do you need it? No?"

"What's it do?" Exis asked.

"It'll double or triple the value of one of your abilities for about thirty minutes. If you get really proficient with it, you'll be able to handle two or three abilities at the same time, but you'll be sluggish for a while after the effect wears off."

Since that tiredness was only a matter of numbers in the world of the game, Cayna was hit with major fatigue after the spell wore off for the first time. She'd tried it out while killing time in Felskeilo. Running around, flying, and jumping had been great, but she realized such a skill had its disadvantages in a protracted battle. There had been at least some value in giving it a whirl.

Quolkeh considered the pros and cons of what Cayna said. Exis thought for a moment as well, then asked, "Can I change it to something else?"

"Sure. You don't need that skill, right? Fine with me. Ask for whatever you like. But keep in mind that if you don't match the prerequisites, you won't be able to learn it even if I give it to you."

"I know. What I want is MP Conversion. You got that?"

"What a dumb question to ask a Skill Master. Still you gotta be pretty hard-core to want a skill like that..."

"Slashin' is faster than magic."

Special Skill: MP Conversion was a skill that warrior-type players consumed often. Rather than a skill, it was more like a one-use item that could be obtained repeatedly. Each time a player used it, it would convert 5 MP into the value of another ability. In other words, it was a unique skill that raised the value of your abilities (with the exception of leveling up).

No other skill could be used to rise up and break through the highest parameters set for each race. In the game world of Leadale, dragoids had the lowest amount of MP, but it wasn't as if they had none at all. Their INT was also low, so aside from casting support magic on themselves, dragoids had a far better chance of inflicting extensive damage on the enemy by slashing as opposed to using Attack Magic.

Dragoids who further excelled in magic were highly praised among players. Of the ones Cayna had met by chance and spoken with, it seemed to her that taking on such a challenge was a thorny path indeed.

Cayna swiftly used Scroll Creation and passed the resulting item to Exis. He immediately used it to convert 5 MP points to STR. What enemy in this world could go up against the level-600+ dragoid now? Frankly, Cayna was under the impression that neither the quest boss they'd gone up against that afternoon nor anything else could lay a scratch on him.

CHAPTER 2

"Have you decided, Quolkeh?"

"Hmm. Even if I ask for something else, it's not like I know every skill out there, y'know... Er, you see. I have no idea what to pick."

Cayna reflected on Quolkeh's battle talents that she just witnessed and had Kee pick out skills that prioritized agility and dexterity.

"Since you focus on physical attacks, how about something like Battle Speed Up, which boosts your attack speed, or Mirage, which improves evasion? The first one will increase your number of moves, while the second will create two clones of the user that move in different patterns to throw off your opponent..."

"Okay, I'll take Battle Speed Up...if you don't mind. It's magic, right?"

"It basically aids one target. Battle Speed Up II will allow you to cast on an entire party, but please complete a trial for that one."

Quolkeh took the scroll Cayna made and quickly activated it. She then opened her menu screen, read the explanation, and began checking how to use the skill.

Exis gave a bored look at the word *trial* and sulked.

"Cayna's tower, huh...? I heard it's way easier than the others. Where's it now?"

"In northeastern Felskeilo, near the Helshper border. I'm also managing other towers right now, so you can use the Battle Arena in Felskeilo and the Crescent Moon Castle in Helshper, too. There's also the Palace of the Dragon King, where I'm headed next. Oh, but the Crescent Moon Castle used to belong to Opus, so I can't say I'd recommend it."

"Geh. That's the House of Murder and Malice, right...? I've seen it before; the gimmicks inside don't match the exterior at all. Still, you're running those now?"

"Ah, well, about that..."

Cayna brought the two up to speed on the thirteen Skill Masters and the management of their towers. Of course, the information she'd discovered included skill exchange as well.

Quolkeh listened with rapt attention. Stuck in an environment where none of her real-life friends played the game, she'd apparently only been able to depend on players she met while logged in for firsthand game info. Exis had pretty much been teaching her the basic facts on his own these past two years, but unfortunately, the two had been so preoccupied with surviving that he hadn't been able to fully go over core parts of the game.

Cayna further told them what she'd hear from Cohral about the mysteriously updating friend list.

"I see. In that case, I wonder if maybe I passed by another player somewhere. Sadly, 'Exis' is a second account, so I haven't been paying attention to stuff like that. It also looks like Quolkeh has a pretty small friend list."

"Here you are, Master."

With an explanatory gesture, Roxilius handed Cayna a wet towel from behind. This was enough for her to realize she'd unwittingly raised her voice to normal volume. She looked down and saw Luka staring at her blearily.

"......Mm...?"

"Oh, sorry, did I wake you?"

Cayna placed a hand to her forehead and moaned in failure. Luka's eyes gradually focused as she stirred. However, she swayed shakily and leaned against Cayna once again. After covering Luka back up with the blanket, Cayna gently sat the girl on her lap and simply asked, "Are you okay?"

"......Mm......"

Luka replied with a downcast gaze, then listlessly locked eyes with Exis and Quolkeh sitting on the other side of the bonfire. Exis's voice was gentle as he nodded and said, "You can go back to sleep."

CHAPTER 2

Quolkeh was unsure of how to respond, and Exis smacked her with an apologetic look.

"Idiot. Don't look so gloomy in front of the kid."

"Ow, that freakin' hurt! That ain't anything to randomly smack me for!"

"Language, Quolkeh, language."

"Uh, well... I-isn't hitting people so suddenly...c-cruel?"

"*Pfft.*"

"...Hey..."

Roxilius poured hot milk from a small kettle cast with an Insulation effect into a wooden cup and handed it to Luka.

Luka looked around at the silent village lit by firelight, her expression distant, and Cayna noticed her gaze cloud over as the girl reaffirmed their situation. Unable to hold back any longer, she squeezed Luka tight.

Exis stood and approached the flustered Luka in Cayna's arms.

"Luka."

"...Mm."

Luka's eyes met those of the gray dragoid as she answered him with a weak nod.

"Cayna says she'll take care of you, but what do you wanna do? Stay here in the village by yourself? Or maybe come with us?"

A few moments passed before she slowly shook her head. Even at her age, Luka naturally understood that orphaned children had no choice but to survive on their own or die by the roadside. If this were the big city, she might have been able to scrape by somehow, but in a rural fishing village far from any metropolis, you had no right to complain if you took one step outside and got attacked by a monster. Not only that, this village was no more and lacked the walls to keep out said monsters.

Luka squirmed around to look at Cayna and nodded as a way of saying *Please take care of me.* Cayna smiled and slowly nodded back;

Li'l Fairy flitted about in midair. From her expression, she seemed to be doing a happy dance.

"There, there. I know it's not gonna happen all at once, but I hope we can become family, Luka. I also have two sons and a daughter back in Felskeilo, and two grandchildren in Helshper. I'll introduce you to them if there's ever a chance."

"……Mm."

Luka's blank-faced nodding aside, Exis, who had returned to his spot on the other side of the bonfire, sat stock-still, breaking into a cold sweat. Quolkeh looked at her speechless partner strangely. "What's wrong? You don't look so good, Exis."

"Th-three kids and two grandkids?! Since when did you get married?!"

Cayna's immediate thought was to freeze Exis in ice, but she didn't want to scare Luka and stopped herself just in time. Instead, Li'l Fairy voluntarily floated over and gave him an upward kick right on the tip of his nose.

"Gyagh?!"

The adorable gesture provoked a not-so-adorable reaction: Exis grabbed his nose and fell over. Li'l Fairy crossed her arms and puffed out her cheeks before swishing her hair as if to say *Hmph!* and returning to Cayna's shoulder.

After lying there trembling and holding his nose for a significant amount of time, Exis finally sat up with tears in his eyes.

"Gaaagh, that huuurt… I—I thought I was gonna die…"

"What'd she do?" Cayna asked.

"She sent a straight line of pain all the way from my nose to my brain. W-wait! I'm sorry, okay?"

Exis apologized to Li'l Fairy, who was leaning forward threateningly from Cayna's shoulder. Cayna herself had no clue why the fairy's actions would cause that much pain. She didn't understand, but considering it was Opus who had left her the fairy, such abilities didn't seem beyond the realm of reason.

"You would have figured it out if you'd been listening to anything I said! My kids are from the Foster System. My grandkids were born the usual way!"

"Nnnghhh. Sorry. I was just messin' with you."

Cayna shot Exis a dirty look as he raised a hand in apology.

"You're totally different from the Tartarus I used to know. You sure that was your true self back then?"

"You got it all wrong. Isn't it obvious from one look at everyone in the Cream Cheese guild? Messin' with tough members like that was pointless. I was happy enough just to keep quiet and stay out of trouble."

He did have a point. There was no question that all the members had a quirk or two. At the time, Tartarus would mediate to prevent discord and act as the voice of reason. Nevertheless, Cayna didn't think he had to be so heavy-handed about it here. After all, it made her all too aware of how much she'd let loose back then, too.

"The heck are you talkin' abo—? Whatever do you mean?"

Quolkeh was the only one still in the dark.

"Basically, the Cream Cheese guild was full of troublemakers," Exis replied.

"I only heard rumors, but apparently when wars broke out, any camp with that guild on their side was a freakin' powerhouse… I mean, had a major advantage," Quolkeh replied.

"We had no choice but to become game addicts if we wanted to keep up with the strongest. And a group of game addicts meant a group of people as far from normal as possible."

Quolkeh tilted her head as Exis answered with an air of self-deprecation. Although since Tartarus himself had been a member of the guild, that made him an addict as well to a degree.

Cayna, too, was well aware of what made her guild so unusual.

Since Cayna could move freely only within the game, logging in was the most fun she ever had the chance to have.

Opus didn't spill every last detail, but he was allegedly a player sent from the administrative company. He would do full investigations of the quests and system for the higher-ups and report any bugs or malfunctions. Thanks to this, he had strangely in-depth knowledge of all the hidden tricks and shortcuts. Cayna remembered how he would often get mixed up in proposals of this nature, and even she would cross countless bridges she never had any intention of crossing.

The guild sub-leader, on the other hand, would go on and on about real-life stories Cayna really didn't want to hear about. Apparently, the woman worked at night and logged in during the day to kill time. Her habit of rambling on and on among mixed company about her graphic IRL experiences earned her the nickname Sin City.

The one Cayna knew the least about was the guild leader. When the evening news came up in conversation, he would cover everything from the legislator who appeared on TV to questions about invasion of privacy. He spoke casually of things that would cause an uproar if the media heard. He walked a dangerously thin line, and it soon became an ironclad rule of the guild that no one could bring up real-life topics in front of him.

Looking back, even Cayna now thought, *We didn't have a single decent soul, did we?*

The biggest mystery was how everyone in a group like that possibly managed to pass the Limit Breaker quest. Cayna had thought that everyone was surprisingly normal deep down, but now the truth would never come to light.

Leaving the three to excitedly chatter on about the old guild, Luka dipped her bread in leftover soup and reluctantly ate it with Roxilius's assistance.

CHAPTER 2

* * *

The next morning.

Since they had laid out capes and blankets to lie on while they slept on the hard ground, Exis and the others worked out all the aches and pains from their bodies as soon as they woke up. Their stretches took an immense amount of effort.

"Damn that Cayna. How come she's the only one who gets to be comfy?"

"N-now, now. We don't have the skills for something like that, so it is what it is," Quolkeh replied.

Cayna was the only one who had pulled out a bed, which she shared with Luka, from somewhere in her Item Box. She'd been thinking of making one for her house back in the remote village and tirelessly worked on it in her free time.

Incidentally, the night guards had been Roxilius, who presumably needed neither rest nor sleep, and Cayna's Night Strix, a two-meter-tall pure-black owl.

After breakfast, Cayna made plans to dive straight into the sea.

Exis volunteered to stay ashore and guard Luka. However, opinions were divided, and Quolkeh insisted they quickly report to the proper authorities that the pair's standard request had ended in a worst-case scenario and the destruction of two fishing villages.

Both appeared to be on the verge of a verbal battle, so Cayna stepped in and offered to send them back to the Helshper capital via magic once she'd done what she needed to do. The conversation was then allowed to continue.

"Come to think of it, *are* you gonna send us back with magic? Shooting us over a parabola?"

"Hell, no! Uh, I mean, of course not."

Exis and Cayna gave looks of *What's with her?* and narrowed their eyes in exasperation at Quolkeh's outrageous reply.

"You can also use Teleport to transport people other than yourself, too," said Cayna. "The destination has to be a place I know, though. Outside Helshper's western gate will work, right?"

"What?! Can't you plop us right in the city? —Ow!"

Exis took a whack at Quolkeh's face.

"You idiot! Sure, let's go ahead and try to suddenly show up in the middle of town even though we've got no clue who's watching!" yelled Exis. "They'll mistake us for some sort of miscreants and toss us in jail before we can even sneak in!"

Sneaking in wasn't a problem if the two didn't get caught, but Cayna, the key figure here, wasn't aware of any place she could send them that was trouble free. That was why she decided to drop them outside the town gate.

"I'm just gonna hop over and activate the Palace of the Dragon King first, so you guys take good care of Luka. *Got it?*"

"Quit starin' me down with those scary, bloodshot eyes! Your butler is here, too, so she'll be fine."

Cayna, who had just been looming over Exis with an ogreish expression, instantly changed her tune when she crouched to Luka's eye level.

"I'm sorry, Luka. I've got some work to do, but just wait here for a little while, okay?"

Luka gripped the edge of Roxilius's pant leg and gave a small, delayed nod as Cayna stood up as fast as lightning.

"Look after her for me, Roxilius."

"I will protect her on my very—"

"If you give your life to protect her, you'll be subjecting Luka to the gruesome sight! Protect her and don't die. Okay?"

"...U-understood."

CHAPTER 2

Cayna's overpowering gaze hit Roxilius like a ton of bricks, and she came within less than an inch of his nose. She only relaxed after watching him nod multiple times.

"Your protective-mommy side is already getting worse...," Exis murmured with an annoyed expression.

Paying him no mind, Cayna walked toward the water's edge and faced what she had summoned.

"I know your magic and summonings are all incredible across the board...but why *that*?" Exis asked.

Taking up a good chunk of the beach was a long, enormous blue creature. Luka, who clung close behind Roxilius, had never seen such a huge, majestic presence, and her eyes widened with shock. Quolkeh, still a *Leadale* newbie, gaped with amazement as well. The only ones who remained unmoved were Exis and Roxilius.

The creature waiting behind Cayna was a fifty-meter-long Blue Dragon. She had just called upon the greatest of the dragons with Summoning Magic: Dragon. Like the Brown Dragon, Leadale's Blue Dragons were unable to fly; instead, they sported an enormous, marlin-like fin that ran from the tip of their heads all the way to the ends of their tails. It was a unique characteristic ideal for gliding through water. The dragon had short horns that began at the bridge of the nose and extended over the eyelids, four solid limbs, and webbed fingers. At first glance, one would think the creature was a streamlined alligator.

"To be honest, I can't swim. Since that means I can't move through the water, I thought I'd hang on to something that'll do the swimming for me."

Quolkeh held her head in her hands as Cayna proudly boasted that she'd be swimming along like a suckerfish. Exis wordlessly patted her shoulder and shook his head with a smile as if to say *Think too hard, and you've already lost*. As Tartarus, he'd been forced to go along with the other Cream Cheese members' outrageous behavior on more than a few occasions, so he knew a thing or two. The main takeaway was *Just smile and ignore it.*

Cayna had switched into her Black Dragon Suit beforehand, and Exis was on the verge of making a comment when her glare speedily silenced him. After stroking Luka's head, she grabbed hold of one of the Blue Dragon's horns and dove into the ocean.

As soon as they saw her off, Exis called to Quolkeh. Of course, they left Luka with Roxilius and moved a distance away so they wouldn't be overheard. The group remained vigilant of their surroundings. Roxilius was level 550 thanks to having Cayna as his summoner, so neither imagined there'd be any slipups.

"Hey, where do you think that Ghost Ship came from?" Exis asked.

"...? It was a Skill Event, wasn't it?"

Quolkeh's response was the most obvious one a player could give. However, such would only be the case if they were still in an MMORPG.

"A Skill Event that wasn't even initiated by an NPC? I don't remember any event involving the destruction of two villages. So where do you think the Ghost Ship sprang up from? I'd heard of events where pirates took over sea trade routes, but based on what we learned while watchin' Cayna, the Ghost Ship event should've only existed as a quest."

"Now that you mention it, the people of this world are pretty wimpy—er, frail. I also noticed there are way less field monsters than back in the game. Must be 'cause this world is nothing like the old one."

The average player level had been between level 400 and level 600. Players over level 900 made up less than 5 percent of the total population. This meant that as long as you kept to most general areas, a maximum of level 600 would more than suffice. Those who wished to go all out typically grinded as much as they could in the Heaven and Underworld Maps, also known as the Advanced Areas. Once you went there, you were officially an addict like Cayna and her crew. *Leadale*'s high degree of difficulty made it a decent game overall, but so many other things made it such a blast to play with friends.

This was also reflected in the quest events, and in all the time Tartarus spent leveling up, he'd seldom seen an event that left as bad a taste in his mouth as the destruction of the two villages had. Originally, two level-400 players should have been more than enough to take on the Ghost Ship. That was what Cayna had said anyway.

"Wanna add this to the report?" Exis asked.

"Won't it end up being a matter of getting them to believe the words of a two-hundred-year-old human?"

The mere fact that Quolkeh was human made her less than convincing. If the person in charge asked her, *How have you been able to live for two hundred years?* she'd be at a loss on how to answer.

"Guess we'll just report we were attacked by the Ghost Ship," Exis concluded.

"If we start going off on a crazy story, they're gonna call in some councillors to question us. I'm not exactly a fan of those guys—they ask the same things over and over again," Quolkeh said as she rubbed her temples with displeasure and turned toward Helshper.

Quolkeh recalled having once run into trouble with the nobility and the subsequent interrogation by several councillors. She'd gotten so sick of hearing the same endless questions.

"Not much helpin' it. Two villages is a big deal. If we don't tell the top brass what's going on, all our work will be for nothing."

"True. There's only so much we can do as adventurers, after all."

As Exis listened to her mild comments, he looked out upon the surface of the sea and wondered if there was anything Cayna couldn't do.

*　　＊　　＊*

Fortified by Underwater Breathing and Underwater Movement, Cayna held on to the Blue Dragon's horn and dove deeper into the sea.

Cayna would have had a hard time without Underwater Movement, a support spell that allowed the user to move in water as they did on land. Otherwise, her stats would decrease by half across the board, and her attack power would be reduced to less than a tenth of its normal strength.

To Cayna, diving beneath the water was like exploring unknown territory. Even with her Black Dragon Suit equipped, she wasn't entirely at ease.

The Blue Dragon's size and Cayna's Intimidate skill scattered the fish obstructing her path. Many looked like those found on Earth, and they came in species of all sorts.

However, even Cayna herself had no time to take in the sights. She'd been unable to obtain information in the village about the location of the Palace of the Dragon King, so with the simultaneous help of Night Vision and Eagle Eyes, she searched for its whereabouts while gauging the reaction of her Guardian Ring. She occasionally had the Blue Dragon stop so she could point the ring in different directions and see which way it lit up.

After a number of primitive search attempts, she finally got a reaction in a shallow area not even twenty meters below the surface. It was the sort of place even fishermen could have discovered while free diving, so she'd overlooked it. The mere name *Palace of the Dragon King* brought to mind the deepest depths of the sea, so her efforts felt horribly wasted when she finally found it.

The area was a flat plain surrounded by coral and glowing with a green light. Within it, the Palace of the Dragon King sat in full view as if to say *Ta-daa!*

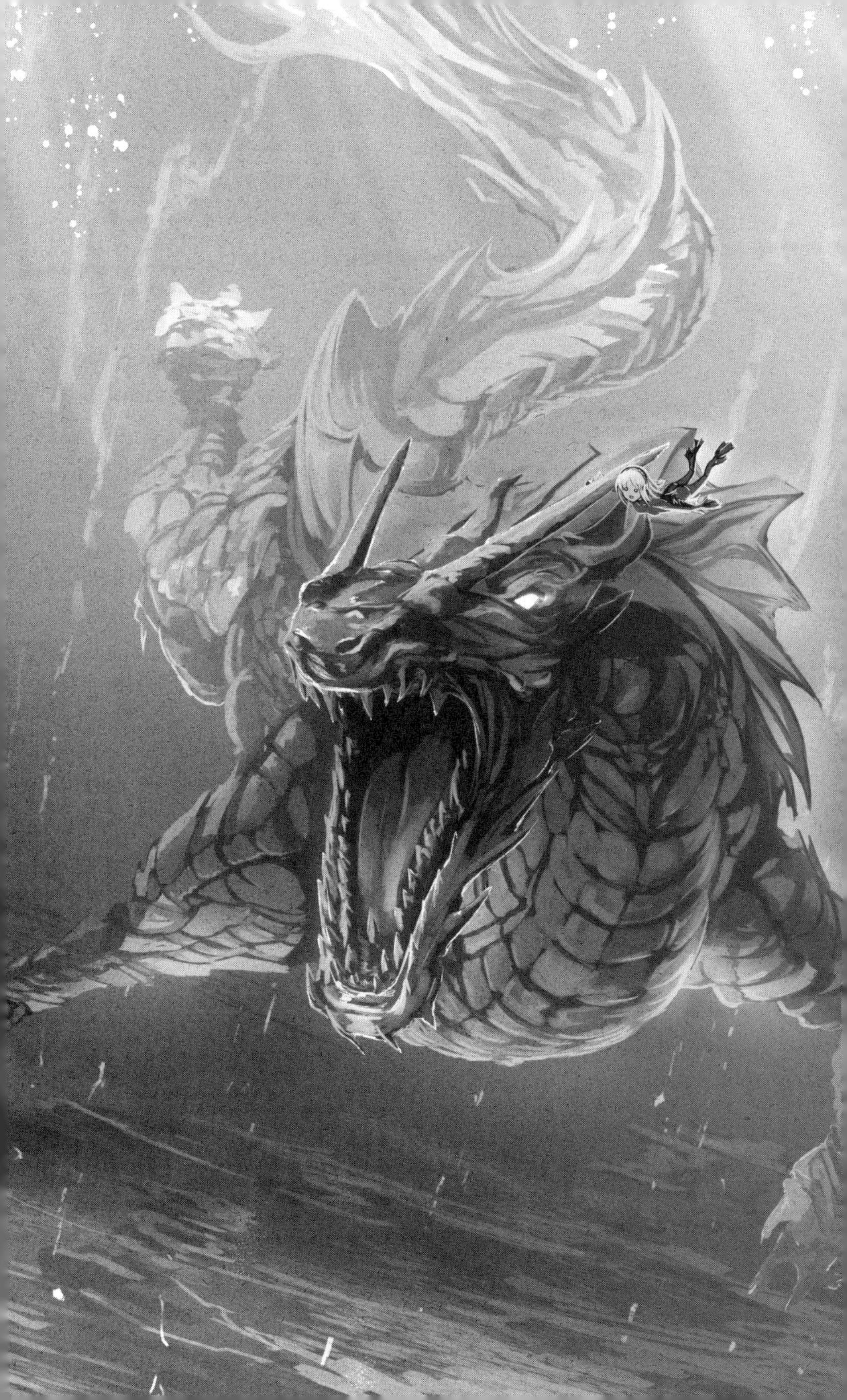

The structure looked like some sort of eye-catching tourist attraction. The foundation was white, and the building was a noticeable red. It was surprisingly compact, like a house you'd find in a sprawling metropolis. From what she had heard, some sort of raging monster protected the palace, but there was no sign of any such creature.

"Perhaps that is a separate feature?"

Kee's hypothesis gave Cayna an overall picture. Since the castle had run out of magic, it could no longer call upon its defensive magical beast.

The Blue Dragon kicked up sand as it landed among the coral reefs.

"Blue Dragon, look around and see if there are any mermaid villages nearby."

The Blue Dragon closed its eyes to signal its acknowledgment, then wriggled its body and moved beyond the shallows that surrounded them to dive deeper into the depths of the sea.

The Guardian Ring shone pink, and Cayna raised it high as she called out the password in a clear voice.

`"One who protects in times of trouble! I beseech you to rescue this depraved world from chaos!"`

Her vision warped, and she passed through a whirlpool that dropped down from above. It wasn't long before Cayna was thrown into a vast space. The instability of her landing caused her to stumble.

The red Chinese-style room was completely covered in water like a lake. Round lotus flowers big enough for a person to ride were floating all over. She had ended up on one of them.

Upon taking a look around, she saw a flower bud as big as a human head sticking out in the center of the lake. Guessing this was the tower's core, Cayna poured half her MP into it. After a short while, its flower petals slowly opened, and a large, light-pink lotus flower bloomed.

CHAPTER 2

"*Phew...* Finally got the third one down. This place sure was far."

Now that everything had turned out like this, Cayna wished she'd asked all the Skill Masters the locations of their towers ahead of time. It was too late for that now, though. The biggest problem was that she didn't even know whether one might be in the sky or another in some unexplored area.

As she pondered all this, a sound came from behind her, and an adorable voice like the peal of bells called out.

"**Hmmmm? Do we have a visitorrrrr?**"

"Yes, are you this tower's Guard— Huh?!"

Cayna was so preoccupied thinking about Luka that she'd inadvertently forgotten the peculiarities of this tower's Skill Master. She turned around and was struck speechless by the enshrined speaker's appearance.

A protruding mouth. Glossy, slimy skin. Dewy eyes that bulged even farther than its mouth. A googly-eyed stare that regarded her with a mixture of black and gold. A body that was more stout than slim. Front feet that gathered beneath its chin. Folded back legs that spread out in opposite directions. A crown between the eyes. It looked just like a toy, and its entire body was so blindingly pink that it hurt to look at. In fact, Cayna didn't *want* to look at it at all.

Gulping back the scream she almost let escape, Cayna gave herself an internal pep talk.

"This isn't an enemy, this isn't an enemy. It's actually on your side."

Frankly, if she hadn't known any better, she probably would have blown the Guardian away with her greatest Fire Magic right then and there. However, there was still the question of whether that would even do anything...

This tower's Guardian was a pink tree frog that stood at Cayna's eye level. It was about the size of a cow.

She made sure to avoid eye contact as she asked it the usual questions in a trembling voice.

"A-are you the Guardian of this tower?"

"Aye, that I ammm. I'm the Sixth Skill Master's Guardiaaan."

"O-okay… I'm Cayna, the Third Skill Master. Pardon my intrusion—I've come here in the hopes you'll let me restart this tower. I'm sorry I'm not your real master, but do you think you could bear with me?"

"Very wellll. After all, I did not expect my masterrr to returrrn. Will youuu be my masterrr from now onnn?"

Cayna assumed from this reaction that Liothek would never visit her Guardian again. She was glad that the frog was able to figure out what she was there for before things got complicated; that saved a lot of time. Its languid speech was a bit of a drawback, but Liothek spoke with a similar affect, so Cayna muttered to herself that it was probably a personal preference.

The bright-pink frog opened its mouth, which was big enough to swallow a person whole, and unfurled its tongue. A Guardian Ring sat at the very tip.

Of course, Cayna's initial reaction was to recoil from the slippery sliminess, but she steeled herself and picked it up. She was relieved to find that, contrary to appearance, it was not dripping with saliva.

"Thank you, I'll take good care of it. Please reach out to my mural Guardian if you need any further information."

"Understooood."

After replenishing herself with a potion and maxing out the core's MP, Cayna left the tower.

She ended up floating in the ocean until her Blue Dragon located her and brought her back to the surface, but that would remain a secret.

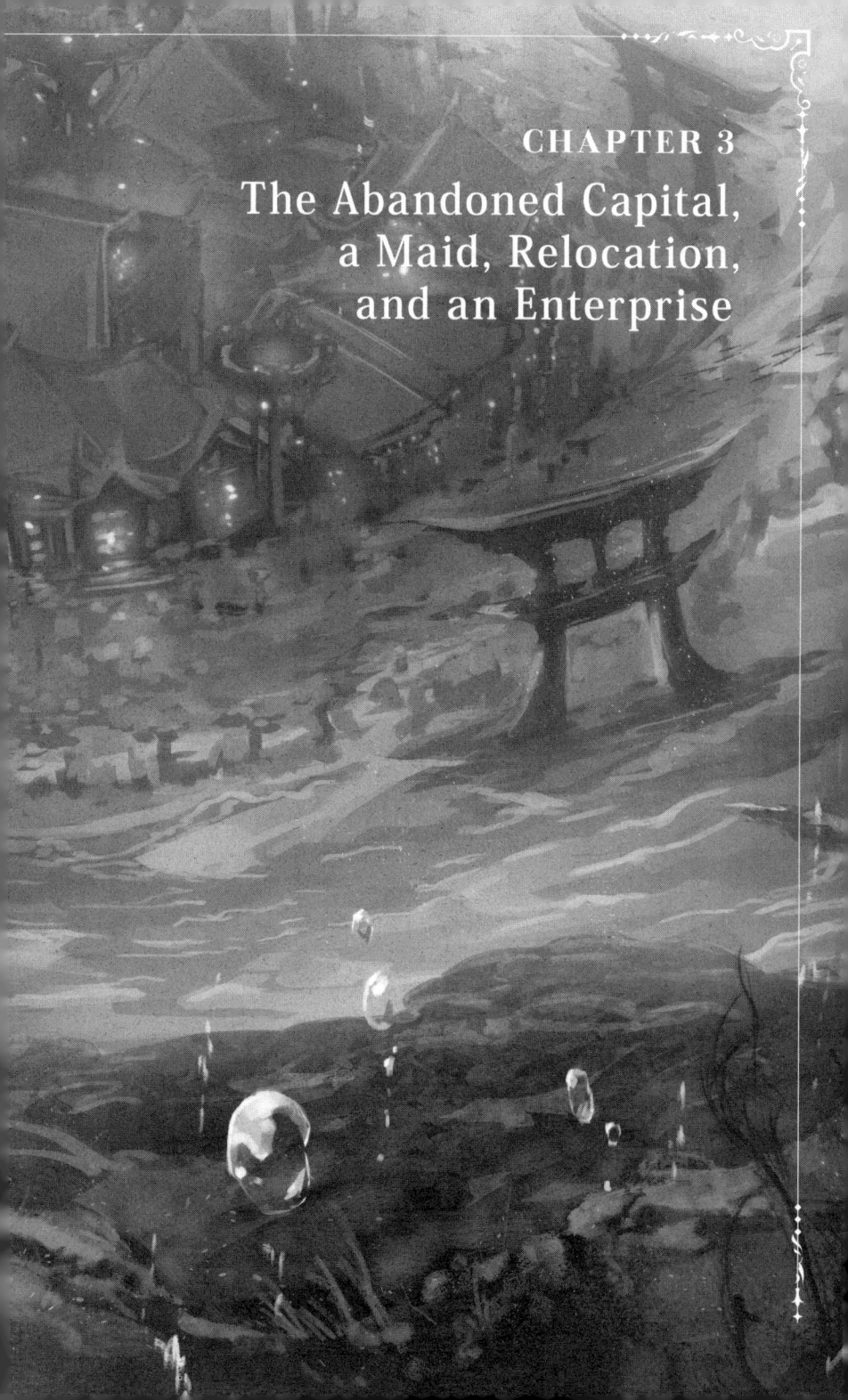

CHAPTER 3
The Abandoned Capital, a Maid, Relocation, and an Enterprise

Luka ran straight to Cayna when she returned to shore after completing her mission. Roxilius stopped the girl just in time so she wouldn't get wet.

"You'll get soaked if you come any closer, so just wait a minute, okay?" Cayna told Luka.

She switched out her dripping wet-suit-type Black Dragon Suit and was back in her normal equipment an instant later. Her hair was still wet, so she cast Dry and Purity. After she finished, she once again took Luka in her arms. She then ordered the Blue Dragon, which peeked its head out from between the waves, to continue looking for any mermaid villages.

She didn't believe there was anything in the area that posed a threat to the dragon, so it could probably linger for several more days as long as it didn't get caught up in a battle. The monster gave a single roar, then grinned as it sank into the sea. The dragon would be able to contact her if it found anything.

"I'm back, Luka. Thanks for looking after her, Rox."

"Think nothing of it. It is my duty."

"...Welcome...back."

Such cheerful conversation made them the very picture of a happy family. Smirking, Exis and Quolkeh approached the trio.

"Looks like we had nothin' to worry about. How was the Palace of the Dragon King? See any porgy and flounder dancing around?" Exis asked.

"...Does a hot-pink frog count...?"

"The heck...?"

Cayna quietly murmured her findings with a somewhat pale expression. "Still," Quolkeh said, a curious expression on her face, "to think there'd be spells like that, too. I wonder if they'd have a lot of uses back in the game?"

"I take it you didn't do offline quests?" said Cayna.

After Cayna gave a simple explanation of skills obtained offline, Quolkeh looked the other way and laughed dryly. Apparently, she'd never realized Offline Mode even existed. The tutorial should have explained this to her when she first started the game, so if Quolkeh never knew, Cayna guessed she must have skipped through the tutorial.

Many of the skills obtained while building one's fortress in Offline Mode were rooted in daily life. Most were useless in the actual game and became prerequisites for Craft Skills. Conversely, you couldn't complete every quest if you didn't use Offline Mode to obtain the online Craft Skills.

"Anyway, I really owe you both one."

"Nah, it was nothin'. Luka was super well-behaved," said Exis.

While they were waiting for Cayna, Roxilius had gone ahead and gathered together all of Luka's personal belongings. These included a few changes of clothes and mementos of her parents. They'd been able to find only her mother's apron and her father's bracelet.

Later on, Quolkeh insisted they create graves. She had piled up a bunch of rocks as a collective headstone by the storehouse outside the village.

"Guess it wasn't a total wasted effort, eh?" said Quolkeh.

"You were gonna make actual headstones?!" exclaimed Cayna.

"Well, *you* definitely could...," added Exis. "Nah, never mind. It looks fine the way it is."

Luka joined them, and all five pressed their hands together in a gesture of prayer.

"Please don't worry. I will raise your daughter well."

"...Mom...D-Dad... Th-thank you."

"......"

"So sorry we couldn't save you."

"May you rest in peace..."

Each murmured their condolences in their own way and departed from the village. When they were a distance away, Cayna left Luka, who kept looking back at the village longingly, with Roxilius. She, Exis, and Quolkeh then added one another to their friend lists.

"Guess that makes four players now."

"I've only got you..."

Cayna sighed while Quolkeh slumped over dejectedly. Exis quickly opened his Command screen and deftly swiped through each window with dizzying speed.

Players couldn't view other users' screens, so he appeared to be typing in midair.

"Hmm. No trace of me even passing by other players," he said.

"And if you haven't seen anyone, then I haven't, either." Quolkeh shrugged in resignation when he saw Exis groan and place a hand on his chin.

"Anyway, you guys tend to wander around more than I do, right? Let me know if you find someone," said Cayna.

"Aren't you an adventurer, too?" Exis pointed out.

"Sorry, but I've got Luka depending on me now, and I'll be retiring to my remote village for a while."

When Cayna spoke of the village she owed so much to, Exis and Quolkeh quickly backed off without complaint. They treaded lightly when the subject of Luka came up and couldn't be too forceful.

At any rate, she decided to send the two back to Helshper like they originally planned.

"Well then, I'll send you on your way."

"What about you guys?" asked Exis.

"We'll work something out. I can't use Teleport now that I have Luka, but I'm guessing it'll be about a three-day journey back home."

"Just so y'know, your name will probably come up when we give our report. That okay?"

"Sure, but be careful."

"Huh?"

If the topic turned to fish distribution, the Merchants Guild would probably get wind of her. And if by some chance this reached Caerick's ears, he'd probably get involved somehow. Cayna felt bad, but sent Exis and Quolkeh on their way with a spell and secretly begged that they get the full Mighty Merchants Guild Leader Caerick experience if that ever happened.

She used a derivative of Teleport known as Transfer, which could be used only to transport other people. Since it was a spell that sent someone flying against their will, it was typically used to get rid of annoyances who wanted to monopolize hunting grounds. It was also used to make enemies in other popular hunting areas. Savvy people like Opus would drop foul-smelling bug monsters right in the middle of an enemy camp during a war. It was a form of harassment.

However, the will of the person sent flying could be ignored only if the sender's level was higher than their own. Since the traveler's consent was required otherwise, every nation had players that specialized in Teleporting people.

A dark curtain rose from Exis's and Quolkeh's feet and covered

CHAPTER 3

them completely. They both waved lightly to Luka and abruptly disappeared. Luka's face fell, and Cayna patted her head and crouched down to meet her at eye level, beaming at Luka to cheer her up.

"All right! Looks like it's you and me, Luka. Those two will be fine on their own, and we're sure to meet again somewhere, right?"

"...Yeah."

Luka's cheeks flushed as she gave a small nod and timidly took Cayna's hand. The corners of Roxilius's mouth naturally lifted as well as he looked upon the charming scene. The girls set off with him not far behind.

However, not even halfway through the day, Cayna summoned a creature while they were on the road. She figured a journey on foot would be difficult for Luka, who was still only a child.

The creature she had called upon was Sleipnir. Radiating majesty, it munched on Luka's hair as way of a greeting and demonstrated its playful love of people. However, Cayna harshly scolded it after Luka instantly burst into tears. This left Sleipnir somewhat depressed, but the creature did its best to keep them safe the whole way. They arrived in Felskeilo the following afternoon, and the horse disappeared after receiving praise from Cayna.

Otaloquess was a lush, forested nation that no one would believe was once half covered in desert. The royal castle was built long ago by a guild praised in this land for their booming prosperity. The guild houses formed by players past had built many a castle that paid no heed to eastern or western styles, and the ones that lasted into the modern day were occupied by royalty and used as mansions by the nobility.

Otaloquess Castle's foundation was buried at the edges and seemed to be part of the forest. The exterior coexisted with the giant trees that surrounded it, and even the interior had been invaded by ivy and foliage. However, the castle's residents weren't inconvenienced in the slightest. After all, this scene of nature was a fusion of the nation's unique magical techniques, and the plants acted as soldiers who eliminated any threat.

Many of those employed at the castle possessed skills that allowed them to communicate with plants like the high elves could. They would hear information from the castle's large, integrated forest and use this to bolster their defenses.

The section that might be called a castle town was spread out across the treetops, and one could travel anywhere they pleased via the suspension bridges between the enormous trees. The citizens lived in the tree trunks and branches, and aside from the dwarves, very few made their homes directly on the ground.

Elves were not the only ones who lived in the treetops; humans and eccentric dwarves were present as well. Even werecats and dragoids took up residence like it was any other town.

Gathered in the castle's throne room were various government officials, with Queen Sahalashade, who had been ruling Otaloquess for the past two hundred years, at the forefront. The purpose of the meeting was to carefully examine the reports their spies had brought back and fulfill the continental mission their nation had undertaken.

Standing before the queen were the three spies—including Cloffe—who had been dispatched to two separate nations for the express purpose of contacting Cayna. Whoever ran into her first in either the Felskeilo capital, the Helshper capital, or the remote village was tasked with negotiating with her.

In a word, the answer Cloffe had brought back from Cayna was "No."

"I see...," came the dull reply from Queen Sahalashade as she played with her waist-length hair that was pure black except for a

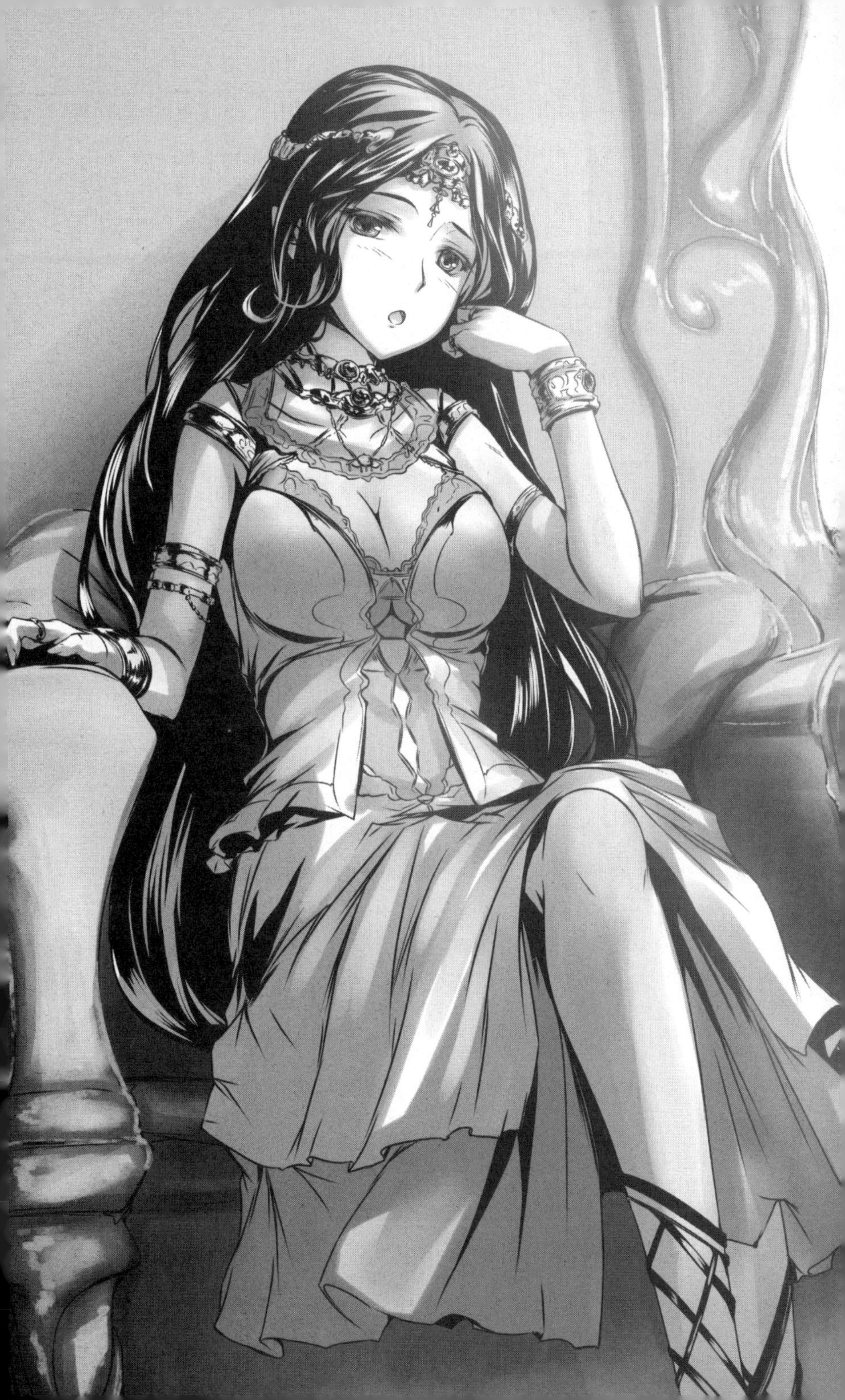

small bit of blue. Unlike Cayna, she was overflowing with womanly charm, and her regal gestures enchanted all.

Most of the vassals thought it too hasty to conclude this "Cayna" was the real deal by name alone. A majority of them were nobles from short-lived races, and amid the debate circling around, they harshly remarked, "She might be some relative from who knows where" and "There's a chance she'll try to steal the throne."

Queen Sahalashade listened with a cool expression as the information went in one ear and out the other, but the captain of the knights and the prime minister standing on either side of her were visibly perturbed.

They were upset, of course, but the main reason for their distress was the significant damage that occurred whenever one displeased a Transcendental.

At over three hundred years old, the captain of the knights was young for a demon. Two hundred years prior, he had witnessed a Transcendental comrade accomplish great things all on his own. This person, a vanguard-oriented melee fighter, rushed forward while the castle was under siege by the enemy and immediately took a swing of his large sword. With a single attack, he sliced both the fortress and the enemy in half. If the person they were now discussing had that same level of power, the word of the queen herself would bend.

Even the elderly dwarf prime minister had seen only two Transcendentals in his long life. The mere recollection of watching them drive out a plain full of monsters in an instant was enough for him to agree with the captain of the knights.

"I cannot agree to inviting a lowly adventurer from who knows where to the palace simply because she is related to the queen. We will stop such discussions in their tracks."

"Indeed. I see hardly any value in bringing her to our nation when we cannot vouch for her abilities."

CHAPTER 3

"Nor is there any guarantee this adventurer will not harm the queen."

Even the dukes and earls did not hold back their criticisms. The queen ignored them entirely.

As Cloffe stared at the officials with contempt, the captain of the knights nodded for him to continue.

"Fear not, for I have measured her abilities," said Cloffe. "I was highly impressed to find that my sister was no match for her."

The knights and soldiers stationed in the room let out admiring cries of "Oh!" and "What the—?!"

Clofia was a bit high-handed and had a wicked tongue, but her strength was well-regarded even among the knights. Now that even someone as promising as her had been beaten single-handedly, gazes of overflowing curiosity and questions of "Just how strong is this person?" flew among those who battled for a living. And the officials' cutting remarks were silenced upon hearing that Cloffe, one of the strongest in the nation, recognized this person and admitted he had no chance of laying a hand on her; it also made them cringe.

The queen watched this exchange among her vassals and recrossed her legs while maintaining her languid position. It wasn't at all a stance a royal ought to display before their subjects, but no one present was going to admonish her.

There was also proof of a strict hierarchical relationship in the room. After all, her attitude wasn't the only thing the prime minister and the captain of the knights weren't reproaching. The lords looked upon the pair's severe expressions and stood at attention as one.

"Well, I'm glad we got the results we did," said Queen Sahalashade. "Good work."

"Yes, thank you very much. In that case, I shall take my leave."

Their missions complete, Cloffe and the other spies bowed, then retreated. Another group dressed in tan robes crossed their path while entering the room. The elf at the forefront was the head Imperial Mage, and two human subordinates followed. The three kneeled just before the throne and dipped their heads to the queen. When Queen Sahalashade gave an exaggerated nod, only the Imperial Mage stood and spread out the scroll they had been carrying.

"I have gathered the results of our observations."

"Speak."

For some reason, the throne room instantly returned to silence. Even the civil officials who had been whispering away strained their ears so as not to miss a single word.

"We believe the barrier is rapidly coming undone."

"…I see." The queen managed to wring out only these words with a worn expression. The prime minister and the captain of the knights grew pale as well and gulped.

There was once a domain in the Brown Kingdom of Hegingium. Thanks to an event two hundred years prior, of which modern people were unrelated, the place became known as the Abandoned Capital. When the three nations were formed, the hands of God crammed together every hazard that would be unnecessary in the modern world. With the Abandoned Capital at its center, God then raised a solid barrier around the area.

…That was the legend anyway.

In truth, although Queen Sahalashade had likely been there, she had no memories of the incident. She had checked with the founding rulers of Helshper and Felskeilo, and they were the same.

Furthermore, other troubles had arisen over the past two hundred years. Otaloquess had been charged with keeping an eye on the Abandoned Capital, and they'd determined over the course of several years that the barrier was coming undone.

Was it a question of God's power lasting for only two hundred years, or was the barrier trembling from the forces sealed within…?

CHAPTER 3

"Either way, it looks like we should ask the other countries for help...," the queen mused.

"It cannot be helped. Those sealed inside possess tremendous power, no matter how diminutive they may appear," the dwarf prime minister said with an assured nod.

No matter how much one mocked these creatures as worthless, an incident had occurred where monsters that leaked out had driven the knights to the edge of ruin. There had been only six goblins, so everyone initially thought one unit of knights would suffice. However, as soon as they went into battle, the six goblins teamed up and swiftly brought about the knights' downfall. If not for the assistance of someone passing by, there would have been fatalities. The person had apparently been a tall demon who beat the goblins with ease and immediately ran off.

"What about whoever helped us?" the captain of the knights asked.

"Yes, about that. It appears they weren't even an adventurer, and their whereabouts are unknown."

The captain of the knights frowned at the prime minister's answer. He thought it was especially unfortunate that he couldn't express his gratitude to the one who saved his precious subordinates.

Since the problematic Abandoned Capital neighbored Felskeilo as well, Felskeilo couldn't label this as someone else's problem. The real issue was Helshper, which shared no direct border with Otaloquess. Unlike back in its founding era, the Merchant Alliance had more influence than the royal family, which meant requesting their cooperation would prove difficult.

After having the prime minister and queen postpone their hemming and hawing over the contents of the letters to be sent to each country, the captain of the knights asked the Imperial Mage about other matters of concern.

"What happened...after that monster ship washed out to sea?"

"Ah, that. My subordinates pursued it, but after it destroyed a fishing village in Helshper, it was apparently subdued by adventurers in a Felskeilo fishing village. The queen's aunt was apparently among them."

"Goodness, what a troublemaker my aunt Cayna is...," Queen Sahalashade grumbled. "Didn't we send warning to both nations ahead of time?"

The queen and her entourage were certain they'd provided plenty of time to respond accordingly. However, that was the exact moment the Felskeilo and Helshper knights had gathered to subjugate the bandits. Since the letter had arrived after the knights already left, both nations had no doubt been stuck twiddling their thumbs. That was Otaloquess's opinion, in any case.

"My subordinates further reported that the queen's aunt apparently has the duty of awakening something called Guardian Towers. If we agreed to aid her in her mission, is it not possible she may likewise help us in this matter of the Abandoned Capital?"

"Now that you mention it, Aunt Cayna is a Skill Master. It seems there were thirteen in the past, but these days the rest ran off somewhere..."

Roxilius was a given, but even Cayna's other spirits had also confirmed the spy's presence. Agaido had his own spies on Cayna's tail as well, so the spirits didn't consider it a threat. However, Roxilius thought otherwise and dispelled the spy from the campsite ever so gently. Even so, he'd simply reported to Cayna that everything was "perfectly fine."

Later on, the Otaloquess party shared details on the information they'd gathered and brought the meeting to an end. Queen Sahalashade watched the officials exit the throne room, and after ushering away her personal guards, she let her body go limp. She then slid off

CHAPTER 3

her throne to sit on the carpet. When she let out an exhausted sigh, the remaining captain of the knights, prime minister, and Imperial Mage gave wry smiles.

"I understand your feelings, Your Majesty, but aren't you acting a bit slovenly?" the captain asked.

"I can't stand all these unanswered problems piling up. I wonder if my aunt will give us a hand..."

"The stories alone give Cayna a stern image, but according to Cloffe's report, it appears she is rather easygoing."

"It's like my aunt has zero awareness that she's a high elf. She immediately makes friends with the townspeople, and you get the sense she's forgotten she possessed any majesty at all."

Rather than concern, Queen Sahalashade's attitude was closer to that of a parent scolding her child. Such statements made one wonder which girl was actually older, and the other three burst into laughter.

However, it wasn't long before they regained their composure and looked at one another seriously.

The Imperial Mage would continue to observe the Abandoned Capital. The captain of the knights would strengthen the army. The prime minister and the queen would work together to keep in close touch with each nation.

"Your Majesty, why don't we finish our break and begin writing those letters together?" the captain offered.

"I'd rather do that with someone more handsome..."

"In that case, shall I procure a fine lad from the knights?"

"...I was joking. Focus on your own job, Captain!"

◆

Meanwhile, back in Felskeilo, on a terrace high atop a castle spire...

The king, Prime Minister Agaido, High Priest Skargo, and Princess Mye—or rather, Myleene Luskeilo—sat around a table.

Despite being so high up, no wind bothered them. This castle used to be the property of some guild or other. The members had a habit of using their extra in-game points to preserve the castle's exterior. Thanks to this, the barrier surrounding the castle was functional even in the modern day.

"I thought something might've happened after a report from the Merchants Guild came in, but...," Agaido began.

"The information substantiates the missive from Otaloquess that we received just beforehand," the king said sullenly as he looked at the two letters on the table.

Agaido frowned at the one letter whose contents included the name of the individual who caused quite a bit of trouble for the nation. This person was easy to get along with on a personal level, but in terms of the country as a whole, it was only natural that you would want to take them seriously.

Skargo muted his usual eccentricities and reviewed the letter from Otaloquess thoughtfully. This was enough to worry Myleene, who called out to him.

"U-um, Master Skargo, is something the matter?"

"Ah, no, it's nothing. Sire, has Otaloquess requested any aid in regard to the Abandoned Capital?"

"No, this time they've only notified us of the threat from the sea and offered counsel. Their country no doubt has more information on the Abandoned Capital than we do. Do you know something, High Priest?"

Overall, the average person was not well-informed on the area known as the Abandoned Capital. At most, it was a fairy-tale place where gods had sealed away evil, and it supposedly didn't exist at all. The fact that it was a reality was mostly restricted to the country's upper echelons.

The Brown Kingdom of Hegingium occupied most of Felskeilo's western sector, but the old capital was slightly to the south. It was

CHAPTER 3

confirmed to currently exist in both southwestern Felskeilo and the western edge of Otaloquess.

At first glance, the place appeared to be a precipitous cliff looking out over the ocean. No one approached it thanks to the barrier that masked its presence. And since the barrier sealed away any trace of the city's existence, average people were unable to sense the barrier itself as well.

Yet even so, evil was seemingly locked inside.

This was the only information passed into present day, so no one had any way of confirming the truth. Based on the monsters they'd seen escaping since the barrier began to break down, they understood its threat level. This series of circumstances could easily be described as unlike anything players had ever experienced.

Skargo shared a connection with the player Cayna, but he also served his country. It wasn't as if he could reveal classified information about the three nations to her simply because she was his mother. Even so, he did think she was the best person from whom to seek wisdom. Since she had declared she wanted nothing to do with government affairs, they'd have to find someone else with whom they could explain and discuss the situation.

Skargo considered who else might be right for the job, and... "Why don't we ask the captain of the knights when he returns?" he offered.

"Him? I don't really see him havin' the brains for this."

The king and Skargo responded to Agaido's cutting remark with wry smiles that said *You can say that because he's not around.* Skargo drew conclusions solely from the information he'd received earlier, and he promised to apologize to the person in question later before revealing a shocking truth.

"Like Mother Dear, Shining Saber is over two hundred years old."

"...What?!" cried Agaido.

"Er...yes, it's true. I heard he previously fought alongside my mother in many a great war."

Prime Minister Agaido had been more shocked than Skargo expected, and Skargo sweated internally over whether he'd said something he shouldn't have. His pearly whites gleamed with a *shing!* as he spoke brazenly, though he wore a conflicted look on his face.

While both Cayna and Shining Saber were players, they were more accurately just from different nations. Skargo hadn't been aware of this. They had, in fact, been pure rivals who blasted each other with magic left and right. Since both saw this only as something that happened back in the game, neither held a shred of resentment against the other.

"Father, be that as it may, we shouldn't simply demand answers of Sir Shining Saber alone," said Mye. "Information on events that occurred before the country's founding might stir national chaos. I understand he works with Lady Cayna often, but I believe her techniques are too disproportionate to our modern world."

"Princess Myleene... Do you see my mother as illegal goods...?"

"If I had to say anything, I'd say she's more like a cute, abandoned dog with a bad personality..."

As the king, Skargo, Agaido, and Myleene formed questions to ask the captain of the knights, Skargo nodded with Myleene's sound reasoning. Anyone would follow along with Cayna if she flattered them, these four included.

For some reason, the topic of Cayna became a source of mutual understanding, and Myleene's heart cried tears of joy. It seemed her love had still yet to blossom.

Then in Helshper, there was some concern over the treatment of a player.

"What happened after that? How is he?"

CHAPTER 3

"Ah, Lady Caerina…"

Caerina had come to the mine where prisoners worked hard labor and asked several dwarf guards about a certain person's actions.

Needless to say, this certain person was the demon bandit leader whom her grandmother had captured. According to reports, his aggression ceased after that, and he swung his pickax with single-minded devotion. However, at night there were times he would moan in his cell and sob. He didn't seem like a murderous villain at all.

The combined knight army still hadn't returned, but from the reports she'd heard prior, it was a terrible scene. The knights eliminated the bandits haunting the fortress, interrogated the survivors, and did a thorough search of the premises. It was also verified that over one hundred travelers, merchants, and adventurers had fallen victim to the bandit leader.

She had sent a report to Felskeilo's captain of the knights, the silver dragoid Shining Saber, that concisely explained the bandit leader's capture. Surprisingly, it seemed he already knew her grandmother and expressed no skepticism over what happened. However, Shining Saber had been highly unnerved when he heard the leader's objective was "leveling up" by "killing players."

Her reason for expressly visiting the bandit in prison to confirm his actions and behavior was due to a conversation she'd had when her grandmother, Cayna, suddenly visited the other day. Caerina had promptly revealed the circumstances surrounding the bandit leader's execution to Cayna, but the discussion she had with Caerick had been a separate matter altogether.

The Merchants Guild, which Caerick had founded, had both a public and private face. She didn't have all the details, but the public side was all about understanding each country's trade network, regulating the value of merchandise, and building distribution channels.

On the private side, Caerick would collect classified information about other nations that his subordinate "merchants" had obtained from the royal families they regularly visited, and then he would sell it to the right sources. He chose his buyers carefully; most were nations, nobility he was friendly with, and relatives.

Naturally, he knew of the turmoil going on in Otaloquess's Abandoned Capital. He didn't yet have information about Otaloquess's response to it, but if things went south, he could tell it'd be necessary for all three nations to mobilize their forces.

He had gathered the following information about the country's struggle:

A team of six goblins had escaped from the Abandoned Capital's barrier and attacked a caravan. Several people barely escaped with their lives, and the matter was brought to the knights' attention. Over fifty knights went to suppress the threat, but they were driven to the verge of destruction by the six goblins. Fortunately, someone powerful stepped in and saved the knights from their predicament.

Caerina's guess was that the person was someone with circumstances very similar to those of her grandmother. Caerick, who had concluded military force would be needed to deal with the problem of the Abandoned Capital, had come up with the scheme to grant the bandit leader partial amnesty or some form of acquittal and have him join the Helshper knights. After all, although the bandit leader had been defeated with ease, Caerick also determined he still had the strength to exchange blows with Cayna.

The problem was the bandit leader's personality. The reports held a tone of dubiousness and spoke of how he regretted his actions so much that he'd break down into tears. To put it simply, he said things even the investigators admitted they didn't understand, so they treated him as if he were crazed. *"Player killers,"* *"level up,"* and *"log out"* were all part of some unknown cipher.

CHAPTER 3

Fortunately, he was very receptive to their will. If told that the plan would allow him to atone for his sins, he'd surely comply.

◆

When Cayna's group arrived in Felskeilo, they first stopped by an inn. It was a slightly pricey place for families, and perhaps because Roxilius was a butler, they were mistaken as nobles in disguise.

Roxilius and Cayna promptly spiffed up Luka in the hotel bathroom. Cayna bathed the flustered girl and combed her hair with Roxilius's help, then used Clothes Creation to make a new outfit for her.

In all honesty, Cayna's knowledge of fashion was limited to hospital clothes and whatever her cousin wore when she came to visit her. Cayna was thankful for the several skill templates available.

Even the simple, minimally designed white dress made Luka so cute that she was nearly unrecognizable. The girl was apparently nervous to wear such an outfit and took great care not to get it dirty as she ate.

While Roxilius efficiently cared for her, Cayna woke the silent Kee.

"Kee, please bring up several skills for me."

"Yes, ma'am."

"Look for object creation skills that are pretty much useless after you obtain them as well as furniture skills. Also find food and drink that are likely to last a long time."

"You intend to buy and sell to compensate for your living expenses, correct? Understood."

After Luka finally looked in the mirror, her mouth dropped when she saw herself as the daughter of a respectable family.

"It suits you quite well, Lady Luka."

"……L-Lady? No, I…"

"You are now the daughter of my master. The title of Lady is only appropriate."

Even Li'l Fairy, who usually refused to show herself, flew around Luka and clapped happily. It was too bad the girl couldn't see her, but the fairy was elated in any case, so all was well.

"I guess I should introduce you to Skargo and the others first, right? I'm sure you're tired, Luka, but come along with me for just a bit."

Cayna decided to bring Luka to the church. Since the little girl could easily get lost in the crowded main street, she didn't bother holding hands and instead carried Luka on her back. Roxilius acted as guard now that his master had her hands full and followed while keeping an eye on the far distance behind them. A female adventurer carrying a small child with a butler in tow was a strange sight indeed.

Perhaps because she wasn't used to seeing so many races in one place, Luka couldn't stop turning her head to gaze around her. When she occasionally asked "What's that?" in a small voice, Cayna would stop and explain.

"That's the market. It's got any kind of food you can imagine. This is the Ejidd River, and if you have money, you can cross it on a boat. That boat over there is a ferry that all sorts of people ride, and that one is used for transporting goods. We'll be going to the white building on the sandbar in the middle of that river."

When they arrived in front of the church on the sandbar, Luka looked up at it in amazement. There had been no church in the village, and apparently, priests had stopped by only on occasion.

When the group entered, Luka was astounded by the high ceiling, and she stood still in front of the stained glass windows. She hid behind Cayna and stared at the goddesses carved into the pillars. Cayna was utterly charmed by Luka's overwhelmed shock and grinned the entire time.

"Master, shall we go see your son now?"

"Oh, oops. Right."

CHAPTER 3

Cayna asked the sister in charge, whom she'd grown friendly with, if she could meet with Skargo. He had just returned from a meeting at the castle, and he invited Cayna and the others to his office as soon as he received word of their arrival. He'd already heard about the fishing village incident, so he nodded sagely when he saw the little girl accompanying Cayna.

"The heck? Just one look at her is good enough for you?"

"Why, I'd expect no less of our Mother Dear. I take it this new family member is my stepsister, yes?"

Skargo had been informed of what happened to the fishing village from Exis and Quolkeh's report to the Merchants Guild. He learned that a little girl had survived the incident and Cayna had taken her in, so he had no qualms about the situation by this point.

Surrounded by Sparkles, Skargo sent a Shooting Star wink at Luka and opened his arms wide in welcome. He glowed as if a spotlight were shining down on him.

"Allow me to formally greet you! Welcome to our family, dear miss!"

Skargo's jubilant display of warmest salutations deeply terrified Luka, and she hid behind Cayna while on the verge of tears.

"......"

It was Roxilius's first time seeing such a sight as well, and he was shocked into speechlessness.

"Oh, *Skaaargo?*"

A rumbling sound roiled behind Cayna, and she swelled with a piercing, murderous aura. Under Cayna's sharp eyes staring him down, Skargo grew pale, canceled out his effects, and hurriedly prostrated himself before her.

"I'm terribly sorry, Mother Dear!"

Cayna dropped her frightening act with an exasperated sigh. After soothing Luka, she reintroduced her son.

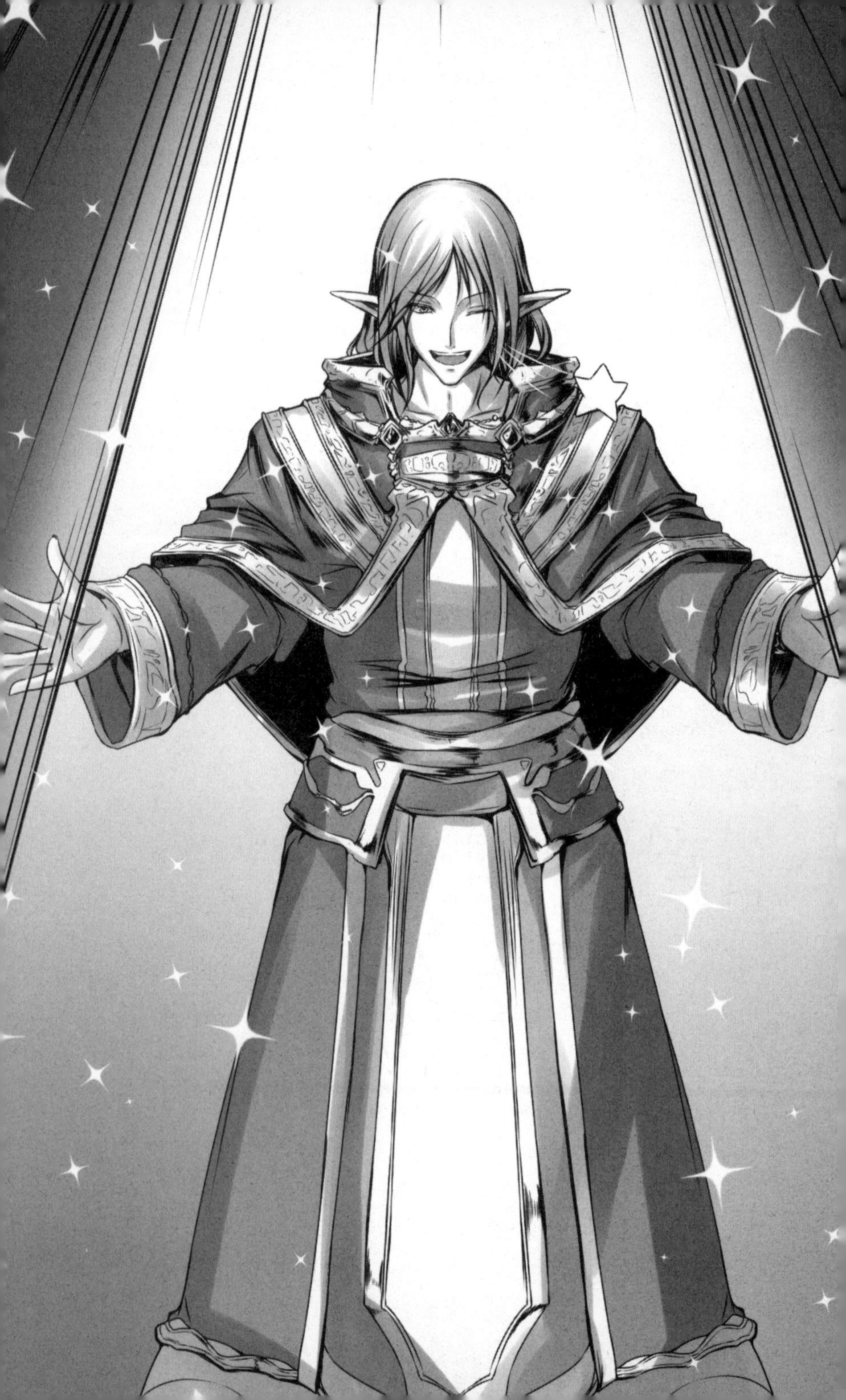

CHAPTER 3

"Anyway, Luka. This is my son Skargo. Think of him as your weird, sad older brother whose only lasting impact is his constant use of effects, despite the fact that he's in a position of power."

"M-Mother Deaaaar..."

He'd already made the worst possible impression on Luka, and his mother's scathing introduction caused Skargo to collapse into a flood of tears. To everyone else, though, he was only reaping what he sowed.

Feeling better after Cayna consoled her and wiped away her tears, Luka timidly came out from behind her and gave a small nod. Now free of his mother's terror, Skargo crouched to meet her eyes, and with a smile, he said, "It's nice to meet you."

"You could've simply done that from the beginning."

"But, Mother Dear, this is just who I am."

"Find a new hobby."

Roxilius offered Luka the cookies and black tea Skargo had provided them, and she took several timid bites.

"In any case," said Skargo, "I heard the report from the Merchants Guild. Not that I believe otherwise, but are you certain all that information was accurate?"

"I'm not sure what kind of report Exis and Quolkeh made or what you heard from Helshper, but yeah, that's the gist of things."

Since Luka was present, they avoided talk of the village and solely discussed the report's credibility. Only the little girl's munching interrupted the silence, followed by Skargo's response of "I understand." Since talk of politics wouldn't benefit Cayna anyway, she switched topics after their main business concluded.

"Anyway, Skargo, I'll be moving to the countryside, so contact me there if anything happens."

"I heard from Mai-Mai, but to think the news would be true... In that case, I shall establish a branch temple!"

"Don't bother."

Skargo drooped his head in crestfallen dejection as his joyous proposal was shot down in one fell swoop. Cayna gave a wry smile, clapped him on the shoulder with a "See you," and left the church.

"Geez, he's always like that when he gets carried away."

"...I see. So that was your son, Master?"

Roxilius realized as much from Cayna's intermittent grumbling and nodded in understanding.

They next headed to Kartatz's workshop so Cayna could pick up the lumber she'd ordered. The jaws of the staff dropped when the huge pile of processed wood instantly disappeared without a trace.

"All righty. I should be able to make a house or two with this. Thanks, Kartatz."

"Sure, no problem. Is that girl our new sister?"

"Word sure travels fast... Oh, right. Telepathy."

Cayna's group had met up with Skargo only a short while before, so Cayna tilted her head quizzically at Kartatz's knowing look. She soon remembered the siblings had a skill that allowed them to exchange information with one another, and she struck her fist against her palm.

Kartatz crouched to Luka's eye level, held out a hand, and greeted her with a simple "It's nice to meet you." Luka put on a smile she hadn't shown since meeting Exis and dipped her head, then barely squeaked out a "Nice...to meet...you." Kartatz gently patted her head and said nothing more. Cayna had secretly been nervous that the stern-looking dwarf would frighten the girl.

"Yup, good ol' Kartatz. Unlike Skargo, you're actually good with people. Maybe it's a wisdom that comes with age? Luka, this is my youngest son, Kartatz. He's your second big brother."

"But you're the older one, Mum... Also, ain't you gonna introduce her to Mai-Mai?"

CHAPTER 3

"Mai-Mai's school is crowded even at the best of times. She already knows what happened, so I was thinking maybe we'd pass."

Kartatz crossed his arms as he thought this through and suddenly gave a dry smile.

"She's crying, y'know," he replied.

He'd apparently contacted her just then with Telepathy.

"Tell her not to skip work just to see me."

"That'd be a mess for her, too. Anyway, haven't seen that boy around before, have I?" Kartatz asked, looking at Roxilius, who'd been standing there attentively the entire time.

"This is my butler summoning. He's super-helpful."

"Your Summoning Magic can even get you a butler?! Didn't see that one coming."

They parted from the highly impressed Kartatz, and Cayna carried Luka on her back as the young girl started nodding off from exhaustion. The three crossed the river to the inn, and Cayna put her to bed.

"I'm gonna go look for some transportation for us, so take care of Luka, okay?"

"Yes. Please leave everything to me."

With Luka in Roxilius's care, Cayna set off once again into town. Her objective was to buy a carriage that could take them to the remote village.

"Since Luka can't officially join my party, it's not like I can directly Teleport us to the village, huh?"

Cayna had already checked on her system screen that Roxilius could be added to her party. Luka's name didn't appear, so Cayna wasn't sure if they could fly together. Even so, she had used magic on Arbiter's entire mercenary crew, so she thought it might be a viable option.

Cayna felt a vague uneasiness, though, so she decided they'd use the main road as usual.

She figured she could also take this opportunity to try out a few things and peddle goods to compensate for their finances. One possible candidate was the prominent skill that allowed one to create decorative equipment for NPCs and others with no level. There were also whiskey and beer creation skills, and finally, there was the Buddha statue creation skill, which had proven successful once before. These were the extent of the skills Kee had picked out.

"That is all."

"Good work. Looks like I'll need to buy plenty of wheat. Maybe some gems, too?"

The usual method of crafting beer and whiskey meant germinating the wheat, utilizing the enzymes composed of those buds to convert it into starch, filtering the starch, and then using the resulting wort to ferment yeast. However, with a Craft Skill, the process wasn't complicated at all. As long as you had water and yeast, you could create either in vast quantities.

Rather than worry, Cayna decided to just give it a shot. She headed to the market and stupefied shopkeepers with her mass purchases. Since there was no place to buy gems, she figured she'd mine the earth for them.

Among her summonings, there was an almost-sixty-meter-tall giant shelled earthworm called a jewel worm. Its natural inclination was to amass jewels and ore in its nest. If she released it into the surrounding earth, she saw no reason why it wouldn't search for an ore vein and dig for her.

Next, Cayna visited the shop Elineh had in the capital. She'd heard about it before but never had the chance to check it out, so she decided to stop by for a chat.

She expected to see a small, compact shop, but what she actually

CHAPTER 3

found was a store located in the best part of town whose size easily rivaled that of Caerick's.

"Whoa? Seriously?"

The main difference here was that the laborers didn't run back and forth across the front of the shop as they did at Caerick's. Furthermore, her grandson's shop was wide, but this one seemed to have ample space in the rear. It was a tidy three-story building, and the sign at the entrance had a suave-looking picture of a dog. She guessed that must be Elineh if he were three hundred times more handsome.

The sign was straightforward enough, yet the shop name was nowhere to be found. The front entrance was wide open, and it seemed that anyone could just walk in. Inside, several housewives as well as travelers and a few possible adventurers scoured the merchandise. From the long tables on either side of the door, amiable-looking female employees sold simple daily necessities.

"Elineh peddles merchandise all over even though he has a shop like this?"

She was both surprised and impressed.

As Cayna stood there gawking at the sign, one lady ushered her in with a "Well now, you won't know how wonderful the shop is by looking from over there. Come on in!"

The moment Cayna entered, a young female employee swiftly approached her.

"Welcome. Is this your first time? Please let me know if there's anything I can help you with. We carry all manner of merchandise from diapers to steel swords," she said with a professional smile.

When Cayna took a look around, she saw that the first floor carried items that produced small sparks, others that created a single bucket of water, and several other magical tools. Swords, spears, and shields were suspended along the wall, and the shelves at the center of the shop were packed with utensils and cookware.

"Ummm, what kind of store is this?"

"We primarily sell a wide variety of home goods as well as products that are helpful to adventurers."

Upon hearing the employee's explanation, Cayna took another glance around and realized it was much like an online store. At least, as someone who used to be more or less bedridden, that was really all she could compare it to.

According to the employee, the shop extended to the second floor, which carried both secondhand and customized clothes and accessories. Since Cayna was interested in such things to begin with, she thought to herself that she could bring Luka with her next time.

Cayna interrupted the woman as she still continued to wax poetic about the shop's offerings, and said, "I'd like to buy a carriage."

"A carriage, you say?"

"Used is fine, and it can have a canopy, but an actual roof would be great."

The woman thought for a moment, then replied, "Right this way." She led Cayna to the back of the shop.

There was a wagon with no roof, a box wagon, and an overly decorated carriage. Each was in fine order, but they were imbued with expensive-looking parts all throughout. What Cayna wanted was the canopied wagon hidden way in the back. The whole thing was slightly dirty, and it was the shabbiest of the bunch. According to the employee, the wagon had been part of a caravan until recently, after falling into disrepair.

Now that the woman mentioned said so, didn't it seem kind of familiar?

"Maybe it's the kind the laigayanma pull...?"

As Cayna crossed her arms and thought back to the scene, the employee's eyes went wide for some reason, and she froze. Her mouth opened and closed wordlessly for some time, but she immediately readjusted her lax air and gave a deep, elegant bow.

"My sincerest apologies. May I presume, dear customer, that you are Lady Cayna?"

"Huh? Um, yeah, that's me."

When Cayna gave an honest yet confused answer, the employee murmured, "I see. Very well." After that, she abruptly gestured to the canopied wagon and said, "In that case, there is no need for you to pay for this product. Please take it with you."

"Whaaaaaaaaaat?!"

Cayna thought for sure the wagon was at least in the gold-coin range, and her eyes flew open in shock at the outrageous proposal. Her cry drew highly curious glances from surrounding employees.

It was apparent that not many customers came this far back into the shop. Those repairing wagons and carrying furniture stopped what they were doing, but as soon as the woman gave a bright smile at them, they quickly looked away and resumed their duties.

"The president instructed me to provide an explanation, since he was certain you would have questions."

"'The president'... You mean Elineh?"

"That's right."

Cayna approached her new canopied wagon and checked it over as she listened to the woman.

"His orders were 'If a female elf adventurer named Cayna visits, make sure her first purchase is free of charge.'"

"...Elineh doesn't seem like the type to just hand something over. Maybe he wants me to owe him?"

As Cayna muttered this bitterly, the woman giggled.

"You're just as my husband said."

"Huh?"

"Ah, my apologies. I'm Elineh's wife, Armuna."

The chestnut-haired woman named Armuna took off the bangle on her arm. Her human visage faded away, and she transformed into a short kobold.

Unlike Elineh, who looked like a Welsh corgi, Armuna was like a black-and-white papillon. She'd apparently been using a magical tool to alter her appearance, and her human form had all been a ruse.

"Ehhhh?!"

The employees around them all secretly watched and nodded in understanding at Cayna's second dose of surprise. It seemed that Armuna had pulled the same trick time and time again, and she'd been looking for a new target recently, since there was no one left to scare. When Cayna suddenly appeared, she knew she struck gold.

However, Armuna's spirits were dampened when she realized the real reason for Cayna's shock centered around the fact that Elineh was married.

Cayna instantly put the canopied wagon in her Item Box, and while she never intended it as payback, this successfully flabbergasted Armuna and all the rest.

"My husband isn't here much, but please do come again."

"Right. Next time I'll do some actual shopping. Tell Elineh I said hi."

"Of course. Thank you for your patronage."

The employees saw her off with a unified bow, and Cayna quickly scurried away from Elineh's shop and the odd amount of special attention. She returned to the inn to find Luka awake, and she explained the next step of their plan. They were going to live in the remote village.

"As far as I can tell, there's a good chance you'll get along with the innkeeper's daughter Lytt, since you're both around the same age."

"What…should I do there…?"

CHAPTER 3

"Help around the house maybe? Can't say I know much about housekeeping myself, though."

Luka tilted her head with a confused expression. For someone like her, who had been helping around the house her entire life, Cayna's statement was unintelligible.

For Cayna, the root of the problem was the all-important *house* part of *housekeeping*. She had absolutely no point of reference for this back when she was Keina, either. And even if she did, at best it would have been nothing more than wiping the dishes while her mother washed.

Ashamed, Cayna considered asking Marelle for a few pointers. Since this world lacked electrical appliances, she'd have to learn the old-fashioned way.

Keina had always been sickly. From her youngest days until elementary school, she didn't really have the all-too-common experience of standing by her mother's side in the kitchen. The accident had occurred before she entered middle school, and she'd been confined to lying in a hospital bed. Her life was nothing more than those scenes she saw in hospital dramas. Rather than a beginner, it was easier to say she was a complete greenhorn. Luka probably knew more about the subject than she did.

After pondering over this to the point of frustration, Cayna consulted her professional housekeeper, who offered a most unexpected proposal.

"Pardon?" said Cayna.

"Why don't *we* manage your household, Lady Cayna?"

"Huh?"

Preparations were complete, and the day they were to set off for the remote village arrived. A magical tool known as a magic rhymestone was taken from the Item Box and used to power the wagon

Cayna had obtained, and a strange horse head sprouted from the driver's seat.

The horse golem and wagon fused together to become a self-running canopied transport that required no actual horse. The eyes of passing adventurers and travelers in carriages laden with products shot open wide as they took in the sight.

The crossbreed of the golem and its magic rhymestone buried within was a Craft Skill that created a semipermanent operational object. In the Game Era, one often saw houses with wheels, houses with feet, and houses that had completely metamorphosed. In worst-case scenarios, there had been confirmed sightings of chaos here and there as castles and fortresses swaggered over the fields. Since quite a few were mobilized in times of war, it wasn't uncommon to see huge, decisive battles being fought in one corner like the passing trend they were. Compared to that, Cayna didn't see the autonomous canopy wagon as any sort of big deal.

However, if she had taken into account only the reactions of those who looked upon it, she wouldn't have gotten into the later mess that she did. Cayna had no way of knowing that on the very day of her departure, rumors were swirling throughout Felskeilo and reaching the ears of those who could cause her a world of trouble.

"But wait. Isn't your statute of limitations coming up, Roxilius?"

Cayna frowned at Roxilius's suggestion. She kept an eye on Luka, making sure the girl didn't fall out of the wagon as she took in the sights, eyes wide with wonder.

"Phrasing it in such a way makes it seems as if I have done some wrongdoing, wouldn't you say?"

To be more precise, Roxilius's work period was drawing to a close. To call him out again, Cayna would have to ring the handbell and give him more money. She had considered doing so from the outset,

CHAPTER 3

if only for Luka's sake. Cayna had enough money in the bank to keep him for two thousand years.

However, for someone like her, who wanted to set the money she'd earned from the game aside and be self-sufficient in this world, it wasn't an ideal solution. That was why she came up with the idea of trading with Elineh's caravan whenever the merchants occasionally stopped by in order to raise money to live in the village.

"You were forced to disappear the last time your clock ran out, right?"

"No, that is only my conjecture. I myself am uncertain of whether or not I can return."

"Huh? What's that supposed to mean...?"

"In all honesty, my memories before coming here have grown hazy. Ever since we last met, Master, it seems the place where I once waited to be summoned has been disappearing. There is no guarantee I can properly return."

That alone was enough for Cayna to understand most of the situation.

"...Ah, I see. Guess it's safe to say that with the Admins no longer up running things, their system has stopped working, too. And maybe the Ghost Ship appeared out of nowhere since it was a quest event?"

In that case, it wouldn't be strange for *all* the quest-event monsters to come pouring out. If something like that happened even once, Cayna didn't expect anyone in this world would make it out alive.

For now, the problem was whether Roxilius would be forced to return. The answer would come with time.

"There is one more matter, if you don't mind..."

"What's that?"

"I was curious if perhaps you could call Roxine. Would it not be better for Lady Luka to have a female attendant? I'm exceedingly reluctant to make such a proposal, but..."

"Cie, huh? She'll liven things up, that's for sure."

Cayna smirked as she recalled the havoc Opus had caused when the game still had NPCs. Rather than *lively*, she had a feeling the better word for their days ahead was *turbulent*. After all, a lot of players ended up getting involved in the chaos back then.

Opus had put out an open call for artwork of NPCs sporting a "maid look," but offered no other requirements. Pro and amateur artists alike logged on in droves, and soon the town became buried in picture frames like some sort of art exhibit. Cayna probably would have enjoyed it more if the theme hadn't been "maid." She was glad it all ended on a fun note but felt the world was perfectly fine without another Personal Maid Extravaganza incident.

Eventually, Roxilius's set time passed while the group was on its travels, and the building where he was to return never appeared. Naturally, Cayna ended up agreeing to the butler's wishes.

And thus, she summoned the maid to join them. After momentarily stopping the carriage midday, Cayna checked to make sure no one was around, then rang the red handbell. A soft *riiiiiing* echoed clearly around them, and light flashed as a large white magic circle opened before them.

Roxilius watched blankly, while Cayna's face slightly twitched. This was Luka's second time witnessing the sight, but she'd been filled with such crushing anxiety the first time that she couldn't remember most of it. So when the rare sight of an enormous magic circle appeared before her, Luka's mouth hung wide open.

White phosphorescent light seeped from the sky and flowed endlessly into the circle. A building slowly rose from within.

It had a red roof and white walls. It was a single house that had a small garden bursting with yellow, white, and blue flowers.

CHAPTER 3

Luka never imagined such a thing could rise up like that, and she remained frozen in shock. Light poured out from a door as it opened of its own accord. A girl in her late teens with brown cat ears and wearing an orange plaid maid outfit appeared. She was a werecat like Roxilius, and she tugged at the edges of her miniskirt as she dipped her head politely.

"It has been quite some time, Lady Cayna. I, Roxine, am at your service."

"Hey there. It's been a while, Cie. You're not feelin' weird anywhere, right?"

"'Weird'? I am in perfect health. I see you have already summoned Rox. Has this halfwit done something so crass as to warrant summoning me as well?"

Roxilius was quietly standing at attention behind Cayna, and a vein of anger popped out at his temple. He held his tongue, but his twinging, trembling body made it clear he had something to say.

Just like the first time Cayna ever summoned Cie, her mouth had a slight twitch to it as well. At any rate, she made sure to introduce the still-dumbfounded Luka and ask the maid to watch after the girl's well-being.

"Understood. I, your humble Roxine, shall raise Lady Luka into a fine woman of society."

"Uh, no, you really don't have to do all that. She's good the way she is."

Roxine had raised her fist high and struck the air as she spoke, but Cayna shook her head and emphasized prudence. Luka had only just lost her parents, so Cayna thought it best that she be allowed some peace and quiet. Just to be safe, she explained as much to Roxine. To prevent Luka from hiding herself away, Cayna thought it best that Roxine offer the young girl this manner of care.

"I see. Very well. I shall provide only the most minimal interference."

"Great. Let her do whatever she wants, since she's not used to all that formal stuff."

Roxine bowed respectfully, but Luka couldn't understand why she was being paired with the maid, and she tugged on Cayna's cloak with worry.

"Um… She'll be…taking care of…me?"

"Roxine will help you with everything from getting changed in the morning to bath time."

As Cayna briefly explained what the maid would be doing, tears wordlessly came to the trembling Luka's eyes. Cayna had squatted down, and Luka clung to Cayna's arm tightly.

"I'm…not important…enough…"

"Hmm. Well then, what if we all took care of you? Would you like that?"

After Cayna thought for a moment and made this proposal, Luka immediately leaped at her with an eager nod. Overcome with emotion, Cayna squeezed her tight.

Meanwhile, a veritable catfight was unfolding right behind them.

"I do wish she had summoned me first instead of this halfwit."

"Who're you calling halfwit? Watch yourself, Roxine. We are Lady Cayna's servants, after all."

"Why should I listen to you, Rox? Who knows what sort of vile creature this young girl might become if made to follow your pitiful example?"

"The only vile thing here is your bitchiness. It's so contagious you might pass it onto the poor girl. Nothing beats germs like a disinfectant."

"Oh? Anyone who treats others like plague-ravaged pests honestly doesn't deserve to see tomorrow."

With a "*Hissss!*" the angry veins on Roxilius's temple multiplied. It was hard to tell whether the two despised each other because they

CHAPTER 3

were so similar or because they didn't get along when summoned simultaneously. Roxilius had been the one to reluctantly make the suggestion, but it was apparently more unbearable than he thought.

The tit for tat raged on, and like feral alley cats, they were on the brink of a scuffle. Cayna gave each one a knuckle sandwich on the head, and the fire was swiftly put out before it could begin.

"All right, all right, break it up. You two are gonna be family from now on, so no fighting, got it? And no toppling roadside trees, destroying houses, and throwing people, either. Don't do anything that would be a bad influence on Luka."

"Yes. As you wish, Lady Cayna."

"...Understood, Master."

Cayna smiled uncomfortably as the two reluctantly obeyed. After all, she'd never been able to interact with them so much back when they were game NPCs.

It was fine if she couldn't read their actions or behavior and that they possessed free speech, but letting these explosive situations continue would only add to her stress.

After all, Roxine spit verbal fire at not only Roxilius but male characters in general. Roxilius shot back at her with sharp turns of phrase rather than a retort. Moreover, Cayna's use of force to make a point didn't exactly work in her favor, either.

Only after summoning both did Cayna learn the hard way that combining them in town would result in massive damage. She was a bit worried, and on this instance alone, even she would allow a little leeway. Cayna made sure to give them a stern warning.

"I owe a lot to this village we're going to be living in, so I'm going to be really angry if you lay a hand on the people or their property!"

""Y-yes, ma'am!""

The two trembled at the dangerous look in Cayna's eyes. Luka, who couldn't sense the unsettling aura, clapped fervently at Cayna's

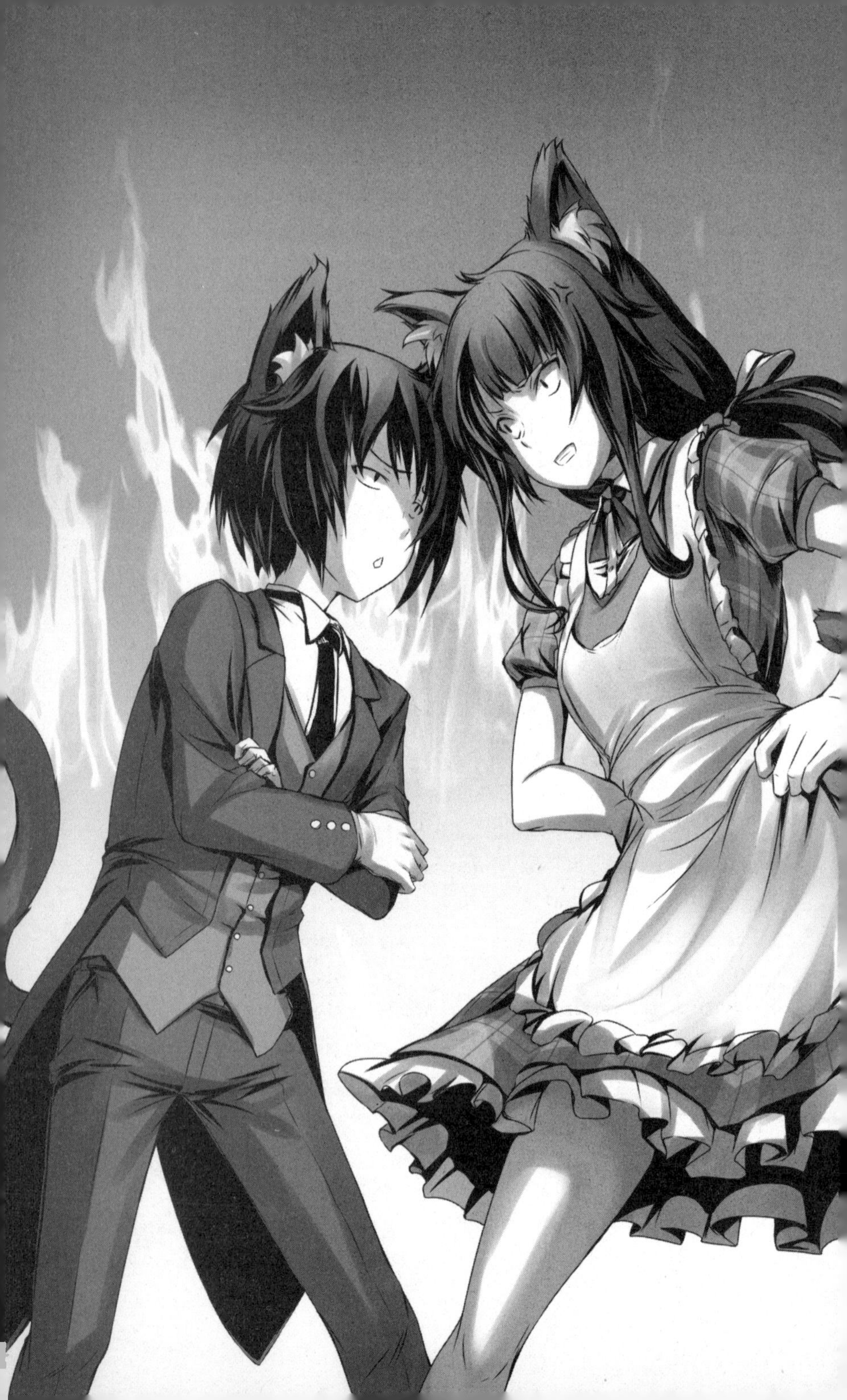

awe-inspiring image. Cayna puffed up haughtily at her adopted daughter's flattery. Only Li'l Fairy on Cayna's shoulder shrugged in a manner of *Good grief.*

The wagon golem listened to the boisterous voices coming from the loading bed and once again set off powerfully down the road toward the village to fulfill its destiny.

"What's this...?"

When they arrived in the remote village, the first sight to greet Cayna was Lux Contracting, which stood where the carriage rest area used to be long ago.

The store itself was fine enough; the problem was the words on the sign out front.

Written in large, flowing script was SAKAIYA BRANCH STORE.

"So Caerick really did open his own branch here. I guess he pushed out Lux and Sunya."

Cayna was a bit concerned Caerick might have mustered up his skills to force them out. It had only been about ten days since she last saw him, so she wasn't sure if she should be amazed by his quick response or angry at his pushy methods. Cayna told herself she'd definitely ask Sunya later and get to the bottom of things.

After she helped Luka down from the canopied wagon and both Roxilius and Roxine disembarked as well, she put the wagon back in her Item Box. They made their way to the inn as Cayna exchanged greetings with the villagers who had heard them arriving and popped out to take a gander.

"What a pretty girl. You got a job?"

"That young man is a tall glass of water, too."

"I am not for drinking."

Roxine and Roxilius were mistaken for people looking for work out of town.

"Who is that little girl?"

"I took her in. She was orphaned after monsters destroyed her village."

"My, how awful."

This village had very few children, and Luka was shocked to find herself surrounded by sympathetic adults. The group continued past the villagers.

Marelle and Lytt were waving and waiting for them at the front of the inn. However, while Marelle appeared more cheerful than usual, her daughter had a terribly panicked look on her face.

"I'm back, Marelle."

"M-M-Miss Cayna! U-um!"

Lytt tried to tell her something, but Marelle's hand was faster, and she latched on to Cayna's head.

"H-huh? Marelle, what's wron—? Ow, ow, ow, ow, ow, ow!"

The grinding force was like a vise, and Cayna let out sharp cries of pain. That hand was proof of Marelle's skill and years of running the inn. She gripped Cayna's skull with a terrifying force. Kee had apparently determined this was a form of bonding, and his barriers didn't go up.

"Gyah!"

As Cayna writhed around, Roxilius and the others stood in frozen shock. Luka was on the verge of tears, and the absurd punishment finally ended when she tugged on Marelle's skirt.

"Ow, ow, ow, ow…"

Luka clung to Cayna, who was now crouched on the ground with her head in her hands, and Roxine handed her a wet towel. Watching this scene, Marelle looked at her quizzically.

"What's goin' on here? Where'd this big family come from?"

"…I should be the one asking what's going on… Why in the world did you suddenly come at me like that?"

CHAPTER 3

"You really don't know?"

Marelle quickly drew her face right up to Cayna's and looked her straight in the eye. The latter recoiled slightly, but unable to come up with anything she should feel such guilt over, she replied, "Well, uh..."

Marelle put her hands on her hips and sighed. "Unbelievable." It was then that Lytt, who could only tremble up until this point, cried out.

"I-I'm sorry, Miss Cayna! She found the bird on the roof!"

As soon as Lytt said this, Cayna finally gave an "Ah!" of realization. Marelle shot Cayna a menacing glare.

Cayna had completely forgotten that she'd left behind a gargoyle. Breaking into a sweat, she bowed her head and gave an apology of "I'm sorry." All the while, Marelle exerted a silent pressure over her.

Incidentally, it was another family who had noticed it. A kindhearted, middle-aged farmer had gone up to the roof of the inn to fix a leak. He thought he saw a monster there and rushed inside to yell for Marelle. Lottor, who was inside at the moment dissecting some game, was tasked with the duty of dispatching it.

However, Lytt couldn't bear the guilt in silence any longer. She confessed everything and kept the entire village from falling into chaos.

"I can't eat a single bite when I think of that scary thing right over my head. Just get rid of it!" Marelle fumed. When she put it that way, even Cayna didn't have much of a choice.

Cayna loved this village, so she had left the object there to prevent it from falling into misfortune when she wasn't around. If she was going to live there as a resident from that point on, there was no reason for the gargoyle to stay as a permanent fighting force. Roxilius alone could take care of any bandits on his own before breakfast.

After Cayna remove the gargoyle with a look of relief on her face, Marelle finally asked about her three companions.

"So what's the story with these kids?"

"This is Luka. A few things happened, so I've taken her in. The werecat boy is Roxilius, and the girl is Roxine. They're my attendants who have been helping me out for a long time. We'll all be living together from now on."

Since the villagers wouldn't understand what summoning a butler and a maid meant even if she explained it to them, Cayna decided to say they worked for her (aka she summoned them a lot) a long time ago (aka in the Game Era).

Marelle acted dubious for some reason and commented, "I knew it. So you really *do* come from a good family, huh?" However, since high elves were considered royalty in this world, she wasn't really wrong.

Even if there were some misunderstandings, as long as it didn't affect how Cayna was treated, then she was perfectly happy.

"So when will you build the house?"

"I figured we'd stay at the inn tonight and build it tomorrow. I wanna relax for a bit."

"I see. In that case, we better get everyone together."

Marelle beamed happily. Cayna, however, turned pale.

"No, it's okay. You've already welcomed me as a villager once."

"You can never do it too many times. Why would a village with nothing else to do for fun pass that up?"

A banquet was all fine and well, but she hoped they'd give her a break and not force her to drink while leading the others in a toast. She was honestly happy for the warm welcome, however.

In any case, Cayna replied vaguely, 'Uh, well, that's true…' and valiantly resigned herself to her fate.

Roxilius and Roxine deftly bowed their heads to Marelle and her husband and to all the villagers present in the dining hall.

CHAPTER 3

"Like Lady Cayna, we shall be in your care from now on as well. My name is Roxilius. I am pleased to make your acquaintance."

"Yes, the likes of him is but a mere servant. You may use him to your heart's content until he is nothing more than a dirty cat-fur rag. Ah, my name is Roxine. The pleasure is all mine."

The villagers let out cries of "Eek!" and stepped back as Roxilius, who had veins popping out on his forehead and a twitching grimace, and Roxine, who looked down on him as always, began to go at it. After that, Cayna angrily put her in an Iron Claw hold, but Roxine defaulted. Cayna immediately yelled "Go to your crate!" and needless to say, the werecat was put away in a room of the inn.

"I'm sorry about that, Marelle. She's a bit of a wild child to deal with but means no harm. *(I think.)* She's just got some tough habits..."

"R-right. Well, don't worry about it. You run into kids like that every now and then."

Cayna looked at the wavering smile of the veteran proprietress (at least that's how Cayna saw her) and vowed to hardly ever allow Roxine outside once the house was finished.

Behind the flustered adults, Lytt approached Luka.

"My name is Lytt. I'm the daughter of the innkeeper. It's nice to meet you!"

Luka's eyes initially darted back and forth at such a straightforward introduction, but she found her resolve and nodded repeatedly. She timidly held out her hand enough to touch Lytt's fingertips and squeaked, "I'm...Luka. It's nice...to meet you."

Lytt, who had been waiting ever so patiently for Luka's response, broke into a smile. She gripped Luka's trembling hand tightly and happily replied, "Yeah! Let's be good friends!"

However, she just as quickly let go.

"Ah, sorry. Did that hurt?" Lytt asked with a sad expression.

"N-no... I'm okay."

Luka shook her head, smiling shyly, and Lytt once again beamed.

Above them, Li'l Fairy watched the two girls' blossoming friendship with a pleased smile, but of course, it is to be remembered that no one except Cayna could see her.

After Luka and Lytt became acquainted, Cayna took her three new family members to the public bathhouse. Roxilius went to the men's area, while Roxine, Luka, and Cayna went to the women's.

After they removed their clothes in the dressing room and proceeded to the bathing area, Mimily, who had been relaxing in the shallow end, noticed the three. Luka was shocked to see a girl whose bottom half was a fish, and she hid behind Cayna. Roxine took a bucket in one hand and prepared for battle.

"Hi there, Mimily. It's been a while."

"Hello, Cayna. Who might these two be?"

As the two greeted each other congenially and called each other by name, Luka looked up at Cayna quizzically. Seeming to put the pieces together, Roxine set down the bucket and stood at attention behind Luka.

"I mentioned living in the village before, right? This is Roxine, my maid, and my foster daughter, Luka. We'll all be living together. There's also a butler named Roxilius. I hope you'll all get along."

"So you have more than three kids..."

Cayna tilted her head at Mimily as the mermaid looked at Luka with utterly hollow eyes. It must have been hard to imagine that despite appearing the same age, Cayna had four children.

After that, Cayna soaked alongside Mimily and washed up while Roxine taught Luka how to use the bath.

"How's the laundry business?"

CHAPTER 3

"It's going quite fine, thanks to your kind patronage," Mimily replied with a giggle. Cayna couldn't help but join in.

At any rate, there was plenty for the mermaid to do each day. If there was a way to cut her time spent doing laundry, Mimily would surely switch to it. The single men had used the service every day but soon noticed that the fees incurred were by no means negligible. They started stockpiling laundry for several days before submitting a request, and thus, Mimily's business was much busier than when it first began.

Doing laundry in winter also became easier, since the other villagers could visit natural hot springs. Cayna heard the people would help Mimily when they could, and the reserved feelings between both parties was thawing.

"Well then, Cayna."

"Hmm? What is it?"

"I know we talked about finding my hometown, but what would you think if I said you didn't have to?"

"What?!"

Cayna let out a surprised yell, but she looked into Mimily's sad eyes and decided to hear the rest of what she had to say.

"I'm fine with it, but are you?"

"Yes. I was a burden in my village. I hardly saw my older sister, who was my only relative, and the others all gossiped about me. Just when I was thinking to myself that I was better off gone, I found myself here. That's why my new circumstances have been such a lifesaver."

The unsettled look in Mimily's eyes left Cayna at a loss for words. Both girls had a shared experience of unexpectedly losing their homes. However, it was up to each person whether they would live a life of pessimism or completely cut their lingering attachments.

To be honest, Cayna couldn't claim to be above it all, since she was still full of regret over her cousin and uncle in the other world.

"...Right. Well, I'll stop the search for now. But absolutely tell me if you change your mind!"

"I will. Please help me if that time comes."

Cayna canceled out the Blue Dragon that was still roaming around the sea. Several days had passed, and yet the dragon, whose sole focus was on the search, had found nothing. She took this to mean that there were no mermaid villages around Leadale.

"If only I had that idiot to talk to at times like these..."

A certain *someone* probably could have given her spot-on advice, but since they weren't around, there wasn't much helping it.

Roxine took Luka out of the bath before Luka got too dizzy, and Cayna followed suit.

"Bye, Cayna."

"It looks like there's going to be a banquet at the inn. Are you coming, Mimily?"

"It's your welcome party, right? But didn't you have one before?"

"Apparently, it's important for small villages to not give up the few pleasures they have..."

"A-are you okay?" Mimily asked with an awkward smile as she looked at Cayna's drooped shoulders and dead eyes.

Cayna, who ended up drinking spirits from a tankard at the party, murmured the Lotus Sutra as she stabilized her mental condition. Showing less-than-stellar enthusiasm, she'd been offered one drink after the other. The latter half of the evening was nothing more than a desolate memory.

"I want to dig a hole and bury myself in it..."

At breakfast, Cayna sat in the dining hall with her head in her hands. Smiling, Marelle patted her from behind.

"What're you talkin' about? Anything that slipped out last night will stay in the village, so no worries!"

"That's not the probleeeem."

The one saving grace was that the banquet had run late, so Luka and Lytt were already asleep by the time it ended. Cayna was certain that if the two had seen her chugging her sorrows away, it would cause even Cayna to explode.

She stuck out a forked snake tongue devilishly and cackled, at which point Roxilius chided her that she'd be a bad influence on Lady Luka's upbringing.

"Please do not push Lady Cayna so," he warned.

"That's right. If she unleashes her power, she can turn this entire village into a crater in one blast," Roxine said.

The butler and maid made appropriate threats while keeping a safe distance. For some reason, they seemed to be in perfect agreement only when defending their master.

Cayna brought Luka and the others to the building site. The village elder, Kohke, had also brought several villagers to help.

"Good morning, Lady Cayna."

"Good morning. It looks like I'll be in your care from now on."

Cayna bowed, and the maid and butler on either side of her gave deep bows in turn. Since the two had introduced themselves at the banquet the night before, they merely stood in silence. Since Cayna had *harshly* warned them not to fight, the two didn't look at each other or say a word.

Some gazed at the pair with deep curiosity, but one glare from Roxine was all it took for them to back off.

"Still, I see ya got a butler and a maid there, Cayna. You some big shot's daughter?"

"Well, I'm catastrophically bad at housekeeping, so I thought I'd leave that to Rox and Cie."

Lottor, likely not expecting such a straight answer, said, "Maybe I shouldn't have said that," and fell silent.

A number of the older women gave incredulous looks of *How is that even possible for a mother?* but it was the unavoidable truth.

Roxilius and Roxine both stepped forward and bowed again.

"Please leave the running of the household to us."

"Lady Cayna, please sit back and reign as undisputed dictator and master of your domain."

"What kind of lady of leisure is that…?"

She appreciated their support, but the option they offered was a little worrisome.

Cayna checked the intended construction site against her Craft Skills and confirmed the space she'd secured. The village elder said she could use her biggest spells anywhere in visible range. The plot alone was large enough to easily fit the castle tourist attraction in Felskeilo that saw crowds of people coming and going daily.

Building: House had several templates available, so this time, Cayna picked the large one. This type could house about eight people, and a single space came with either two floors or one floor and a basement. There was more than enough room for a yard, but since she was worried about it blocking the village roads, she stopped just before the edge of the homestead. She planned on building a largish bungalow, so part of the house would be underground.

Once the materials she'd bought from Kartatz earlier noisily appeared, her preparations were complete. Cayna summoned the Earth and Wind Spirits and quickly set to work on construction. The ground caved in without warning, and the stones that would serve as the foundation rose up from within. After first digging out the basement, she stuck the lumber floating in midair into the ground in sequential order to form pillars and walls. Beams were suspended, and the roof came together of its own accord; the bungalow was complete in a matter of minutes.

The villagers, who were already used to such sights, clapped and cheered at this feat, which ignored all common sense. The shock only extended to everyone from Lux Contracting and Mimily.

Afterward, the women of the village came with baskets to decorate the entrance and windows with white flower petals.

Thinking it was some sort of charm, Cayna watched them with curiosity. Kohke the Elder offered an explanation.

"It is a custom of our village that occurs whenever a new house is built. It is meant to help the building grow accustomed to the land."

"Ah, I see. You have traditions like that?"

"I don't believe the blossoms will be especially bothersome, so please treat them as decoration until they wilt away."

"If that's a village rule, then sure. Please take care of that for me, Cie."

"Understood."

The werecat girl, who had already been appointed head housekeeper, nodded. She would see to all indoor affairs, while Roxilius would be in charge of outdoor matters. Roxine was the type to snap at every little thing, so Cayna was concerned that having her out and about would sow discord with the villagers. This setup put her mind at ease.

After greeting each villager who had gathered to watch, she was relieved that the first step went smoothly. However, Lux rushed up to her in bewilderment and asked, "The techniques of the gods can do that, too?!"

"Uh, well, yeah. You can more or less create buildings."

"That's incredible! Can you build not only houses but castles and fortresses as well?!"

"You can, but you need the necessary materials. You won't know how long your supply will last just scraping things together."

Not surprisingly, it was impossible for anyone to gather several hundred tons of material on their own, so Cayna shrugged. While possible back in the game, it would be next to hopeless for anyone to create a castle that way in this world. Felskeilo had made one in their redevelopment area by converting the materials from local ruins, but it was much smaller than average size.

After Lux's repetitive cries of "Incredible!" and "Amazing!" went on for some time, Sunya whacked him on the head and returned him to himself.

"I'm terribly sorry my husband has caused you such trouble, Miss Cayna…"

Sunya grabbed Lux's head and forced him into a bow. Her expression was completely composed, and one would never guess she possessed the strength to physically outmatch her dwarf husband.

Thinking they were quite the married duo, Cayna replied that Lux's behavior was no doubt out of intellectual curiosity, and she quickly forgave him.

"Come to think of it, I saw that your sign out front says Sakaiya Branch Store."

Figuring this was as good an opportunity as any, Cayna brought up the topic of the sign.

"Ah, the master simply asked us to open a service counter."

"It might have somethin' to do with the fact that we'll probably be handling more Sakaiya goods. Hey! That's all I said!"

Sunya quickly cut Lux off. To keep him from saying anything else unnecessary, she dug her elbow into his side and silenced him. She waved her hand in a gesture of *Oh, just ignore that*, and they left.

"…That was weird."

"If he said more than he should have, is it safe to assume your intuition has picked up on it?"

"A window counter means people can place orders without going to Helshper."

She didn't know yet whether they'd be going to pick up the goods

CHAPTER 3

or sending them out, but Cayna thought it sounded a lot like online shopping.

While Cayna was answering Lux's questions, Roxilius and the others finished checking the details of the house's interior. They confirmed nothing was warped, there were no gaps anywhere, and the doors opened and closed properly.

At Roxine's request, Cayna took out premade furniture from her Item Box. Roxilius placed the beds, dressers, tables, and chairs in each of the rooms.

The layout had a dining room/Western-style living room with large glass windows at the central south side. There was also a fireplace along the wall. To the west of this were the wash and prep areas—the bath and the kitchen—though they would use the public bathhouse for most bathing. Two rooms were situated to the east of the living room, and another six rooms and a half bath were to the north, off a hallway that stretched through the eastern, western, and central corners of the house.

Each room was about nine square feet, and each one came furnished with a bed and dresser. At Cayna's request, Roxine put a small table and chair in her room. Cayna and Luka would use the two rooms to the south, and Roxilius would be stationed across from the kitchen. Roxine chose to be directly opposite of Luka. Currently unoccupied rooms would be used for storage. The basement was right beneath Roxilius's room and had an entrance from the hall.

After Cayna placed several shelves in the basement, she installed a small number of lighting fixtures with magic rhymestones. She then placed a magic crystal—an item that could temporarily house spirits—farther within the cellar. After summoning an Ice Spirit and installing it within the crystal, Cayna checked that the basement was now appropriately chilly and removed all the vegetables and fruits from her Item Box. With Roxilius's help, Cayna put the produce away on the shelves for storage.

After they roughly finished their preparations and returned upstairs, Roxine immediately put on water for tea. Luka's room had been readied for her in short order, and the question of wallpaper and the like had apparently been asked. However, Roxine was the only one doing the talking.

"Luka," Cayna called.

"...Yes?"

"If you don't want to stay in a room all by yourself, you can come stay with me or Cie in our rooms anytime, okay?"

A cup in her hand, Luka stared blankly outside—or maybe at the window itself. She looked up at Cayna and slowly nodded.

After patting Luka on the head, Cayna finished her tea and stood.

"I'm gonna go out to make a few stops," she said. "Watch things here, okay? And no fighting."

"Please leave it to us," Roxine answered.

"Well then, I shall be off in search of firewood," Roxilius stated.

Roxilius headed outside first and left the door open for her. When Cayna exited, he bowed and saw her off.

Just as he tried to close the door, he stopped for a beat. Luka hurried over the threshold to catch up to Cayna, and only then did he shut it behind him. After Roxilius gave the two one more bow, he went in search of villagers who found their calling in the forest in order to ask where they might obtain wood. Since he could possibly chop it on his own depending on the situation, he would have to ask about that, too. As a member of the village, he would surely be a part of rotational jobs.

Luka dashed from the house and clung to Cayna's waist; Cayna patted her on the head to calm her down, then took her by the hand as they headed for the inn. It looked like Cayna wouldn't be doing

CHAPTER 3

much by herself for a while. She hoped that befriending Lytt would put Luka at ease even a little.

It was already past noon; Cayna and Luka went straight to the inn and ordered lunch from Marelle. Lytt brought out water, and Cayna reintroduced Luka.

"Lytt, you make nice with Luka here, okay?"

"Sure thing, Miss Cayna. Luka, let's play together!"

Luka, who sat next to Cayna and stuck to her like glue, stared at the beaming Lytt. She then looked up at Cayna's smiling face, slowly got down from her chair, and faced Lytt to give her a small bow.

"...Okay... Some...other time..."

They looked the same age, since they were the same height, but Luka was probably about two years younger. Whether it was thanks to the family business or Marelle's policies, Lytt had a dependable attitude that made her seem like a big sister.

Lytt tried to invite Luka to join her, but Luka shook her head and refused to leave Cayna's side.

"Thanks for the invite, Lytt. Could you wait a little longer until Luka gets a bit more adjusted?"

"Okay!" Lytt replied with an earnest nod.

Marelle came in with soup and bread to take her daughter's place. The woman grinned as she watched Luka nibble at her meal. She leaned toward Cayna and asked quietly, "Pretty mild kid, ain't she?"

"Her village was destroyed not too long ago. She was the only survivor."

"How tragic..."

Marelle frowned for a moment. Then as if to dispel the dark atmosphere between them, she patted Cayna's shoulder, saying, "Hang in there."

"Ow! Hey, that hurts!"

As Cayna trembled in pain, she suddenly remembered something. She caught Marelle as the woman made her way back to the kitchen.

"Ah! Hold on a second, Marelle. There's something I want everyone to taste."

"You want us to try something?"

"I was thinking about making and selling alcohol, but I don't really know much about how it should taste."

"Sure, I don't mind. That means it's on the house, right?"

"Yes, it is. Let's see… How does one barrel sound?"

Cayna remembered all the villagers seated in the dining hall at the previous banquet. She thought the quantity would probably be enough, but she wasn't sure if the taste would be up to their standards.

Marelle patted Cayna's back reassuringly.

"No worries. If there ain't enough, we've got my own stock," Marelle said, thumping her chest in full confidence that Cayna had nothing to worry about.

And so she took out the cask from her Item Box.

"Here you go."

"Where are you always pulling this stuff out from? A lot about you really doesn't make a lick of sense."

After they finished eating, Cayna returned home with Luka and called for the other two members of the household.

"…So, since I'll be having dinner and a sample party at the inn, you don't need to prepare me dinner. Sorry if you already got started."

"Understood. It seems I will only be cooking for two, then," Roxine replied.

"………"

Roxine gave a light nod to which Roxilius responded with a shifty stare.

"Why are you so suspicious of everything?" Roxine demanded. "Don't worry; I'll make you dinner, too. You like kitty chow, right?"

CHAPTER 3

"Oh, don't bother going out of your way for me. I'd rather have fish straight from the river than whatever you make."

Tension crackled in the air between them.

Luka held Cayna's robe from behind, and as soon as she looked up to see her foster mother holding her head in her hands, the girl waved her hands between the two werecats in an attempt to intervene. Their eyes turned to dots at this unexpected mediator.

""Lady Luka?""

"Fighting is...bad..."

Upon catching a glimpse of strong will in the gaze of this little girl, who almost always kept her head down, the two distanced themselves with apologetic looks.

After Cayna confirmed there was no longer any danger of another war breaking out, she wrapped Luka in an emotional embrace and held her tightly to her modest chest.

"What?"

"That was so moving! You're such a dependable girl, Luka. You can be our Minister of Mediation from now on!"

"...Meedee...ashun?"

"Please step in whenever these two start fighting. You're totally right for the job, Luka!"

The doting parent side of their master was already peeking through, and Roxilius and Roxine sweat bullets. Cayna then gave them a piercing stare. The two Rs stood up straight and awaited her orders.

"You two are going out to dinner with us!" said Cayna.

"What? No, that's quite all right," Roxilius insisted. "We are only servants. There's no need for us to take part in such an affair..."

"You're going out to dinner, got it?"

""Yes, ma'am!!""

Her terrifying tone told them if they shook their heads no, that would likely be the last thing they ever did. Roxilius and Roxine answered her swiftly, visible stiffness in their expressions.

Cayna gave a nod of "All right, then" before taking Luka's hand and resuming her village errands. After the two werecats saw them off, they sighed and fell to the ground.

""*Pheeeeeew…*""

"Th-that was terrifying…"

"The apple might not fall far from the tree… The young lady will be a force to be reckoned with in the future."

"This was mostly your fault, Rox."

"You started saying weird stuff first, Cie."

Just as the two were about to go at it again, they sensed eyes peeking in on them from the properly closed entrance and simultaneously stiffened.

"…Hey, Rox."

"…Yeah, Cie?"

"I have a feeling we've had a terrible rapport so far. I was thinking we might try to fix that now. Can't say I'm thrilled about it, though."

"What a coincidence. I was just thinking the same thing. It goes against every fiber of my being, however."

"………"

"………"

They both nodded at each other seriously, then returned to their work as if nothing ever happened. It is to be noted that neither took the slightest glance at the entranceway.

Cayna watched the swaying ears of wheat as she greeted the villagers tending the fields; later on, she met with Lottor to discuss hunting. The village wasn't big, but its people were so warm that she made her rounds ever so slowly. Soon enough, evening was upon them.

CHAPTER 3

Luka's cautious heart had softened a bit, and while she stuck close to Cayna, they simply held hands. Cayna was smiling from ear to ear.

Their last stop was Lux Contracting with its Sakaiya Branch Store sign out front. The owner, Lux, was in, but his apprentice, Dogai, was apparently out of town delivering some goods. Lux's wife, Sunya, and their son, Latem, were present as well.

"Hello, Cayna," said Sunya. "I look forward to having you and the young lady here as our neighbors."

"We feel the same way. Luka, why don't you introduce yourself?"

Luka timidly stepped forward at Cayna's insistence but naturally kept her head down. Cayna wondered if maybe the girl was being a bit impolite, but Sunya and Latem smiled.

"Also, I want to apologize. It looks like Caerick asked a lot of you."

"Ah, no, it's not like we're dissatisfied. In fact, you might say we're honored to display the Sakaiya name."

Cayna had apparently come at just the right time, and Sunya explained Caerick's aim. The merchant had informed the workshop that they could freely create items for him that seemed likely to sell well, since he would be providing the materials.

"Create with abandon… I wonder what Caerick is planning to have you make?"

"At any rate, to think you would be the master's grandmother… I was quite surprised."

"Ha-ha, Caerick is actually the impressive one. Go ahead and treat me the same as always," Cayna said with a wave of her hand and an awkward laugh.

Caerick had informed Sunya that his grandmother was unlikely to want special treatment. Canya did indeed respond this way, and the favorable impression it left on Sunya made her think they could continue building their friendship.

"Ah, well then, would you mind if I gave you a sample product to show him and see if it'll sell?" Sunya asked.

To be honest, Cayna could have used Teleport to do so herself. However, since she couldn't leave Luka alone for very long, she decided to leave the promotion of her new product entirely to Sakaiya.

From a jute bag, she took out three sacks of wheat that held about sixty kilograms each. She then cast Craft Skill: Whiskey Creation and Craft Skill: Beer Creation. The wheat, bags and all, disappeared into a swirl of fire and water; an instant later, each had turned into a ninety-liter barrel.

Cayna looked at the barrel of whiskey and the barrel of beer and internally grabbed her head.

"The alcohol is one thing, but where did these barrels come from?!"

"Perhaps they're from the jute bag and outer husks of wheat?"

"I feel like no one in real life would understand how this stuff just pops out of nowhere…"

Sunya watched with concern as Cayna mumbled strange things to herself.

"I'll just have a taste, then," said Sunya. She poured a small amount of the whiskey into a cup and took a taste. They'd save the barrel of beer for the sample party later and introduce it there.

While the adults talked, Latem gave Luka a balancing *yajirobe* toy made from a block of wood and tree nuts. She didn't stray far from Cayna's side but had fun placing it here and there. Feeling pleased, Latem took out all the models, wooden animals, and toy carriages he'd made and explained them to Luka.

As for the whiskey, Sunya found it to be rather good; it was "very smooth" and possessed a flavor she'd never experienced.

You usually add water or ice to whiskey, right?

CHAPTER 3

Cayna faintly remembered how her father used to drink it long ago.

However, this was the wife of a heavy-drinking dwarf who knew his stuff. Sunya drank it straight and held her own against Lux with ease. When asked if it would sell, she replied, "A dwarf would have no complaints drinking several of these."

"I'll take responsibility for this and make sure our boss gets it," said Lux.

"Don't drink it all on the way."

"………"

Lux stiffened at Sunya's warning. If she hadn't reminded him, Caerick would have probably received an empty barrel.

"Should I make one more?"

"…Please do."

Sunya nodded at Cayna's question with a wry look on her face.

◆

The beer Cayna brought to the dining hall of the inn that night was meant for just a sample party, but in the end, the affair turned into a full-on banquet. The flavor was a hit, and the barrel was emptied within the night. It was *so* popular that the men of the village fell down dead drunk. They lay across the floor with red faces, and here and there, you could hear someone snore with a cup in their hand.

Marelle stared at the empty barrel in shock.

"Sheesh, these louts are a handful."

As always, families came to collect their drunken loved ones. Most were wives and siblings. Lonely, single drunks were left were they lay.

"Shouldn't we bring blankets or something?"

"Nah, leave 'em. If they're going to learn their lesson the hard way like this, then they might as well settle down already."

While Marelle helped those who came to pick up their drunks, her own family cleaned the dining hall. Cayna helped as well, and she asked Roxilius, whom she'd brought along, to join her. Since Luka became sleepy after she ate, Roxine had taken her home.

"Sorry for puttin' you to work like this," Marelle said.

"No, I apologize terribly for the trouble I have caused you."

Roxilius spoke politely with everyone, and even Marelle wasn't sure how to interact with him. Feeling bothered by this, she whispered to Cayna in secret.

"Can't he act a bit more casual?"

"I'm sorry, but he's always been that way. Please try to put it out of your mind."

"Is…is that so?"

Since Cayna couldn't tell her he was specifically made that way, it was easier for people to think he came from a service-minded family. Roxilius quickly learned Marelle and her family's usual work routine, and the cleanup was finished in the blink of an eye. Cayna gathered all the uncollected drunks into one place.

"If possible, why don't you sell that alcohol to me wholesale on a regular basis?"

"I like the idea, but I haven't settled on a price yet."

That was the biggest issue running through her mind. She'd been creating without calculating the profit to be made from her stockpile. Since she'd already converted half her ingredients into beer and whiskey, she had no idea what the actual value of a single barrel was. Cayna had bought them along with quite a number of other things, so she had only the faintest memory of asking herself how much wheat was.

"In any case, we can just guess this time around."

"You can't do that, Cayna. What about your business?"

"I'll take it to Sakaiya and have them settle on a price for me, but if you'd like to buy it cheap, then now's your chance."

CHAPTER 3

"You really are too much. Guess I should take a good deal when I see one."

Although just this one time, Marelle paid Cayna a small fee, and the dining hall became a supplier of beer.

Despite ale and beer being fundamentally the same, in this world devoid of brewing techniques and Craft Skills, the difference was like heaven and earth. The drunks were absolutely floored when she drank her own beer and reported that "it tastes like wheat." Although her looks were misrepresentative of her actual age, they wanted to yell, *Young people should watch their mouth!*

Dogai returned two days later, but he turned right back around to Helshper with Lux and the promotional whiskey. After the product was accepted, Cayna was scheduled to receive large quantities of wheat.

And it was thus that Cayna's job in the village was decided. It felt like somewhere out there, someone was yelling *Blasphemy!* over the idea that a nondrinker was creating and selling alcohol.

"...I sure hope that's true."

"It has already been decided, so let's accept our fate."

Kee's support was more akin to a bullet wound, and Cayna wasn't sure how to feel about it.

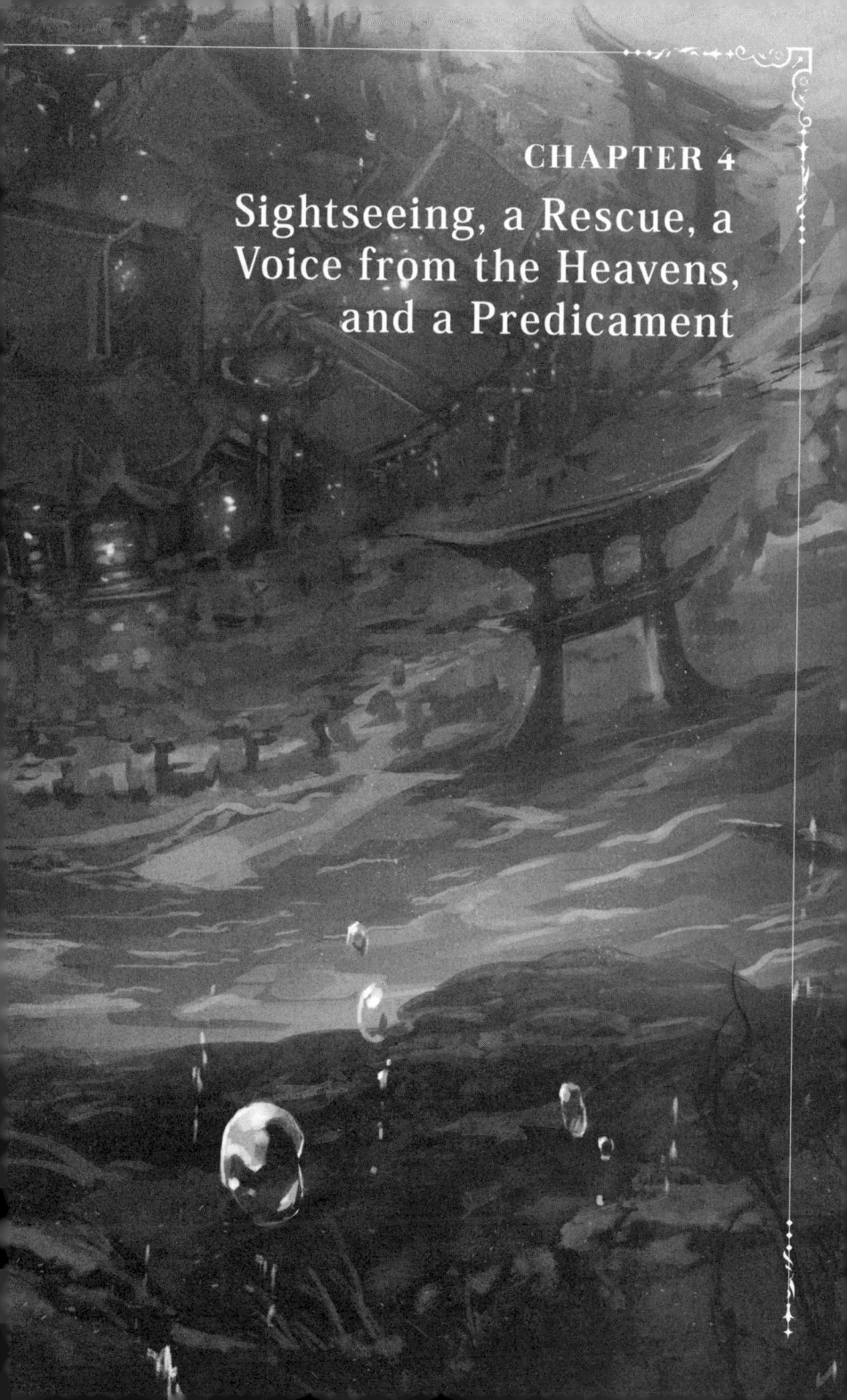

CHAPTER 4
Sightseeing, a Rescue, a Voice from the Heavens, and a Predicament

Then five days after Cayna and her group moved to the village...

Luka's usual way of tottering around after Cayna like a little chick became a daily occurrence. A mere glimpse of Cayna brought a smile to the little girl's face, and she immediately grew anxious the moment Cayna disappeared. She climbed into Cayna's bed at night and slept with her regularly.

Even so, as long as Cayna was in the corner of Luka's eye, there were no obvious issues. When not helping around the house, Luka would play with Lytt and Latem.

Latem was three years older than Luka. Apparently he was put to work at the shop only when the owner, Lux—his father—was present. The boy's primary job in the village's engineering firm involved repairs and servicing. He would fix houses and furniture. Most of the requests that came in were for new furniture. Since the master and his apprentice were away, Cayna had heard Sunya could only accept orders.

And thus, Latem was assigned to managing the children. Latem and Lytt's job was to play with Luka and help her grow accustomed to the village.

Climbing trees. Games of tag. Working the fields. Some activities were a bit puzzling, but there was only so much the three could do together. Cayna herself wasn't familiar with many games, and those that she did know required the wonders of modern civilization, so they weren't all that helpful.

When it came to playtime professionals, it was the adults of the village who answered the call. Cayna tried asking what sort of games they played as kids, and many of the aforementioned activities arose.

Incidentally, since Luka had cried after she fell from a low branch while climbing trees, that idea was quickly nixed. She was also fatally slow, so tag was nixed, too. After ruling out activities deemed too physical, there were plenty of other fun options. Latem taught her simple wood-carving, and she wove flower crowns with Lytt. Children were also an incredible source of labor, so they were sometimes sent to work the fields on occasion. It wasn't yet harvest time, so the majority of the tasks involved weeding.

There was also plowing to be done, so Cayna took this upon herself. She did the work of several, and her intense bulldozing power in the fields shocked the villagers. Since simply striking with the hoe would cause the ground to explode, she used an Earth Spirit as a last resort to rumble through the ground *tatami-gaeshi* style. After that, she picked up the loose stones and roots that rose to the surface and plowed in one day what would have taken multiple people several days. This, too, caused the villagers' jaws to drop.

That day, the three children were making flower crowns in the shadow of a large, lush tree.

"All right! This looks pretty good. Next… H-huh? Why won't it come together?"

"Where? Latem, you messed it up a while back!"

"I'll…attach it here…like this. I just…have to untie it…first…"

The trio were at the edge of the field making flower crowns.

CHAPTER 4

Cayna leaned against the fence and naturally smiled at their conversation. (She more or less tried to ignore the plants' screams.)

Roxine, who made a rare appearance outside, brought them a basket of snacks and stood at attention nearby. In the morning, the children would meet just before noon, and in the afternoon, they would meet after lunch and play until early evening. Essentially, it was a pattern that fit Lytt's schedule, since she often had to help with the family business.

"All right! It's done… Aaagh?!"

"Uh-oh…"

As Latem raised his finished product high, the flower crown fell to pieces. He had apparently messed up somewhere.

"I'm…done…"

"Ooh, very pretty," said Cayna.

Lytt and Luka both happily put their flower crowns on their heads. Li'l Fairy enjoyed trying to pick the scattered petals from Latem's out of midair, even if they passed right through her.

After that, everyone ate the cookies Roxine had made and called it a day. This course of events had become the children's typical schedule as of late. When Lux returned and Latem had to help with the family business once again, the trio's playtime would undoubtedly decrease.

Cayna taught Luka a bit of reading and writing in the mornings, but when Luka, who was learning a number of things at home, had showed her friends how she wrote her own name, Cayna gained two more students within the day.

Thanks to that, from the next day forward, she spent time teaching open-air classes both to the three children and to the occasional villagers with free time on their hands. Since it was a village far removed from the capital, the literacy rate was practically zero. The village elder could just barely read hiragana, and Marelle and her husband, Gatt, could only do three-digit addition and subtraction.

"Never could have guessed I'd come out all this way and end up a teacher, huh?" she murmured with a wry smile as she considered her circumstances. People really never knew in what ways they could be of use to others.

Roxine, who had been listening to her, simply nodded as if this were only natural.

"The common people are eternally grateful to have you so kindly extend your wealth of knowledge to them, Lady Cayna."

The maid's usual lack of consideration was a particularly headache-inducing problem.

"I seriously wonder how Opus made you…"

The NPC aides summoned from the handbells had to be created according to a wide array of standard character settings. Cayna's interests had created Roxilius the young werecat butler, but Opus had decided to cause trouble and throw Roxine together without much thought.

Aides came with two personality settings, so Cayna chose "sincere" and "loyal" for Roxilius. Roxine listened to Opus and Opus alone; he'd probably chosen "uninhibited" and "free-spirited" or something similar. Opus's black-haired elf maid had been set to "graceful" and "kind," so there was a high chance he'd gone with the direct opposite of that.

"Give it a rest, okay, Cie? We aren't above the villagers. You can't say stuff like that to people."

"…I apologize. My comment was uncalled for." Roxine bowed her head at Cayna's chiding. The werecat's body language didn't seem especially remorseful, and Cayna gave an exasperated sigh of "It's no good…"

Roxine probably had some setting that caused her to have undying loyalty to her master. This made her more difficult to deal with than Skargo and the others. Her speedy housework made her very

CHAPTER 4

helpful as long as she kept quiet. For some reason, her destructiveness had something to do with her fellow werecat, Roxilius. This had been going on since the Game Era, so it probably had something to do with conflicting character settings.

She would have liked to get more evidence on this, but *those* were the conditions for obtaining the handbells. Unless one threw their life away and played ten thousand hours like a true addict the way Cayna had, it was an impossible task. Based on Roxilius's remarks on his former residence, most players only had a decent number of hours. As far as Cayna knew, Opus was the only one who had managed to keep up.

"Lady Cayna, if you have a spare moment, do you think could you make me a weapon?"

"Huh? You don't have one?"

Cayna listened to Roxine's rare request as, smiling, she watched Latem fix his flower crown and the two girls lambaste him. She remembered how she'd equipped Roxine in the game the first time she summoned her. Nevertheless, both Roxilius and Roxine had only the clothes on their backs now. Since Cayna had freshened them up with Purity during their travels, she hadn't given their inventory much thought.

"It's been this way since you summoned me."

"If you'd told me that when we arrived in Felskeilo, I could've stocked up. Why'd you wait until now?!"

Cayna suddenly raised her voice, and Luka and the others froze with shocked expressions. When she apologized with a "Sorry, sorry" and explained they were just having a discussion, the kids returned to their peaceful flower crown–making.

Cayna put a hand to her forehead with a "Geez," and Roxine bowed her head in remorse.

"I'm sorry. I didn't think it necessary at the time. I didn't think I'd be living in some backwoods village…"

Roxine's tone was meek, but she apparently still couldn't hide her sharp tongue.

Nevertheless, the quality of her maid outfit was fine enough to be a national treasure. None of the local shops could readily provide anything of its magnitude. On the whole, most clothes sold in this world were secondhand. Ready-made, mass-produced goods weren't exactly a thing, either. If one wanted custom clothes, they had to go to the merchants frequented by nobles.

If that was the case, it would be faster to buy the fabric and make it themselves.

"Guess I'll have to ask Caerick or Elineh."

"If we have fabric, Roxilius and I can use Sewing *(the prerequisite skill for Clothes Creation).*"

"In that case, all I'll have to do is add protection to the finished product. All right, let's do it."

As the two continued to converse smoothly, the three children looked up at them strangely.

"Huh, what's wrong?" Cayna asked.

"This lady can make clothes?" Lytt's eyes sparkled, and she drew near to Roxine. Seeing as Cayna was right next to her, the werecat responded with an inoffensive "Well, I guess so."

A helper NPC's skills were 12.5 percent of the skills possessed by the summoner. Roxine and Roxilius, who had been summoned by Cayna, both had a maximum of five hundred skills. Roxilius's skillset was geared toward battle and butler work, while Roxine's consisted of housekeeping tasks such as cleaning, laundry, and cooking. She could fight, although she wasn't nearly as capable as Roxilius was in combat.

"I know, why don't we make plush toys next time?" Cayna proposed to the three children since Roxine had fallen silent.

Roxine would surely teach Luka a great number of things. But if Lytt and Latem joined in, it'd be a pain, since Cayna would have

CHAPTER 4

to get involved as well. Thus, it would be easier for Cayna to do the teaching from the outset. If she taught Luka first, even the other two in their jealousy would be roused to action.

Sure enough, Lytt and Latem raised their hands in agreement. Luka nodded a bit slower than the rest, but she looked pleased. Everyone would no doubt enjoy thinking about what they were going to make.

Even most people in this world who learned sewing from their mothers stopped at simply mending clothes. After all, there was no economic wiggle room to learn how to create something new. It was for this same reason that Cayna's language classes were popular among the villagers.

"Master, why don't you take things a bit easier? I believe it will be beneficial for you to sleep the day away while thinking of nothing at all."

Having determined from the height of the sun that her timing was appropriate, Roxine brought out warm hand towels as she called to Cayna and the children. She distributed the towels and spoke with concern as she handed Cayna hers.

"Please leave the home and Lady Luka to myself and that stray cat."

"...You still haven't made up?"

"No, we've simply reached a mutual understanding. We haven't reconciled. After all, he and I are sworn enemies."

Roxine spoke with such forthrightness that Cayna could only tilt her head in wonder over what could have caused such bad blood.

"Anyway, I should take it easy, huh?" she murmured as she looked at the sky. Well, the screams of the plants sacrificed to the flower crowns alone were awfully hard on her sanity.

Out of the corner of her eye, she saw Li'l Fairy chasing butterflies. As if she couldn't leave Cayna past a certain distance, Li'l Fairy didn't try to go beyond a certain point. Cayna could touch her, but Li'l Fairy passed through everything else.

Even in the house, Cayna often saw her passing through walls like it was nothing. Neither the villagers nor her helper NPCs Roxilius and Roxine could see her. Kartatz and the others were the same way. The players were the only other people who could, and the fairy didn't seem to want anything to do with them. Kee also seemed to notice the fairy, but Cayna didn't know if the same could be said the other way around. After all, a Divine Spirit like Kee was plenty mysterious all on his own.

The fairy conveyed her will only through gestures and expression; she had yet to ever speak. She never even tried, so she likely had no words at all. Even so, Cayna somehow managed to understand her. She wasn't sure if it was intuition, but the words would pop into her head.

This hadn't been the case when the fairy initially came out of the book, but now she occasionally pointed out things Cayna had forgotten. Cayna thought if these instances grew, the fairy might give her hints on how to meet Opus.

Cayna recalled a promise she'd made thanks to the fairy's suggestion. Just as she started thinking about taking Lytt through the skies, someone held a flower crown out to her.

"This...is for you...Cayna."

"Oh my. Thank you, Luka."

Cayna put Luka's flower crown on her head. Lytt praised how pretty she looked, which made Cayna hug Luka in gratitude. Perhaps because they were in front of everyone, Luka became profusely embarrassed.

Since she'd anticipated bringing only Lytt, Cayna thought strolling through the sky with Flight would be a simple affair. Now that

CHAPTER 4

there were three children involved, she'd have to come up with a few safety precautions.

"Have anything for me, Kee?"

"What about a carpet to ride on?"

Kee was talking about an item known as a Magic Carpet. It could fit one to five people, hover about a meter above the ground, and travel at the running speed of an average human.

"That'll take a while to make, though..."

Since she would need thread filled with monster magic, gathering the materials would likely take some time. Cayna wasn't even sure the monsters from back in the Game Era still existed. She could make the thread herself, but that would take a tremendous amount of time, too.

"That's a hard pass. Next!"

"Well, the only other option is summoning, but..."

"Right..."

There were several possible summonings that could carry the children. However, since the griffins and dragons weren't the most friendly-looking, anyone who didn't know better would be terrified. In fact, since the village was right along the border, there would likely be endless trouble if the soldiers spotted them.

"Maybe something low-flying that doesn't go past the treetops?"

Cayna had to think of the children's safety first and foremost. With crumbs of Roxine's cookies on their cheeks, the three looked at Cayna quizzically as she glared at the empty sky mumbling to herself.

"Miss Cayna doesn't look very happy, does she?" Lytt said.

"Uh-huh... Maybe...she's sad...?"

"Come to think of it, I heard my dad say somethin' about how high elves can hear plants' voices."

""What?!""

Shocked, both Lytt and Luka turned around to stare at where

they'd all just been sitting. It was a nameless flower field filled with white, purple, and yellow blossoms. Thanks to the children's thorough plucking, all that remained of one section was pitiful leaves.

As the two girls gazed downward sorrowfully, Roxine poured them the tea she'd brewed and spoke in reassurance.

"Lady Cayna would never blame you for something so insignificant. She's much too forgiving. If you prefer, you could make these somewhere else, where she cannot see you."

"Somewhere else...," said Lytt.

"Where she...can't...see us...?" asked Luka.

"Does the village even have a flower field like that?" Latem wondered aloud.

Roxine giggled as she watched the children hem and haw, putting their heads together to talk it over. After all, since Cayna was more focused on wowing the children than anything else, they had nothing to worry about.

The next day, Cayna discussed her plan of action with Marelle and Sunya and informed them of the risk involved. However, since the three kids would be with Cayna—an adventurer who had made even Arbiter howl—it seemed more than safe to trust her with their children. Cayna, who had spent the morning teaching the kids to read and write as usual, told them to meet in front of Lux Contracting in the afternoon.

"Well then, ready to take to the skies today?"

""""What?""""

The three tilted their heads, not understanding. With a smirk, Cayna cast a spell she hadn't used in quite some time.

Summoning Magic: Double Load: Griffin

A shining green line drew a magic circle in the air a few meters above her. It was a double-layer hexagram, and mysterious writing

CHAPTER 4

wrapped around the inner layer. Two complete circles formed side by side, and a thick green light came pouring down.

Slowly slipping through that gallery of light were two mythical beasts whose top halves were pure-white eagles and bottom halves were majestic lions.

"*"KWRARARA!!*""

The griffins' sharp talons pierced the ground, and their high-pitched shrills echoed in every corner of the village. Once the circles disappeared, they unfurled their mighty wings in an ostentatious display. They were slightly larger than an African elephant, and their presence caused a stir among the villagers.

Summoning Magic: Load: Earth Spirit Thog Level 5

Next to the griffins appeared a chess piece that stood twice as tall as them. Thicker than a pawn, it was a rook with uneven protrusions on its brick surface. It was white from top to bottom, and it looked like a work of art carved from marble.

Seeing in the flesh a mythical beast found only fairy tales, legends, and the songs of minstrels left most villagers once again slack-jawed and bug-eyed.

The two griffins rubbed their feathers and beaks against Cayna's outstretched hand, and they purred lovingly. To outsiders, it was an act far beyond any wild Beast Master. The scene conversely forfeited all hope for Beast Masters across the board.

In regard to their original purpose, all summonings were created for battle. Thus, on that note, the beasts had ever-present skills that made the very sight of them overwhelmingly terrifying… That was how the game had made them, anyway.

Cayna had summoned them several times before and saw the beasts not as tools but as friends. The griffins seemed to respond to this, and they took control of their skills out of respect for her. Taking the villagers, who Cayna saw as dear neighbors, into account, they moderated their harsh skills so they wouldn't appear scarier than they actually were.

"*Grararagh.*"

"*Krawgh.*"

Luka had clung to Cayna, and she thus ended up ruffling the soft feathers of a griffin's neck without running away. High above her, a head with a sharp beak big enough to tear apart an adult looked down at her with its round, golden eyes. She initially froze in fear, but her heart let down its walls once the griffin enveloped her in its fluffy feathers.

Seeing that Luka had recovered from her paralyzing fear, Cayna held the girl up in her arms and introduced her daughter to the two griffins.

"Okay, guys, this is my daughter Luka. If anything happens, protect her above all else, got it?"

Up close, the two beasts truly were frightening. Luka let out a small yelp, and the two retreated a few steps to bow to her. They did so simultaneously, and the rumbling coming from their throats was reminiscent of pet parakeets.

Taken aback by these comical actions, the little girl timidly held out her hand and touched one of the griffin's soft feathers. It narrowed its eyes comfortably, and Luka gave a small smile.

Lytt and Latem had escaped behind Roxilius, who stood a bit away from Cayna. When they saw Luka petting the griffins, they finally approached Cayna, too.

"Miss Cayna… C-can we pet them?"

"I-is it really okay?"

Cayna chuckled when it was clear Latem was less adventurous compared to Lytt. Irritated by this, he forced himself to race up to one of the griffins.

However, because of his height, Latem was only able to place his

CHAPTER 4

hand on a rough joint on its front claw. Just as the suspicious griffin bent its head to seeming stab Latem with its beak, he ran away screaming.

"UWAAAAAAGH?!"

"".......""

"Um…" Cayna was shocked; she'd never expected a boy to be the first to head for the hills. She secretly decided to not leave Luka with him going forward.

Of course, the rest of the villagers watching laughed, and his mother, Sunya, was surprised as well. The griffin no doubt found the whole ordeal more outrageous than anyone else, since it had merely bowed its head. The boy had run away screaming away despite the griffins' attempt to drop their intimidation factor, and they felt like they'd lost face. One dropped its head sadly, while the other wrapped its wings over its companion and stroked in apparent consolation.

"They're pretty cute creatures once you take away the menace."

"It is rather evident their master played a vital role in that, wouldn't you say?"

As soon as Latem escaped, his mother, Sunya, dragged him straight back by the ear.

"Ow, ow, ow, ow, ow, ow!"

"Nothing is more embarrassing than a boy like you being too afraid to touch something a girl can with ease!"

She plopped him in front of the griffins, and he averted his gaze as two pairs of large, round eyes stared at him. Finally, he said, "Sorry," and the griffin that had been doing the consoling batted Latem with its wings as punishment.

After Cayna confirmed with relief that she could go on with her preparations, she took a thick rope from her Item Box.

"We're flying with that?"

"With rope?"

Lytt and Latem seemed to be under the impression the rope would fly through the sky on its own, but Cayna hadn't explained everything just yet.

"My plan is to get the two griffins to pull us on the floating Earth Spirit."

An Earth Spirit could control gravity, but you wouldn't be able to gain enough altitude to soar that way. Plus, it was incredibly slow. Her idea was to attach it to the griffins and turn it into a flying carriage.

Initially, the plan was to suspend the golem carriage from the griffins. However, everyone would be in trouble if the rope snapped. She then considered restructuring the golem carriage to make it float, but she soon realized she'd never have enough magic rhymestones and gave up. Finally, as a last resort, there was one remaining option: the Earth Spirit, which they could use as a solid basis. This method would allow them to float on their own power if the rope was severed, and even if Cayna separated from it for whatever reason, the Earth Spirit could act in self-defense. Since its protective powers were a cut above the rest, the risk to the children would be minimized.

"Just to be safe, please take these as well."

Roxilius brought out heavy coats, cloaks, and the like, and he passed them to the children.

"We're not gonna fly *that* high, you know."

She planned on taking them just a little higher than the treetops as well as casting Invisibility on the griffins. That way, no one at the border would recognize their group as anything more than specks.

"It will be cold in the sky, so please be sure to dress properly," said Roxilius.

"C'mon. Hop aboard, you three," Cayna urged.

Cayna and Roxilius urged the children forward as they made sure the ropes were properly fastened around the griffins' torsos. A disturbance erupted along the rook's surface, and a spiral staircase sprouted

CHAPTER 4

around the outer circumference. It looked like a pure-white marble chess piece on the outside, but since it was packed with firm sediment inside, it could change its shape at will. The rope would be tightly held within the Earth Spirit itself, so there was hardly any chance of it getting cut off.

Lytt and Latem gingerly climbed up and were captivated by the view they had over the village rooftops. Luka alone was unwilling to rush to such a high place on her own, and she clung tightly to Cayna's cloak. Cayna lightly lifted Luka princess-style and carried her upward.

"I'm so jealous, Luka."

"Well then, I'll be sure to carry you on the way back down, Lytt."

"Yay! That's okay, right, Luka?"

"…Uh-huh."

Luka nodded, and Lytt jumped for joy. Cayna tilted her head, thinking *Girls really like the princess hold, huh?* as she totally missed the point.

Cayna held tight to the three children bundled up in coats. The protrusions at the top of the Earth Spirit (which were set in sawlike intervals) were shorter than the children's heads, but if she cast Fence, they wouldn't fall outside. Roxilius confirmed the rope's security, and the griffins took off at Cayna's signal.

The beasts cried out with a slow beating of their wings, then began to rise upward. At the same time, Cayna's Invisibility spell made sure those wings didn't make a sound. The group switched directions and turned as they passed the village's tallest tree, making a big circle around the village.

Although timid at first, the children seemed to grow more comfortable, giving cheers of "Wow!" and "Ooh!" As usual, Luka stayed by Cayna's side, but she seemed to enjoy watching Lytt and Latem while also slowly taking in her surroundings.

Seeing this, Cayna gave a huge smile and ordered the griffins to speed up.

"These two are going to go a little faster. You're not scared, right?"

"Nope, I'm totally fine!" Lytt chirped.

"This is awesome! Awesome! AWESOOOOOME!"

Latem's ways of expressing his excitement were apparently rather limited; he'd been saying nothing except "awesome" for a while. Cayna then thought that she ought to work on expanding their vocabulary during their reading and writing classes.

As Cayna listened to their cheerful voices on the wind, she determined that all was well and instructed the two griffins to head east toward the mountain range, as she'd intended. The plan was to circle around her Guardian Tower, pass over the Ejidd River, and head back to the village.

The others waved and saw them off with cries of "Have fun!" and "Take care!"

The wind wasn't too strong thanks to her Fence spell, so Cayna put her hands on Luka's shoulders and turned her 180 degrees.

"Here, Luka. Don't look down, but check out what's up ahead."

"...Um, o-okay..."

Although Luka said this, Cayna could tell her body was tense, and her eyes were shut tight. Lytt grabbed Luka's hand gently, while Latem squeezed the other hand tight.

"It's okay, Luka. We're not swaying, and the wind isn't all that strong."

"We'll be right here with ya, so open your eyes at least once. Just one time."

Perhaps thanks to their encouragement, Luka slowly relaxed. Finally, Cayna heard her give the slightest "W-wow..."

"Right?! Isn't it amazing?! It is, isn't it?"

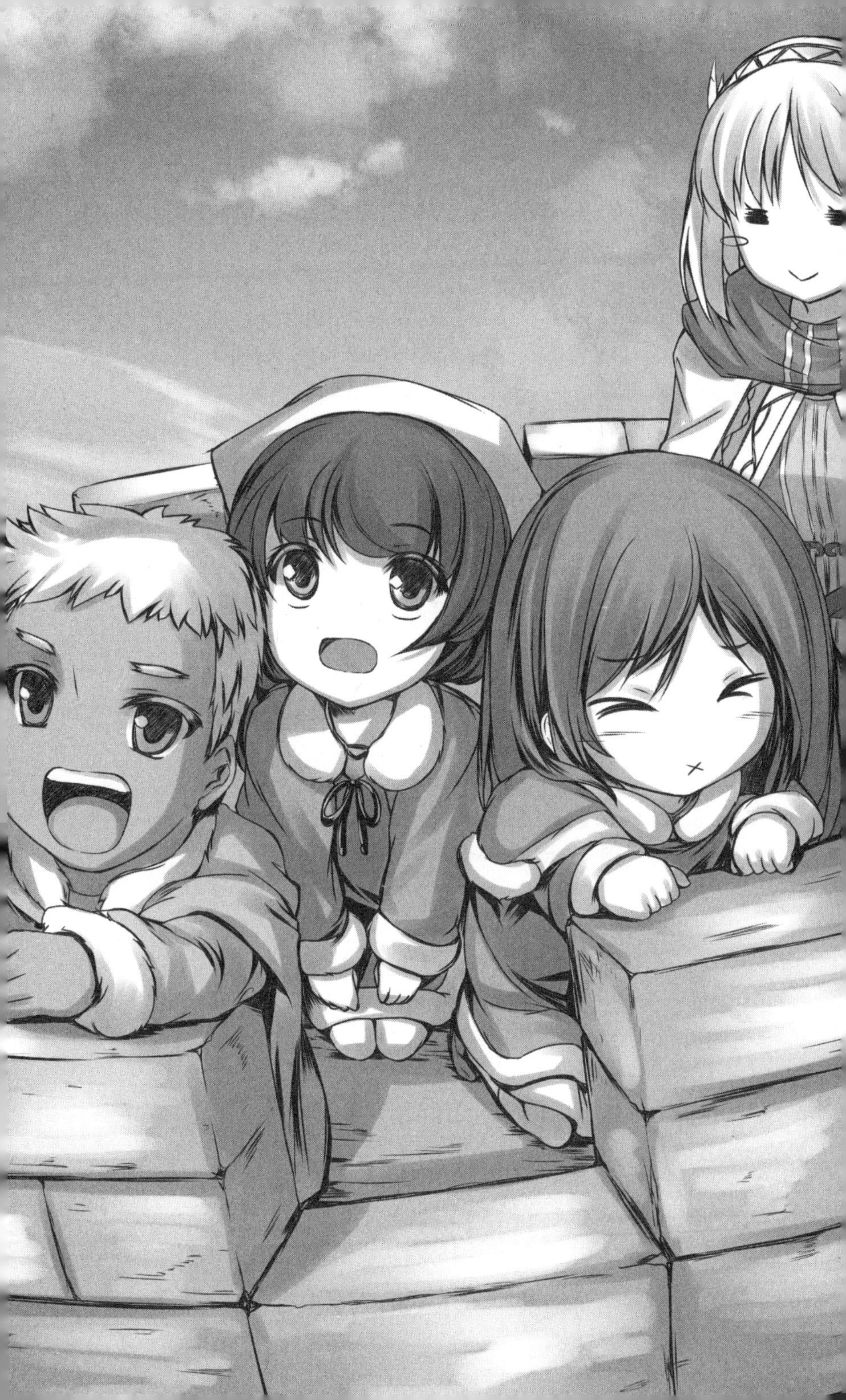

"Hey! Look, look! That silver pole over there… What do you think it is?!"

To the ecstatic Latem, it was indeed a silver pole. However, in reality, it was the tower of a very bad witch. Since getting too close would kick in the Nullification Barrier and cancel her summoning, Cayna gave the griffins plenty of time to make a long detour.

The children's eyes locked onto the silver tower that reflected the sun's rays and sent particles glimmering all around them. Lytt was the only one who whispered in Cayna's ear.

"Is that yours, Miss Cayna?"

"Yup, that's it. The home of the big bad witch."

As they grinned at each other, Latem began to feel left out, and he pouted.

"Hey, what gives? Somethin' going on?"

"Nope, nothing at all."

"That's right," said Cayna. "It's our little secret."

"Heeeey, that's no fair. Tell me, too!" Latem demanded, but reluctantly gave up after being told it was a girls-only secret. After all, he was outnumbered three against one.

Luka looked up at Cayna and asked, "What about…me?" Lytt met Cayna's gaze, and the two of them had a brief, wordless exchange.

Lytt nodded, then hugged Luka and happily declared, "I'll tell you when we get home."

Flying was tiring business, Cayna had planned on relaxing and enjoying the scenery the rest of the way, so she was shocked to find Lytt and Latem so unexpectedly energetic.

"Cayna! I wanna go to that tower!" Latem insisted.

"Y-you can't, Latem! A veeeery scary witch lives there!"

He was apparently excited either way. Just when she thought he was a boy of some discretion, she turned out to be wrong. He was now a loose cannon—or perhaps something that had been freed of its shackles. In any case, he was entirely focused on the one thing that had caught his eye.

"I wonder if this is how kids act on roller coasters."

"...? Roller...what?"

"Ahhh, don't mind me. It's nothing for you to worry about, Luka."

"Okay..."

Latem's eyes shone with a fierce fire, and he seemed utterly infatuated with the silver tower. Cayna ordered the griffins to briefly slow down after they moved farther away from it.

"Tch. I wanted to go see that tower."

Latem clicked his tongue as he looked toward the tower that was now the size of a toothpick, and Cayna couldn't hide her irritation.

"Don't be stupid. Even the griffins wouldn't have been able to hold their own in there. It's not the type of place worth risking Lytt's and Luka's safety just to satisfy your curiosity." Cayna gave Latem a dead-serious look that turned him into a trembling mess of fear right where he stood.

While there wasn't anything that could be called a *monster* in Cayna's tower, the surrounding area was full of wild, invisible ones. Any average person who even approached her tower would be in for a mess of trouble. If they managed to make it inside, they would be forcefully thrown back out the moment they stopped moving. The monsters would attack as soon as they found themselves panicking in an unfamiliar place and dropping their guard.

There was no way Cayna would ever allow children to go near a place like that. They'd be like lambs to the slaughter. Even she had a responsibility to care for other people's children. Cayna didn't necessarily want to say this, but she wanted them to understand this world wasn't so kind that a mere desire to go outside would help them survive.

"Now, now. Act your age, Cayna."

Kee gave her a warning as she was about to unwittingly unleash Intimidate. Just as she swallowed her words and considered how to admonish Latem, someone else spoke for her and stepped on his foot.

"Owwwww!"

"Don't be selfish! Miss Cayna brought us all the way here out of the goodness of her heart!"

In front of Latem, who now held his foot in a crouch, Lytt stood like a fierce guardian god. The boy frowned, and tears welled in his eyes. That stomp must have held a ton of force.

"If Luka wasn't here, she probably never would have taken you! Miss Cayna has already done so much for everyone. After all, we're never flown before!"

As Lytt put her hands on her hips and silenced Latem, Cayna bowed her head and gathered her thoughts.

Lytt really is incredible.

If someone else had been there, they would have thrown in a comment of *Hey now, you're praising someone?* Somewhere out there beneath the sky, her terrible friend was holding his face in his hands.

"S-sorry…for makin' you so mad…"

Lytt looked angry enough to bite him, and Latem at last bowed his head.

"What are you apologizing to me for?! You should be apologizing to Miss Cayna!"

A wave of intimidation rolled off her, and he hurriedly turned to Cayna with a bowed head.

"U-um. I-I'm sorry."

Cayna was used to never hearing any selfishness from the children she met at the hospital, even though they surely once had selfish desires and opinions like anyone else.

Back in the hospital, a lot of us, myself included, had given up…

CHAPTER 4

Pushing sentimentality aside, Cayna switched her attention back to Latem, whose head was still bowed.

"What are you apologizing for?"

Even if he'd done some reflection, it'd be problematic if he was unaware of the root cause.

Latem then responded in a loud voice, "Huh? Ummm. I-I'm sorry for being selfish!"

Cayna lightly bonked his head and forgave him.

"If you understand, then that'll do."

She continued. "If we get too close to that tower, both the griffins and this Earth Spirit will disappear." Cayna knocked her heel against the rook that served as the ground beneath their feet to prove her point. "If you three were suddenly thrown into the air, what would save you?"

"U-um..."

They were currently more than ten meters above the ground. When they took the long detour around the tower, they'd been flying at about a hundred meters. As they recalled this, not only Latem's but also Lytt's and Luka's faces became instantly strained.

"Even if I caught you, I sadly wouldn't be able to use magic, so you'd just fall. I'm pretty confident I could grab Luka to save her, but what about you two?"

If the children were now aware of the cause, it was best they be properly aware of the effect. Her words were probably a bit harsh, but the experience would no doubt be useful later.

"W-we'd fall?" Lytt questioned. Her face was pale, and she clung to Cayna alongside Luka.

Cayna didn't plan on adding more detail beyond that, but considering the height from which the kids would fall, it obviously wasn't necessary.

"I'm sorry! Really, really sorry!"

This time, ashen-faced Latem apologized to Lytt and Luka. He seemed to have finally realized how much danger he'd put them all in.

Cayna heaved a sigh. *I'll never get used to this scolding thing*, she thought.

"It's just not my forte."

With a dry smile, she thought of the many members in her old guild who would have had a smart comment about that. Since they'd referred to themselves as "a bunch of no-good adults," reprimand had mostly fallen to Opus and Ebelope.

If only they were here at a time like this was too far-fetched a wish even for Cayna.

"*Gyararagh!*"

As they continued flying above the forest, one of the griffins let out a warning cry. Since Cayna was the summoner, she understood it was telling them to be careful.

The children were looking at the far-off mountain range and watching the clouds pass, so they didn't notice anything amiss. Cayna had completely forgotten one had to keep an eye out for monsters soaring in the skies as well. Originally, the griffins would emit an aura that said *Back off* whenever they appeared, so the weak monsters would typically stay away. However, the beasts now had no presence, since they had shut off their Intimidate system for the sake of the children. They were now floating defenselessly in the sky (or so it seemed), and it didn't take long for monsters to see them as easy pickings.

Wham!

A monster crashed right into the Earth Spirit's Fence. Although the method of arrival was a *wham!* the actual sound of the crash came out more like a *whomp*.

Before they realized it, the Earth Spirit was surrounded by a flock of black crows. When packed together in such a way, their fierce attack was comparable to that of a horned bear. The birds were known as Caro Bears, and they scavenged for dead meat like condors. The monster birds circled the area with loud squawks of "*Caw, caw*" and "*Gyah, gyah*" as they threatened Cayna and her group.

Lytt and Luka were absolutely terrified, and they huddled under Cayna's cloak. Latem was just barely standing, but his face was paler than ever before.

"M-Miss Cayna..."

"...?!" Luka gulped audibly.

"Ah, don't worry. Chumps like that can't break the Earth Spirit's barrier."

Cayna said this with a light wave of her hand, but by the children's tragic faces, they clearly thought it was the end of the world.

In the meantime, a number of Caro Bears tried to attack, but it was a suicide mission. The Fence forced them back in droves. Their adamant refusal to learn better and give up had to be some monster instinct.

"Guess scaring kids isn't really their goal, huh?"

She thought maybe they'd go away on their own, but there seemed to be little chance of that.

Cayna swung her right arm over her head. In that instant, sparkles appeared outside the spirit's Fence and solidified into multiple layers.

It was a low-level ice-type attack spell, Shattering Ice Arrow Gira Giga. The intense spell didn't stop at just freezing the target; it immediately shattered it. Each arrow was about the size of a pen and generated endlessly around the Fence. There had to be several hundred already. There were probably ten hits for each Caro Bear.

Despite seeing this right before their eyes, whether the Caro Bears were unfazed because they were literal bird brains or because they didn't see it as a threat was unclear. Already pretty sick of being shadowed, Cayna uttered a quick "Fire," and the pathetic flock of Caro Bears were eliminated in three seconds. After their clamorous cries died away, Cayna waited for a moment before turning back to Lytt and the others.

"...Are the scary birds gone?" Lytt asked.

"I took care of 'em, so you're nice and safe now. You come on out, too, Luka!"

Cayna patted Luka's back with encouragement, and the little girl finally popped her head out. Her body was still tucked into Cayna's cloak, but she didn't seem to be trembling anymore.

"Th-that's an adventurer for ya. Awesome."

Only Latem, who had managed to remain standing, saw the Caro Bears' entire demise. He looked at her with admiration and envy, but he was better off not regarding her as a normal mage. Someone like Cayna, who could cast magic with a flip of her hand, was the epitome of illogical. A normal mage could never go up against a horde of Caro Bears alone or fire hundreds of shots at once. If one were to use Cayna as a standard, any Imperial Mage who met her would be tormented by dejection and despair.

Latem's excitement piqued Lytt's interest, and she joined in the discussion of Cayna's valor. Since Cayna herself could say nothing more than "I hit them, and they fell," Latem spoke for her.

"It was crazy. These shiny things surrounded us, and just when they disappeared, the monsters all got taken out!"

Having someone else explain was a little embarrassing, so Cayna could only smirk as she listened to his retelling. Seeming to feel he wasn't giving the whole story, Lytt and Luka demanded he be more specific.

"Uh, well..."

"That didn't tell me anything! Miss Cayna, what did you do?"

"Coming to the source, huh? Hmm. I shot lots of ice magic."

CHAPTER 4

"What? That was ice magic?! Never seen that before."

"Cayna's magic...is amazing..."

"You've seen it, too, Luka?!" said Lytt.

Luka had also seen Cayna's Summoning Magic, so a giant Blue Dragon was the sort of thing she considered impressive. Lytt, on the other hand, had only ever seen Cayna use a bit of magic to make daily life easier, which generally couldn't be called *amazing*. Even so, in the eyes of people who spent their entire lives in the same village, such magic was nothing short of extraordinary.

"Heads up, everyone. We'll be passing over the Ejidd River next. It's super-wide, so make sure you get a good look."

It'd be problematic if the kids got *too* interested in magic and started saying things like *Teach me!* Therefore, she decided to try to sway them from the subject and bring attention to their surroundings instead.

"I know lots about the Ejidd River. It's a loooong way to the other side," Latem stated.

He'd likely seen it if his family had crossed over the bridge Cayna and Kartatz had built. But they wouldn't be walking alongside it this time. Instead, Cayna thought they could follow the stream downriver. Since they'd end up in the Felskeilo capital if they went too far, she planned on stopping just beyond the bridge.

There were also waterfalls with some nearby mountain streams on the way; it must have been difficult for craftsmen of the past to float their lumber along them. The guards at the Helshper border were unlikely to see the group, but in the event their group *was* discovered, she had every intention of pulling some connections with her grandson.

Cayna had initially considered grazing just above the river's surface as they flew, but she thought it'd be pretty bad if they got stuck on the bridge she and the others had constructed. Rising as high as possible, they sped along the river at top speed. Both sides of the river were covered in sprawling forest, and the flight had a trail-like ambience that delighted the children.

As she listened to their cheers, she remembered one war where she dove into the water and ambushed guys from the Red Kingdom from behind. Since she didn't know what might be living in the river now, the last thing she wanted to do was dive in. It wasn't like she thought she would lose a fight, but if she happened to come across a daioyanma dragonfly, she was confident she'd panic and blast it away with zero discretion. Doing so would probably change the flow of the river or create an avalanche of debris. The consequences would be undoubtedly scary.

As she gazed into the far distance, harkening back to old memories, the group suddenly passed right over the bridge that mother and son had built.

"Huh…?"

Flying over it was fine enough, but at the same time, Cayna felt she'd seen something strange, and she cocked her head in bewilderment. She'd been so mindful of the children's safety that she hadn't been able to properly notice a scene occurring on the bridge.

Just when she thought she was thinking too much, Lytt tugged at her clothes.

"Miss Cayna! There were carriages on the bridge just now!"

Latem also started crying out "The bridge! The bridge!" in a fluster.

Left with not much choice, she consulted her third eye.

"Kee, what's going on with the bridge?"

"It appears carriages are being attacked by monsters."

"Right. Carriages are being attacked by mons— WHAAAAAAT?!"

She could have hurriedly ordered the griffins to stop, but landing wasn't the right move, and it was impossible to suddenly halt. Having

CHAPTER 4

heard their summoner's orders, the griffins bravely gained altitude and went around in a circle.

Meanwhile, Cayna used Farsight to check out the situation on the bridge and spotted several carriages at a standstill. Ogres and goblins locked the group in on both sides, and it was obvious they were in a pinch. She felt like she'd seen several of the carriages before. They were most likely part of Elineh's caravan.

However, she still had the children with her, and Cayna's thoughts came to an impasse.

◆

"Oh dear, we're in a bit of a tight spot, aren't we?"

In the middle of the bridge, Elineh admitted their hopeless situation and narrowed his eyes as if to prepare for the worst.

There were ogres at their front door and goblins at their back. Despite having the aid of the mercenary group the Flame Spears, who were led by the battle-renowned Arbiter, their leader was absent, and only half the group's numbers were present. Protecting even three carriages would be a struggle.

"Just when I thought that luck was on our side…," Elineh murmured as he glanced at the small wooden crates piled atop the carriage beds. He didn't let his resignation show on his face even once.

This merchandise, ordered directly from Sakaiya himself, was addressed to Cayna, who had decided to live in the remote village. Even an amount of this size rivaled the transport cost of other completely packed wagons. It was likely just as profitable, too.

It was hard to believe that only a little while ago he'd been casually laughing with Arbiter, who joked that Cayna "sure wears a lot of hats." The situation had quickly taken a turn for a worse; Elineh couldn't help but click his tongue at how utterly unfair the world was.

A monster attack had driven Elineh and his caravan into this corner. They'd experienced a similar dilemma not too long ago when

Kenison ended up seriously wounded, although a lack of vigilance wasn't to blame.

This attack began shortly after the caravan crossed the Helshper border. One ogre and three goblins had appeared from behind, and Arbiter left with half his men to take care of them. The plan was for the caravan to wait a short distance away.

However, this turned out to be a diversion meant to divide Arbiter's forces. Five goblins appeared from the nearby forest, leaving the caravan no choice but to keep moving. The co-captain then decided it was best to drive the carriages faster and outdistance the monsters.

Just as they were about to give the tenacious goblins the slip, the caravan arrived at the bridge. When the caravan had almost crossed, three ogres appeared on the opposite side. Even though the remaining mercenaries managed to fend them off, the goblins drew ever closer. In all likelihood, Arbiter wouldn't be able to return to the caravan no matter how long they waited. Monster reinforcements would arrive and keep his group from getting back to the bridge.

This wasn't a strategy ogres or goblins, with their limited intelligence, could cook up—someone had to be pulling the strings in secret. The thought made Elineh shudder.

At that moment, a giant creature passed over his head, and Elineh wondered if something outrageous might be happening behind the scenes.

…With extreme unease, he questioned if he was thinking too much. They were still holding out within the limited confines of the bridge, but if monster reinforcements arrived here as well, the caravan would never last.

```
Magic Skill: Load: Boa Lu Ludo: Strike, 0
Lightning
```

It was then that salvation lent an outstretched hand. Several

CHAPTER 4

serpents of lightning crackled through the air from downstream, avoiding the bridge and carriages before striking three ogres that were fighting the co-captain and his men.

Its destructive power was mind-blowing. The ogre that was struck at the shoulder instantly turned to ash from the waist up. The ogre struck in the stomach had its torso turned to ash, and it crumbled away; its only remains were the head and anything below the knee. Several bolts struck the last ogre all at once and left nothing but charcoal.

When the co-captain, Elineh, and the others turned in the direction the spell had come from, they found Cayna floating in mid-air nearby.

""Lady Cayna?!""

But there was no time to be shocked: Another bizarre incident occurred toward the back of the caravan. The surface of the river bulged, and pillars of water large enough to soak the entire line of carriages came bursting forth. Cayna had anticipated this, of course, and cast a barrier spell on the caravan, keeping things completely dry.

The only ones affected were the goblins in the back row that had been causing trouble. Five were blasted into the river by water cannons before getting swept downstream and drowning. Even those remaining on the bridge were trampled by the water giants that appeared from the river. Not a happy ending for the goblins, either way.

"Lady Cayna! I have a favor to ask!" the co-captain called when Cayna set foot on the bridge and kicked at the ogres that had turned to ash.

"Oh, it's the co-captain. You okay?"

"I'm terribly sorry, Lady Cayna. Might I ask you to protect the caravan for a short while?"

"Uh, sure, no problem."

Cayna wasn't really sure what was going on, but she nodded. The co-captain spoke briefly to Elineh, then took his remaining men to race back the way they came. He shouted hoarsely, "Captain, please be saaaafe!!"

Cayna saw them off while looking perplexed, and Elineh bowed his head.

"Thank you very much, Lady Cayna. Because of you, both our people and goods are safe."

"Huh? Oh, yeah. I'm glad I just happened to be passing by."

"Gyaaararagh."

"Gyarararagh."

The two griffins screeched as they flew over to Cayna with the giant chess piece in tow. The creatures remained airborne, but the three children peeked out from the top of the chess piece. Among them was Lytt, who Elineh recognized.

"So that's what passed by us just now...," he said.

"We were on a bit of a sightseeing flight. Good thing we made it here in time," Cayna replied.

Elineh squinted at the airborne griffins. "Some rather frightening creatures you've brought sightseeing with you."

"They're not scary at all. I think they have you beat in fluffiness, Elineh."

"...'Fluffiness'?"

Cayna's eyes glinted with a light like that of a bird of prey. Every strand of fur on Elineh's body stood up in fear, and he instinctively backed away.

"...Ah."

Cayna's face fell in disappointment, and she didn't push it any further than that.

They couldn't stay on the bridge forever, so the caravan crossed to the other side for the time being. They stopped the carriages in an open area, and Cayna heard the rundown of events. Afterward, she introduced Elineh to Luka. Lytt and Latem stayed on top of the chess piece since they had no idea what was going on, while the griffins rested their wings nearby.

"Oh, are you Lady Cayna's daughter?" Elineh asked.

"...I'm...Luka," the girl mumbled softly. She dipped her head and stuck close behind Cayna.

"My name is Elineh. It's a pleasure to meet you."

Cayna was pleased to see Luka giving a rare introduction without prompting. Elineh could sense her deep, doting adoration of the girl, and the corners of his mouth lifted.

"At any rate, is it rare for ogres to do this sort of thing?" Cayna asked.

"Well, they don't typically employ such advanced tactics. But let's discuss it further when Sir Arbiter returns and everything has calmed down."

In the game, monsters commonly worked in groups during certain types of quests. Elineh's explanation contradicted that, so Cayna wasn't quite sure what was going on.

"*Gyararagh.*"

As she pondered, one of the griffins standing guard for its master let out a warning cry. It had spotted the raucous mercenaries crossing the bridge.

At the head of the group was Arbiter, who stiffened when he saw the creature. He approached the caravan hesitantly, but the tension on his face drained in relief when he caught sight of Cayna. Luka hid behind her, frightened by the rough-looking men.

"Nice work, Arbiter," said Cayna.

"H-hey, miss."

"Thank you so much, Lady Cayna. I appreciate your help."

The co-captain expressed his gratitude, sent the men to their stations, and prepared for the caravan to advance. Arbiter took notice of Luka but didn't force any introductions on her.

"Was anyone injured?" Cayna asked.

"Nah, we're all doin' just fine. Barely even a scratch on us."

The most severely injured seemed to be Kenison, whose left arm was wrapped in bandages. When Cayna approached him with a look of *You again?* he stuck out both arms and waved them around to prove how okay he really was.

Having determined the caravan and mercenaries would be fine without her, Cayna took Luka back to the top of the chess piece.

"I'll be waiting at the village, so let's save our discussion for then," she called out to Elineh after giving the griffins the order to take off.

The beasts obeyed their summoner's command and produced powerful gusts of wind as they ascended. Cayna's group set off for the remote village, and Arbiter watched them leave with a noticeably disgruntled expression on his face.

"The heck? She's not nearly as chummy as usual…"

"I'm afraid that little girl has us beat."

Elineh burst into laughter, not the least bit surprised at how much of a mother hen Cayna turned out to be. Arbiter was left bewildered.

The number of scouts increased, and vigilance was heightened, so they were prepared in the event of a second attack by the same monsters. Thus, the caravan was already in the village by the time night fell. Before it grew too late, Elineh set off to pass his goods to their recipients at Lux Contracting and did a double take when he saw the sign proudly displayed out front.

Cayna stopped by the inn that night and, for some reason, brought Roxine with her. Luka had fallen asleep early from the day's adventure, and Roxilius had stayed behind to mind the house. Roxine

CHAPTER 4

decided to join Cayna for more violent purposes: "No one will dare make a pass if I pummel them first."

Roxine was strikingly attractive, so naturally, a few brazen mercenaries attempted to pick her up. However, she pummeled any triers one by one without a shred of emotion.

Her responses were as follows:

"Try again once you've got a new brain."

"Are you only able to talk to women when you're that drunk?"

"Don't come near me with your disgusting breath. How utterly filthy."

"It appears to me you don't have the funds to support a wife and child."

And so on.

Each barb had a grain of truth to it, and that only crushed the men's hearts further. Roxine didn't pummel them so much as skewer them straight through. The suitors' ships sank like rocks.

"Hey, miss. This maid of yours some sorta demon?"

Arbiter had initially cautioned his men not to "go overboard" as he watched the drunken spectacle unfold, but Roxine ended up freaking him out after she had verbally harpooned his subordinates into a pile of corpses.

"Ah, she's related to a friend of mine," Cayna explained. "They're basically cut from the same cloth."

Roxine's spitfire spread until the village's bachelors were clutching their hearts with hung heads as well. Some even hurried home without even a drink, claiming their mothers were super-strict. Marelle was exasperated by the carnage.

"Honestly! You're all a bunch of cowards if this is what a little rejection does to you," she griped.

Rather, she seemed more exasperated with the men themselves.

Cayna put a hand to her heart in relief that Marelle didn't say Roxine was obstructing business.

"Hey, innkeeper! Keep that ale flowin'!" Arbiter called.

"It's not ale—it's beer. I got it from Cayna," Marelle replied.

Arbiter seemed to take a great liking to the beer, and when he demanded more of it, Marelle explained its origins.

"What did you say?!" Elineh yelled. "Lady Cayna, I ask that you tell me every detail!"

"I'd expect no less of you, Elineh. You're always quick on the draw." Cayna could only smirk at how Elineh instantly jumped at this. "Sorry, Elineh. I'm already discussing sales and materials with Caerick."

"Hmm, the Sakaiya owner himself, you say…? In that case, I'd simply like to request priority rights."

Apparently, he expected to be one of Sakaiya's retail outlets.

"Isn't that a bit hasty?"

"Whatever do you mean? Your ale has a clean taste the likes of which has not been seen before. There will undeniably be a demand for it."

"It's not ale—it's beer."

Elineh seemed highly interested. He wasn't the only one, either; given how his caravan companions and the members of the Flame Spears were guzzling it down, it was obvious they felt the same way.

Roxine's sharp tongue sent home a number of the villagers who had come in for an evening drink, and the caravan was doing a great job of making up for any lost customers. There were endless orders of snacks and side dishes to go along with the alcohol, so Luine and Lytt were swamped running back and forth between the counter and seats.

Even this calmed down once people started getting smashed. And like the previous day's proceedings, Cayna helped send the drunks to their rooms.

CHAPTER 4

* * *

"Now then, these packages are for you, Lady Cayna."

Five wooden boxes the size of orange crates from Elineh's caravan had been brought to Cayna's doorstep. The contents made a stiff rattling noise and were unbelievably heavy. She stopped Roxilius from fetching the pliers and instead unsheathed her Rune Blade, cutting off one of the lids with a single slash.

Shocked at the sudden show of such incredible skill, Elineh smirked and said, "Well, you *are* Lady Cayna, after all." No matter what came flying at him, he was likely to just go along with it. His attitude reminded Cayna of her veteran gaming friends who'd quit *Leadale*; her gaze grew distant.

The boxes were packed with small, dark-gray pieces of ore. Based on the magical reactions, the rest of the boxes were all filled with the same thing.

"Stones?" Elineh said curiously.

"Wow, I mentioned only a couple of specifics and just look at how much he got! Goes to show how skilled Caerick is at this."

Cayna stared in admiration at the five boxes filled with magic rhymestones. She'd told Caerick nothing more than *"It needs to be able to hold magic"* and *"It needs to react to magic,"* yet he'd been able to gather this many. How could she not be impressed by such talent?

Even to Elineh's trained eye, they appeared to be no different than the stones one would find by the roadside. He'd never imagined a product with such a high transport fee would be a bunch of rocks, and he grew a bit dejected. Cayna, however, was becoming more excited with every lid she opened, so he concluded there had to be something unusual about them.

To distinguish these from any other stone, one needed Magic Skill: Appraisal. Caerick must have had players, or at least those of similar standing, in his employ. That alone had made it simple for Cayna to obtain these magic rhymestones, and her opinion of her grandson rose drastically.

She took a magic rhymestone out from one of the boxes, performed Synthesis to expel its impurities, and transformed it into a drab, perfectly round ball about five centimeters in diameter.

`Craft Skill: Install: Flame`

The ball instantaneously turned red in Cayna's hand, and both Elineh and Arbiter watched with puzzled looks on their faces. She plopped the ball on the ground and asked Elineh a question.

"Elineh, could you give a command for me? Please don't look at me when you do."

"Ah yes. Ummm, what should I say?"

"*'God, please grant us fire.'*"

Elineh faced the ball with some dubiousness and said the phrase as Cayna requested. The moment he did so, a pillar of fire nearly three meters tall came bursting forth. It was a simplified magic circle that would set an attribute and password in a single step and activate with a set amount of MP. It was an extremely versatile item that could be used in weaponry and armor for battle or in objects to help make daily life easier. A good example of this was the wand she had recently obtained from the bandits, which could release up to ten balls of fire. Many creators of such weapons would set a password and, since the MP couldn't be recharged, treat them as disposable.

However, the item's power changed depending on the level of its creator. As someone whose magic was unparalleled within the game, Cayna created weapons whose value were nothing to sneeze at. The magic rhymestones had also been very handy in the dungeons and her guild home as well as in different seasons and environments. One drawback was that there were some who thought it was a good idea to recreate a lava zone or the Arctic.

CHAPTER 4

The highest caliber of this magic rhymestone was embedded in the Guardian Towers. Players had unlimited design choices, but since their construction was manually controlled by the Admins, the magic rhymestones had a permanent effect. However, only those with the title of Skill Master could use magic rhymestones of this caliber. The Admins couldn't have known they would be brought to a different world.

The lighting in Cayna's home also used these and could be turned on and off at a snap of the fingers.

The caravan workers and mercenaries who brought the boxes were shocked to see the tower of fire rise before them. They fearfully peeked at it as they took cover and put distance between themselves and the ball.

She hadn't added that much MP to it, so the fire was quick to extinguish. However, Cayna realized her error and said, "Sorry for startling you."

There were indeed many uses for the magic rhymestones, but people like Cayna had *too* many uses for them. She would go to Caerick for guidance on how they might be marketed. Cayna then asked Roxilius to put them away in the storeroom.

"I see. So items such as these were widely distributed long ago?" Elineh asked.

"The stones were often put into swords and equipment. People mostly used them in…dungeons, I guess?"

Elineh grimaced and made a strange expression that said he wasn't familiar with every word in that sentence.

Just then, Lytt and Latem skipped in. They had probably come to invite Luka to play as usual.

"Good morning, Miss Cayna! Is Luka here?" Lytt asked.

"Good morning, you two. She's almost ready, so wait just a minute."

"I want her to teach us how to make flower crowns again. I hate bein' the only one that doesn't get it," said Latem.

When the top half of Luka peeked from the doorway, the two ran to her in greeting. They then took her hands and headed for the well at the center of the village. Although Cayna would be out of her sight, the children would give Luka a crash course in going solo.

Cayna wasn't entirely sure whether she was sad or happy Luka was learning to play without her nearby. She had no clue that, only a few hours later, she'd deeply regret letting them go.

"Well then, Lady Cayna, please sign this receipt."

"You'll be taking this all the way back to Caerick, right? That's almost a month's round trip. Don't you find that difficult?"

"The process is indeed taxing. However, this is the sort of work I'm best suited for."

"But you have such a nice shop," Cayna said as she passed him the signed receipt.

"Oh, so you paid us a visit," he replied, beaming. "Thank you very much."

"What'd you think, miss? The boss's place is pretty great, right?"

Arbiter cut in and ruffled Cayna's hair. After prying his hand off, she grinned and told Elineh, "I did some lovely shopping."

"Wonderful, wonderful. Customer satisfaction is our top priority," Elineh said with a sprightly nod. Behind him, Arbiter was gripping his hand in agony. The other members who had been watching agreed that tearing off his skin was a most suitable form of payback.

Afterward, they discussed the recent state of product distribution and the possibility of Sakaiya transporting casks of alcohol. The co-captain, village elder, and Lottor soon joined them.

"Finally here, eh?" said Arbiter.

"It's rare for you to be early, Captain…," his co-captain replied.

"Ain't it worrying we got ambushed again?" said the elder.

"My apologies for making you wait," added Lottor.

CHAPTER 4

Since they hadn't been able to come up with countermeasures against the ogres the day before, even the village elder was called to join the discussion. After all, on top of the caravan being attacked a second time, it was confirmed that the monsters were moving systematically. Depending on the circumstances, the plan was for the Flame Spears and Cayna to work together to subjugate them.

"We shall leave some of our own men here to keep watch outside the village," the co-captain explained.

"I have Rox and Cie, so we'll be fine, right?"

"Those two kitties won't be able to handle a whole horde of monsters. The problem here is that we've got no clue how many are left," Arbiter argued.

"You defeated three ogres and five goblins yesterday, Lady Cayna," said Elineh. "The rest retreated when you injured their boss."

For some reason, they were holding the meeting in front of Cayna's house. Roxilius brought out a table, and Roxine provided tea. After a noisy debate, it was decided who would go subjugate the monsters and who would stay to protect the village.

Arbiter and his most elite forces would be the subjugation group, while the co-captain and remaining men would serve as defense. When Cayna proudly boasted that Roxilius and Roxine would be more than enough protection, the mercenaries flared up and shouted, "What can a little boy and girl do?!" After Arbiter replied with "Let's hurry up and put 'em to the test," a mock battle was set between Roxilius and the men who had been quick to lash out.

The group moved to the village entrance, and everyone gathered in droves. Their stage would be a spot some distance away from Lux Contracting. There was nothing in the area except for, well, the caravan wagons.

"What do you think, Cie?"

"Obviously that stupid cat will be victorious. I know all too well just how strong he is. And these shrimps think they stand a chance against that foolish feline? Such an utterly pathetic spectacle. If left to me, I would send those men's heads flying."

"Uh, well, it's a mock battle. Taking each other's heads isn't the point."

This conversation infuriated some of the mercenaries who overheard, but they kept their mouths shut after witnessing the results of the mock battle.

It was an overwhelming victory for Roxilius. Each opponent who went toe-to-toe with him lost in only moments as he held them down with his short sword pointed a hairsbreadth away from their necks and hearts. Understanding now that the village needed these two, Arbiter decided he would leave with his select elites, including those who had lost the mock battle.

As far as Arbiter was concerned, Cayna was just a young lady who happened to be moderately skilled in magic and close combat. But in truth, she had enough magic power to destroy a nation; if she used any of the fearsome techniques she gained from Opus, she could decimate the entire mercenary squad in combat. Cayna was choosy when it came to revealing the full extent of her capabilities.

"...Say, Sir Aribiter—I have a question for you," Elineh said.

"You're not gonna tell me you wanna come, too, are ya, boss?"

"Do you know where to find our foes from earlier?"

"""".........""""

At Elineh's simple question, the mercenaries who had thus far been in high spirits fell into silence. Arbiter very obviously averted his gaze.

They didn't know the answer to one of their most crucial remaining problems: the location of the ogre stronghold in question.

"Arbiter, were you going to leave without knowing where their

CHAPTER 4

hideout was...?" Cayna asked. She thought to herself with horror, *I'm right, aren't I?*

"We were so busy runnin' around yesterday that I didn't have time to think that far," he answered.

Cayna had been focused on her sightseeing flight and prioritizing the children's safety. Naturally, she wouldn't have thought to look for some hideout in the woods.

"Do you have any leads, Lottor?" she questioned.

"I've never stepped that far into the woods myself."

Since Lottor had only been as far as the forest entrance, he couldn't begin to guess where it might be. The villagers had only their bows, traps, and own two hands, so it would be harsh to expect any more of them.

Elineh took out a map, and Arbiter and the others gave their guesses. They concluded the hideout was someplace surrounded by trees with an easy water source and free from prying eyes. This led them to a riverbank deep in the forest right in front of the tower of the evil witch (to Cayna's tears and dismay).

It was indeed a location that made it easy to attack people crossing the bridge while staying hidden.

Just to be sure, Cayna tried confirming this with her own skill.

Special Skill: Oracle

Will this even work with the Admins gone?

She tilted her head in puzzlement, but this was the best skill to use when dealing with murky information.

For some reason, Li'l Fairy flew out right in front of her. She held out her hands and kept her feet perfectly together to form a cross pose. With a serious expression, she then closed her eyes and began glowing with a faint phosphorescence.

Cayna had no idea what was going on, but she didn't think she'd get an answer even if she asked. For the time being, she decided to let the fairy do as she pleased. Of course, no one else saw what was happening.

"Please bear with me for a minute, everyone."

"What's goin' on? Can you read the future now, miss?" Arbiter asked.

"Ha-ha-ha... Well, something like that. Some strange things might happen, but please don't let it get to you."

""''Strange things?''""

They all looked at Cayna in wonder as she produced a crystal ball the size of a human head from out of nowhere.

In the old game world, it was a skill said to have the strangeness of Special Skill: Oscar—Roses Scatter with Beauty in reverse.

It would answer five of a player's questions. As for how it responded...

"Is there an ogre nest within about sixty kilometers of here?"

Ding!

The happy little electronic noise that suddenly rang over their heads flustered all present. Anyone would be taken aback when an unfamiliar sound popped right over their head from the blue sky above. It was programmed to be audible to anyone around the player. As a function in the game, it was used by many to check crossword puzzles they'd completed in the real world. Why anyone would bring a physical game to kill time inside a VRMMORPG was another question altogether...

In other words, it was a skill one could ask questions. To use it, there were several conditions.

First, the caster had to ask a clear question.

Second, they had to use the crystal ball.

Third, they had to ask under a blue sky.

Incidentally, she had specified sixty kilometers because that was

CHAPTER 4

the approximate distance between the village and her Guardian Tower.

"Is it to the south?"

Bzzzt!

"Is it north of here?"

Ding!

"Is it a cave?"

Ding!

"I've always wondered: I don't actually need the crystal ball for this skill, do I?"

Boooooo—!

"......What the heck? That was scary."

Cayna had continued asking her questions while paying little attention to everyone staring up at the empty sky in confusion. In the end, it only further supported Arbiter's guess. Roxine, however, seemed to get a kick out of that last answer, and she trembled with laughter.

As the skill ended, Li'l Fairy wiped the sweat off her forehead with a look that said her work was done. It seemed a bit like she'd done long years of hard labor.

Although Cayna had asked for a sixty-kilometer radius, they were hardly nineteen kilometers from the Ejidd River. By her estimation, the hideout wasn't far away at all. In Arbiter's opinion, with Cayna's help, they'd arrive by the afternoon.

"Arbiter, you sure are quick to treat people as your personal handymen..."

"Nah, it's not like that at all. I just go with all my options. That's only natural for an adventurer, right?"

"Sure, but it would have been nice if you planned on using those many methods in the first place."

After she sent a Wind Spirit on patrol, Cayna then summoned a kirin that looked exactly like the logo of a certain beer. Incidentally, the hiragana in its name, which were normally hidden in the mane and tail, were gone. It was about the size of a donkey, and its feet strangely hovered above the ground.

Naturally, Arbiter and the others had never seen one before. The creature had a majestic presence, so they surrounded it from a distance.

"What's that, Miss Cayna?"

Nudged on by his fellows, Kenison asked what they all were wondering. Although he'd be staying behind to protect the village, next to Arbiter, he was one of the mercenaries Cayna got along with best. Whenever Cayna did something, the poor soul was the first one put in the line of fire to ask questions.

As Cayna stroked the kirin's mane and told it "I'm counting on you," she tilted her head at everyone's wariness.

"This is a kirin. You don't know them?"

The mercenaries, Elineh, and Lottor all shook their heads.

Back in the Game Era, the kirin was categorized as a Rare Monster, but it wasn't all that well-known now. After all, not only did it inhabit the special Heaven area, it also a noncombatant character with no level. However, it had a number of unique skills unavailable to players and was highly useful in the right time and place. Since it was so special, the downside was that players who summoned it had to deal with a number of limitations. Even so, the truth was that completing its search quest on one's own proved extremely helpful.

After going over their predeparture checklist, Cayna parted with Arbiter, who was preparing his men to split up, and left with Roxine to look for Luka.

They soon found the children whispering to one another at the back of the bathhouse.

"Luka?"

CHAPTER 4

"...?!"

"Uwagh?!"

"Kyaah?!"

As soon as Cayna called out to them, the three jumped into the air before falling on their bottoms. She helped them up and apologized.

"Sorry about that." She looked Luka in the eyes and crouched to pat her head. "I'm afraid I'll be away for a little bit. If anything happens, go to Cie, okay?" Cayna said slowly with a regretful look.

Luka's eyes grew round with shock, and she trembled as she looked at Roxine behind Cayna.

"I cannot say I am as capable as my master, but please come to me at any time, my lady."

"D-don't worry, Miss Cayna!"

"Y-yeah! She has both of us."

Lytt and Latem hurriedly took both of Luka's hands and nodded repeatedly.

Cayna gave Luka another hug and a light pat on the back before asking the other two to look after her. She then set out.

Lytt and Latem gave deeeeep, simultaneous sighs. When they noticed the chilly stare coming from Roxine, who had remained behind, they repeatedly said, "It's nothing," and led Luka to the shadow of the building. Roxine, who essentially didn't care about anyone except her master and Luka, returned home to finish her chores.

"Okay, Rox, watch after the village for me."

"Right. Please leave the young lady to me as well."

Roxilius, the village elder, and Marelle saw part of the mercenary group off at the entrance. The rest were already scattered here and there throughout the village. Arbiter and the others were well-prepared as usual, and those who would be acting as shields were dressed in full plate armor.

In addition to her same old Fairy King Robe, Cayna had the

magic staff affixed to her ear as usual and the Seven-Colored Crystal Ball floating next to her. Since one single orb alone released tremendous magic, Arbiter trembled at the thought that it might be some equipment saved for the most decisive of battles.

The Seven-Colored Crystal Ball automatically amplified one's magic. It was created with the Silver Ring in mind but was an item that could be used only for defense related to cost and specs.

As long as their foe wasn't a player, this would likely be enough. Probably...

"True north is that way."

"Well then, kirin, lead us on."

Cayna compared her intended route to the map of the area she'd drawn up with Kee earlier. The Ejidd River cut the continent in half diagonally, so her Guardian Tower was toward the southern end of the river. The main road to Helshper continued northwest, so the path leading true north would cut straight through the forest. That was Cayna's aim, and she showed the kirin which way to advance. The creature did as it was bidden with a nod and ignored all existing roads as it set off for the forest. Her plan was to compile the information the Wind Spirit had gathered from its patrol and continuously alter their course.

"H-hey, miss. You plan on cuttin' straight through the forest?! That'll take forever," said Arbiter.

"Well, I'll figure it out as I go along, so please follow very close behind me."

Arbiter and the others certainly had their doubts, but their eyes grew large when the forest avoided the kirin's footstep and split apart. As they continued on as a group, the foliage behind them returned to normal. Large trees, thorny shrubs, even weeds and underbrush opened a path for them. To the men, the girl putting this kirin to work was more of an illusionary angel than the beast itself.

CHAPTER 4

"Kirin, please use March."

The kirin nodded at her command, and a green wind blew from its body and enveloped everyone. One might say it was as if they were being pressed forward inside a hollow tube or caught in a wind tunnel. Her magic seemed to have evolved since last time, and there was no question they were quickly blowing past their surroundings.

It felt like they were in a wind tunnel that carried their troops forward, and Arbiter wondered in panic what they'd do if they couldn't escape.

"What? You found it?!"

Those feelings were blasted away by the harried voice of the very person who had put them in this situation.

◆

Shortly before the subjugation unit left the village:

Lytt and Latem had suddenly swept Luka away, and after speaking with Cayna, the trio held a secret strategy meeting in the shadow of the bathhouse.

"I found it yesterday," said Latem. "It wasn't that far from the village."

"We can check it out and be back in no time!"

"?"

Latem and Lytt were strangely excited; Luka, meanwhile, had no idea what they were talking about. She felt bad raining on their parade, but tugged on Lytt's clothes and cocked her head curiously.

Luka never said much to begin with, but the two had been spending so much time with her recently that they knew all her quirks. They patted her shoulders in reassurance.

"Hey, we were told earlier to find a spot where Cayna can't see us, right?" said Latem.

"We saw one when everyone was flying yesterday. It's a field full of flowers," said Lytt.

"Let's go there for just a bit while Cayna's away and make some pretty flower crowns!"

"...But...it's dangerous," Luka murmured with her head hung low. Latem showed her a blue, tear-shaped jewel. Lytt had never seen it before, either and peered in wonder.

"Heh-heh-heh. I took it from the shop without asking. It's for charms."

And it was a popular charm item, too. Walk into any town, and you'd see a commodity like this one carried everywhere from small tool shops to open-air stalls. You needed at least five of these jewels just to draw a pentagram; alternatively, you could create a safety dome around a specific area using many of these charm jewels. A single jewel had the power to temporarily ward off monsters, but it wasn't very potent. Shops normally sold these in sets, but children who never left their village couldn't discern what a single piece entailed. Latem had taken trips outside the village before, but he had never handled such an item and had no clue as to how it worked.

Lytt and Latem had never personally experienced the threat of a monster, so they took an optimistic approach. They knew Cayna would be mad Latem took the jewel charm but never once thought their ignorance would put them in danger.

A calm had settled over the villagers ever since Cayna, their all-important, unbeatable protector, had moved in; with her around, they felt the monsters wouldn't dare try anything. Of course, the village elder disapproved of such sentiments, and hunters like Lottor, who experienced the dangers lurking beyond the village firsthand, remonstrated the adults. However, the children themselves dealt with none of this. After a string of coincidental misfortunes, Latem and Lytt's pride had manifested as baseless confidence.

Only Luka, whose home had been destroyed, feared the monsters.

CHAPTER 4

Thus, she realized something about Latem and Lytt's plan to "make crowns in a flower field where Cayna won't find us" didn't add up:

If Cayna isn't in the village right now, why can't we make flower crowns here?

Latem and Lytt were blinded by their excitement, but Luka could do nothing to stop them, and she simply watched them prepare. In the end, Latem forcefully insisted, "No telling the adults!" so Luka couldn't even say anything to Roxine. Lytt pushed her forward, and they sneaked out of the village.

Luka gripped the pendant she'd received from Cayna, who had told her to ask it for help if anything happened. The girl prayed Cayna would protect her friends as well.

Roxilius returned home from his routine morning and evening patrols of the village to find a displeased Roxine standing at the entrance. He frowned. Her expression was dark, her arms were crossed, and her stance was that of a wrathful god. She was looking around sharply for no apparent reason. That piercing glare was enough to take out the chickens roaming freely about the village.

"What's wrong?"

"I had plans to cook with Lady Luka, but I don't see her anywhere. You've been going around the village as usual, right? Didn't your stupid eyes see her?"

Like always, it was hard to tell whether she was asking him for help or making fun of him. However, considering this was her default mode, pressing further was a fruitless endeavor.

Roxilius thought back to the route he'd taken that morning. He had cleaned the men's section of the bathhouse and repaired the roof of one house as requested. He had received simple snacks as thanks. He'd also done a round of patrol outside the village but spotted nothing more than a few small monsters. When they made eye contact with him, they trembled and ran away. He also visited the usual fields but neither heard nor saw the children playing about as they normally did.

"Come to think of it, I haven't seen her, either."

"Our master just left, and you've already messed up? We have to find her quickly and make sure she's safe. You're the only one getting punished for this, Rox."

If Luka wasn't in the village, it was possible she had gone outside. Even if the danger in the area was minimal, that wasn't to say there weren't any monsters at all. Roxilius went around each house to check again when Mimily called to him from her bathtub golem.

"Ah, there you are. Hey, mister! You live with Cayna, don't you?"

"That is correct. Am I right to assume you are Lady Mimily, the mermaid laundress?"

"Uh, well, yes. That whole I-don't-care-about-anyone-but-my-master attitude is no good, though! Even if you speak politely, I get the message!"

He could handle Roxine well enough but hearing such comments vexed Roxilius. He treated all the villagers with reverence, but deep down, he never had any intention of getting to know them. For better or for worse, Roxilius and Roxine were created to serve Cayna. Even so, he had never expected those feelings to be uncovered after only a few encounters.

"Is that all you wished to tell me? I'm in quite a rush, so if you'll excuse me…"

"Ah! Wait, wait!" Mimily called to Roxilius as he was leaving. "You're looking for Lytt and the others, right?!"

Mimily flailed in a panic, and the water from the bathtub splashed around everywhere.

"That's correct. Do you know where they might have gone?"

CHAPTER 4

"I heard voices coming from near the bathhouse not long ago. They said something about 'flowers' and 'going outside.' It sounded like a conversation between three people. I had a bad feeling and tried calling to stop them, but they were gone. I thought I had no choice but to go to them directly, then I saw you running around..."

Mimily's voice trailed off. Roxilius felt utmost respect for her; even though mermaids couldn't walk on land, she had left the bathhouse out of concern for the children.

"I appreciate the information, Lady Mimily."

"Huh? Sure..."

Roxilius faced her again and bowed low. It was the sincere bow of a butler. After all, he had the feeling he owed her the greatest of thanks.

Mimily froze, taken aback by his elegant gesture.

Just as Roxilius switched directions and was about to set off, he said, "Ah yes," and added a caveat.

"It's nice of you to search for the children, but I suggest you do not leave the village in that golem."

"...Huh?"

"It is a creation of Lady Cayna's in some way. There is a high chance it will transform in order to protect you."

"......What?!"

That was the moment when the differences in their understanding of Cayna became evident. Mimily froze and stared at the tub she occupied as if it were something strange, and Roxilius ran off. If Cayna had been there, she would have no doubt loudly proclaimed, *It's just a transport golem!* Moreover, this misunderstanding wouldn't be dispelled until she returned to the village.

As Roxilius moved to meet with Roxine, he was stopped by Marelle and Sunya, who were talking in front of Lux Contracting.

"Hey there, what's the big hurry? Somethin' up?" Marelle asked.

"A major and rather urgent incident has occurred. Have you seen Lady Luka?"

In that instant, the two housewives' faces fell. Their reactions further confirmed the information Roxilius had obtained from Mimily.

"I haven't seen Lytt around, even though it's already almost noon."

"I'm terribly sorry. It seems my son Latem took a charm stone with him, so he's likely using it…," Sunya said, explaining that when it came to barrier-type charms, a single stone didn't do much at all.

Before she left, Cayna had instructed Roxilius and Roxine to help the villagers. After conferring with Roxine, Roxilius promised Marelle and Sunya that they would bring the children back home safely, then raced out of the village.

The remainder of the Flame Spears who had been left behind paired up in groups of two and primarily guarded the village entrance and the outer perimeter. They never noticed the children cut through the thicket behind the engineering firm, wait for the perfect timing, and cross the main road. The three entered the forest on the opposite side and gingerly continued through the dim lighting. The atmosphere when actually entering the forest was completely different from looking at it from the sky above.

The children's path and footsteps were muddled, and the sun was at its zenith by the time they arrived at their destined flower field. It was a relatively open space, and in one corner, white and blue flowers grew everywhere. Yellow and red flowers could be found a short distance away. There was evidence that the center of the field had been dug up, and piles of dirt were already covered in weeds, grass, and ferns. This was where Cayna had sent the horned bear flying, its giant body mowing down trees and shrubs in a domino effect.

After Latem made sure there were no dangerous creatures around

CHAPTER 4

the field, the three moved forward in a huddle. At the time, they took no notice of the upward and downward drafts of wind that any expert would have taken into account. Incidentally, it was an upward draft.

Unaware of the situation they were in, the three formed a circle and began making flower crowns. They had to at least assign someone to be the lookout. However, expecting that much of clueless children would be rather cruel. Luka alone glanced around, but as she began instructing Latem, even she gradually grew lax. Captivated by the large, colorful flowers not found in the village, the three began making flower crowns in earnest.

By the time they felt chills travel down their spines, it was too late. Hordes of beasts surrounded the field.

Letting out screeches as they appeared from the trees to corner their prey were monsters known as gaur lizards, which had tan scales on their backs and stomachs. There were eight of them. These tawny lizards had long, slender legs like dogs, and they hunted in packs. Although the wings on their backs had only thin membranes, they were able to glide like flying squirrels. They primarily targeted weak creatures, so they didn't approach clusters like the village. However, they didn't stray far, either, and both people and animals would often meet their fate if they went astray.

It would be very difficult for the children to escape a group of eight gaur lizards. And even if they did manage to do so, the monsters were fast enough to catch up with them.

Now cornered, Latem bravely brandished a knife. However, his body was trembling badly.

Lytt had never really left the village before, and while she did hear things from Lottor and Cayna, this was the first time she was actually seeing a monster in person. She felt fear course through her body; her face turned pale, and she stood frozen in place.

Like the other two, Luka had turned white as a sheet and was shivering from head to toe. She instinctively gripped the pendant around her neck. She was very fond of it; Cayna had given it to her after they arrived in the village, and Roxilius and the others praised how cute it looked on her. Cayna had then told her, "*If anything happens, ask that pendant for help, okay? It holds my greatest guardian.*"

With this embodiment of fear now upon them, Luka clutched the pendant tightly in a final, desperate hope.

She prayed for help to come.

"Help…us…Mommy Cayna…!" she whispered.

―――*Understood.*

The next moment, a powerful voice suddenly echoed in the children's minds. At the very same time, a white light surged from the pendant in Luka's hand and engulfed the area. Its warmth washed over the children without burning their eyes.

For the gaur lizards that had followed their natural instincts in search of prey, that light would spell their doom.

No one knew if the moment lasted for a second or a minute.

After the light settled, the children found themselves in the shadow of something enormous. They timidly looked up to find a large, white body towering over them protectively.

The head was long enough to crush a whole house with ease, and silvery-white horns protruded from its temples. Its sturdy forelimbs had four sharp claws each that looked as if they might snap a large tree in half just from picking it up. Two legs that supported its massive size were firmly planted on the ground, and a thick, long tail grew between them. Its entire body was covered not in scales but in glistening white feathers.

This was the guardian that Cayna, the overindulgent mother, had sealed within the pendant. A level-990 White Dragon.

CHAPTER 4

Four wings in sets of two unfurled from the massive dragon's back; when measured from head to tail, the creature was as big as a castle. The eyes in its narrow sockets looked upon the children kindly, and the corners of its mouth lifted in a grin as if to say *I'll take care of this.*

Unlike the children, who were taken aback with shock, the gaur lizards had their tails between their legs in terror. The dragon was so huge that when they looked up at their opponent, they couldn't get the whole picture. Even the magic power that enveloped the guardian was great enough to blur out the gaur lizards' very presence. In fact, there was no point in even comparing them.

The gaur lizards feebly cried out as they began retreating. The second the dragon took its eyes off them, they turned tail and dashed off.

However, the White Dragon, which had been sealed inside the magical accessory, had been ordered to "eliminate anything that threatens Luka," with "eliminate" being the operative word.

The behemoth wasted no time in unleashing a mighty attack that would be considered *savage* for this modern era. With an enormous intake of breath, the light surrounding the dragon warped and converged inside its mouth. Rainbow light flashed between the gaps of the sharp fangs of its slightly open maw. The dragon dipped its head, extended its neck, and took aim at the small, pathetic animals (at least, from the White Dragon's POV) that were attempting to flee.

An instant later, its gaping mouth released an explosive beam of light—an attack called Prism Buster—and decimated everything in its path.

An endless hail of rainbow-colored bullets about ten meters in diameter struck the ground, gouging out the earth and uprooting the trees. The light beams that trailed behind became an aurora that rose above the treetops and practically split the forest in two.

The horde of gaur lizards desperate to escape were devoured by

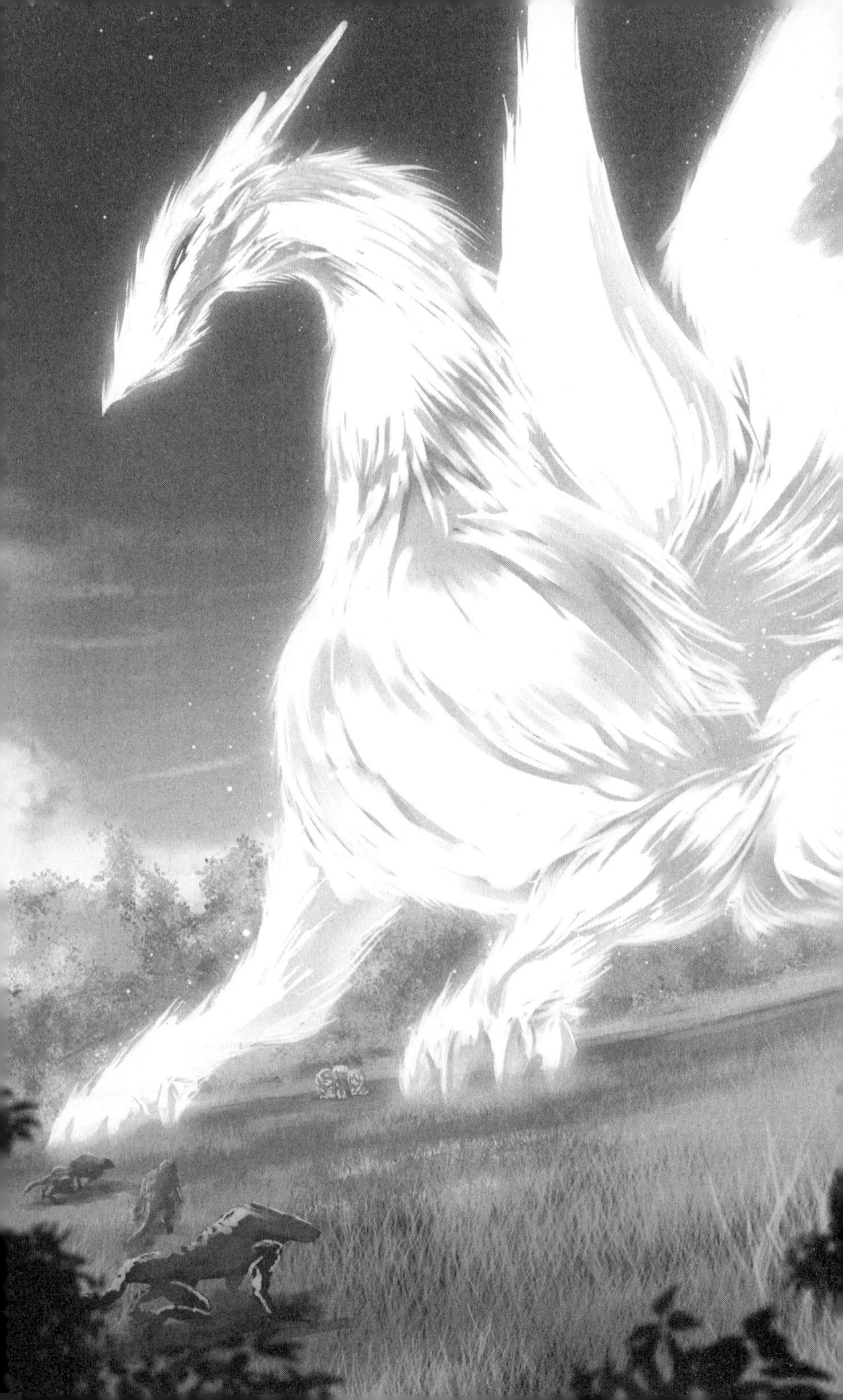

CHAPTER 4

the rainbow bullets and vanished without time to let out anguished cries. Even though the targets had been destroyed, the bullets continued their trajectory through the forest for several more kilometers before growing smaller in diameter. Finally, their power ebbed, and they faded away.

The White Dragon's primary purpose was to engulf the targets and blast them to pieces, but it had toned down its attack to prevent the children from getting harmed.

From what Luka and the others could see, valleys had appeared in the forest in a matter of seconds.

"……A-awesome…"

"…Y-yeah…"

"………"

Witnessing such unprecedented, ferocious might had left Latem, Lytt, and Luka at a loss for words. Cayna's exceptionality as the creator of Luka's pendant was a part of this as well.

As far as Latem knew, even Helshper didn't have anyone who could accomplish such a feat.

The White Dragon above them slowly surveyed their surroundings. Its silhouette gradually faded to phosphorescence, then disappeared. At that very same moment, a crack formed in the pendant in Luka's hand. The magic that had given it form turned to small particles of light reminiscent of fireflies and dispersed.

Almost simultaneously, Roxine and Roxilius came rushing toward the children. When something as enormous as a White Dragon appeared, the pair knew that was where they would find who they were looking for. The creature was so massive that it could be seen from the village, and subsequently caused a huge uproar.

CHAPTER 5
An Assault, a Lamentation, a Doting Parent, and a Request

The subjugation team, meanwhile, was in the middle of an invasion...

"Hey, miss. Is somethin' goin' on? I heard a weird scream outta nowhere," said Arbiter.

Floating above Cayna's head was a doll-sized girl with her fingers pressed together and an apologetic expression on her face. This was the Wind Spirit patrol Cayna had sent out earlier. The beautiful girl was a transparent green, but Arbiter and his men were unable to see spirits.

With her arms crossed and a conflicted look on her face, Cayna offered a simple explanation.

"The spirit I sent out on reconnaissance found our foe. Seems they've got a mage among their ranks. An assault might be reckless."

"An ogre mage?!" one of the mercenaries shouted.

Those three words set the rest of the group on edge. After all, if extremely rare mages were born among the ogres, they possessed shrewdness beyond the rest of their species. There might even be an ogre king that led the others around by the nose and commanded hordes to raid villages. Cayna hadn't yet heard of ogres destroying villages, so that was still just the stuff of urban legend.

"Can we leave the mage to you, miss?" Arbiter asked.

"Yes, I'll handle it."

It seemed that Arbiter was going to fight fire with fire and use Cayna as the strong arm in his battle strategy. Indeed, Cayna wouldn't likely be able to improvise cooperation with the mercenaries if they followed Arbiter's capricious orders. Thus, the most constructive thing to do would be to carry out a search-and-destroy mission and send her to take on the strongest enemy.

I get the feeling this mage is tougher than an ogre.

Besides, the Wind Spirit never said the mage was an ogre. It was mostly likely an elf or other similar race that had the ability to see spirits.

When they arrived at their destination, Cayna canceled all additional magic and sent the kirin away. Arbiter watched reluctantly as the majestic beast licked Cayna's cheek before departing.

"Ain't that thing gonna help us?" he asked, his expression dubious.

"See, there's one downside to summoning the kirin. As long as it's active, all my attacks are sealed."

A kirin was pretty much only used for searches and moving at high speeds—extremely helpful if that's all you had in mind, but a total pain in the butt otherwise.

Arbiter grimaced at Cayna's explanation and murmured, "Summonings sure do seem like a damn nuisance." He was the type that, when noticed by the enemy, would rather charge in first than get ambushed. You couldn't give your foe time to think.

Cayna did as instructed and cast spells on everyone to amplify their defense and magic resistance by several times. Also considering the possibility of a trap, she stood at the front of the group and blasted at the cave area with a direct stream of water magic.

Magic Skill: Load: Torrential Bullet Wave Qua Drohga: Ready Set

A mass of water materialized in midair before Cayna, enveloping her in a watery sphere that noisily transformed into a cannon. The

CHAPTER 5

turret was fitted with ammo that looked like a bundle of ten or so spears twisted together.

"Dig!"

Countless water spears spiraled out of the barrel at high speed like snakes going after their prey the moment Cayna struck her hand forward. Several tons of torrential waves mowed down trees and dug up the earth, flattening everything in its path.

While the mercenaries were indeed shocked, they also told themselves, "Well, it *is* Cayna," in understanding.

Each member ran forward as directed, while Cayna crouched down and put her hands over her ears. This was, of course, because the forest was assailing her with protests of *You're terrible! Savage! Monster!* and *You demon!*

"Wh-what's wrong, miss?"

"Yes, I know. I heard you, okay? ...Ah, please don't mind me. It's a personal matter."

Arbiter wasn't aware of high elves' quirks, and he gave her a funny look as she bowed her head to the surrounding trees. They couldn't lose momentum now, so he harshly spurred on his subordinates and headed for the front of the enemy hideout.

As they rushed over, they arrived at an area surrounded by rocky mountains jutting several meters into the air. Cayna's most recent spell had left a gaping mark on what was supposedly the entrance. Or rather, what was thought to be rocky mountains were actually cave-ins, and the supposed entrance was completely buried under the rubble that had fallen from above. Arbiter and his men's enthusiasm ended in shocking disappointment that hit them hard.

When they looked around, they saw a wide area right in front of them where several people could partake in a melee.

The spot was carpeted in short weeds, and within it stood five ogres in crude leather armor. They were huddled together to a certain degree, and it seemed as if they had been ready to ambush Arbiter's group. However, Cayna's magic had pierced straight through them. The survivors had apparently avoided the danger by running to the left and right; proof of this was written in the area directly in front of the rocky rubble, which was scattered with ogre blood, gore, and bones.

As soon as the ogres saw Arbiter and the others rush in, the monsters looked at one another, quickly readied their clubs and short swords, and let out mighty war cries.

This was all simply part of the job for Arbiter and his mercenaries, so their response was as cool as could be.

"I'll take one, and y'all get the rest! Don't screw up!"

"Yeah, yeah, we got it, boss."

The mercenaries took that as his signal and dispersed all at once. It was two-on-one, and the men vigilantly slayed the monsters without fail. Arbiter faced one of them all on his own, dodging and repelling it with his spear before ensnaring his opponent's weapon and tossing it into the sky. Aiming for the moment his enemy's eyes watched it dance through the air, he ripped the ogre's throat to shreds. The monster had lost focus for only a second, but it gripped its throat as blood came gushing out. Unable to muster even a roar of anger, the foe fell to the ground.

The other mercenaries likewise went with the meticulous strategy of defending against the enemy's attack as they either found a vital point to shred or aimed for the openings the ogres left in their rage. The men didn't have quite as much flair as Arbiter, but they suffered only the most minor of scratches.

"Yo, you guys finally done? Damn, that took forever."

"We weren't slow at all. You're just weird!"

The mercenaries voiced their grievances while Arbiter stared at them indifferently with his spear in one hand.

"They're ogres, aren't they? Spears can't pierce through their tough skin and solid muscle that easily!"

CHAPTER 5

"What're you talkin' about? It's 'cause y'all cut corners during training."

"Nghhh?! How is there this big a difference between us when our magic weapons are pretty much the same level?!"

"Where does his strength come from when he drinks like a fish...?"

There was no obvious difference in attack power between Arbiter's Flame Lance and the other mercenaries' magical weapons (which were long swords, short swords, and the like.) Although those whom Arbiter had chosen to join him on this mission had been with him since he was with the knights, they wanted to stamp their feet in frustration every time they watched him surpass them by no small amount.

Watching the subordinates grind their teeth in frustration, Arbiter finally realized that Cayna, who had been in the rear guard, hadn't followed from behind.

"Hey, where's the miss?"

"She's been behind us the whole— Oh, she's gone."

Looking back at the forest the group had come from, the mercenaries tilted their heads and looked at one another. Indeed, although Cayna had been with them since they exited the forest, she was now nowhere to be seen.

Cayna received a warning while bowing to the trees and plants. She picked up a rock and threw it behind her with all she had. Just as she heard a presence gasp, the stone sent ripples across the empty space. As if breaking an illusion, a blurry human figure appeared from the other side of the distorted background. She was a female elf with dusky skin and dressed in well-made armor and a cloak. She wielded a wand that appeared to be a bow with a knuckle guard attached to it. The woman had a more mature air about her than Cayna, but her graceful features were currently marked with rage.

"Tch, so you sensed me…"

"Ohhh, it was a D. elf all along."

The elf grimaced even more at Cayna's word choice. The abbreviation D. elf (dark elf), together with R. elf (red elf) and B. elf (blue elf), was a summary of skin colors and put one in the "eccentric" category.

Among players, there were those who made their characters colors like red and blue. Needless to say, those unfamiliar with such a sight shunned and avoided them and said things like *Gross* and *Seriously?* Of course, these novel colors would trend for several months after release before naturally fading out of fashion.

If Arbiter had been present, he would have undoubtedly gone on red alert. In this world, dark creatures were said to have sold their souls to evil (the demon race excluded) and were detested as taboo. Nevertheless, when picking color schemes in *Leadale*'s character creator, it was only natural that one could create dark elves, dark dwarves, and dark dragoids, so players didn't have a tradition of shunning the shade. Furthermore, Cayna was out of the loop and had no way of knowing such practices existed in this modern world.

At first, Cayna thought the dark elf was one of the locals. However, her suspicions rose when she used Search and saw the elf was referred to as the Roar of Sinawev. Cayna immediately had Kee investigate further, and he confirmed the dark elf was an event boss she had defeated back in the game.

The same thing happened with the Ghost Ship. Why are event bosses activating when there's no more Admins, NPCs, or quests?

"Perhaps she was left behind when the game ended service and someone abandoned their mission halfway?"

As the dark elf nocked electric magic into her wand-bow (a bow that also cast magic), Cayna zigzagged through the forest to put distance between them. The dark elf shot several lightning arrows without a care; they grazed the trees, which weakened the bolts' power, as they homed

CHAPTER 5

in on their target. Unable to withstand Cayna's anti-magic defenses, the arrows stopped just short of her and vanished.

"Tch, you're a tough one!"

Cayna heard cursing on the other side of the trees, and soon several more lightning arrows came flying her way.

Magic Skill: Rapid Lightning Zan Lezi Sos

Cayna murmured a spell and pointed her right arm at the lightning arrow flying toward her. An instant later, a flash surged from the band around her arm, and the head of a *shishi* lion burst forth to crush the arrow between its teeth.

"What?!"

The lightning lion wrapped around Cayna's arm and crackled with electricity. Its eyes gleamed savagely at the dark elf.

"You there, D. elf! Quietly toss your weapons and surrender!"

"An elf like you, fraternizing with humans?! Damn traitor!"

Cayna had intended to form a connection with her after peaceful negotiations, but the dark elf had nothing for Cayna but abuse. Humans and elves had never been antagonistic against each other when *Leadale* was just a game.

"Ummm, I'm not really sure what she's getting at."

"Perhaps she is merely doing whatever her assigned event has laid out?"

"Ah, gotcha. Still, I don't remember any events having such a chatty NPC."

"We do not yet know the full picture. Therefore, we cannot make any assertions."

"What are you mumbling to yourself about?!"

Having obviously lost her temper, the dark elf fired off a spell. She cast it instantly, meaning she had to be using some kind of magical tool. Her outstretched hands held an orb of lightning, which then extended into a large spear; she raised it held high over her head and immediately unleashed it. The thick lightning spear charged straight at Cayna, smashing trees and incinerating underbrush in its path.

Not fazed in the least, Cayna calmly threw forward the lion head wrapped around her right arm. The moment it left her, the lion was no longer just a head; it grew a body, four legs, and a tail as well. The lion was only about as large as a medium-size dog; it hardly even compared to the opponent's enormous spear. To the untrained eye, the question over who would win was clear as day.

The dark elf seemed to be thinking the same thing, because she gave a pleased laugh that suggested Cayna's time was up.

"Ha-ha-ha-ha! You think that little kitty cat can hold up against my greatest weapon?!"

Faced with that delighted, twisted smile, Cayna remained unmoved as she awaited the spell's outcome.

Not far away from Cayna, the spear and the lion violently clashed, and electricity flew every which way. The ensuing collision flashed like a strobe light, so it was hard to make out the details. Nevertheless, that equilibrium lasted for barely a moment. It wasn't even a second.

From within the pure-white brightness came a lightning lion that had ballooned to the size of an elephant and pierced straight through its opponent.

"Wh-whaaaaaaaat?!"

The dark elf's gleeful sneer vanished, replaced by a shocked expression.

A lightning attack like that was mere fodder for the Lightning Spirit. Cayna had called upon her weakest lion spirit, but it was more than enough to best the dark elf.

The dark elf raised her bow-wand over her as a shield, but she held out for only the shortest second. She managed to save herself because she threw something in her hand at the lightning lion. The beast batted it with one swipe of its front paw, alighted to the ground, and started chewing on it. Cayna could hear a crunch.

"It ate the magic device…"

"It does seem that way…"

When Cayna stuck out her right arm to the side, the lion transformed into a single horizontal bolt of lightning and returned to the ring.

"Dammit! Dammit, dammit, dammit, dammit, dammit! Dammittt!"

The dark elf had fallen to her knees, trembling, and when she shot back up, her voice held a resentment for the world and everything in it. Although there was no questioning she was actually very beautiful, her expression was as distorted as ever. She glared spitefully, unsheathed the blade at her side, and charged at Cayna.

Cayna was shocked by the deep-seated hatred on the dark elf's face, but she took the magic staff out of her earring, returned it to its normal size, and squared off against her opponent.

The dark elf had gone for a direct charge but changed her trajectory at the last second. She stepped to the left and thrust her blade at Cayna's neck in a poorly timed attempt. Cayna, who spun her magic staff to repel this, met the dark elf with the opposite end of her quickly revolving weapon.

"Phew, that was close!" said Cayna.

"You're too soft!"

The dark elf twisted her upper half to avoid the blow, then spun her body, sword and all, like a top to slash at the right side of Cayna's head.

Rather, she *tried* to slash at Cayna's head. The dark elf's arm was struck hard by Cayna's spinning staff, and she dropped her sword. When the dark elf saw Cayna's sinister grin, she quickly tried to put distance between them. However, something stopped her, and she fell before she could take another step. When she swiftly raised her head and stared at the ground awash in dead leaves, she saw both her legs were caught by earth-colored hands protruding from the ground.

The dark elf looked up and found herself face-to-face with a wicked witch twirling her magic staff.

"All righty, then. Ready to surrender?" Cayna asked.

"Pretty fast for a mage! You won't get that lucky again!"

The dark elf tossed a weapon forward, striking the bottom of the hilt with her palm to send the sword flying at Cayna—an incredible ambush attack. The dark elf tried going against the eternally composed enemy before her, but she felt the thick magic radiating off Cayna and was rooted where she stood.

The sword fell to the ground, useless. A green glimmer, far more powerful than her own earlier lightning spear and likely to level the entire area if fully unleashed, slowly converged in Cayna's right hand.

`Magic Skill: Load: Type II Raging Storm, Dan la Giga: Ready Set`

"Blast her away!"

A basketball-sized ball of air pressure released from Cayna's hand. This vertically striped melon sphere was a hyper-condensed hurricane that contained enough power to mercilessly cause as much damage to people's lives as any natural disaster.

The melon storm traveled at a languid pace before hitting the dark elf. An instant later, it demonstrated its recoil power and sent the target flying. Under this momentum, the dark elf's back snapped scores of trees as she disappeared from sight. The force of it was like being taken out by a wrecking ball.

The noises her body made were unpleasantly fatal-sounding, and the dark elf crashed into a large tree deeper within the forest. Without time to let out even a cry of agony, the dark elf's body flashed with static as it gradually began to fade away. Finally, her entire image grew blurry and then dissolved into pixels until nothing was left.

CHAPTER 5

Cayna's expression loosened slightly as she watched. This was a common sight in the game whenever one defeated an enemy character.

"......Agh, geez! I don't know anything anymore!"

"Huh? Miss, are you okay?!"

As Cayna gripped her hair and wailed in cluelessness, Arbiter appeared from the other side of the trees. A number of his men had been wounded, but everyone was more or less okay. With an accomplished look on his face, Arbiter asked about Cayna's situation and the disastrous scene around her.

"We're all done on our end. How's it going over…here…?"

Burnt foliage. Sections of earth completely gouged out. Trees that looked as if something solid had blasted straight through them. Parts of the forest was completely flattened, and it seemed like a terrible force of nature had passed through.

Arbiter had been worried Cayna had run into some detached flying forces, since she didn't follow after them. However, Cayna herself seemed perfectly fine, so he gave up on pressing her further.

"At any rate, I beat the ringleader," she announced.

"We've only got five ogres left to take care of. We struck oil and embers in the cave just to be safe, though."

"Seriously, why'd something like that have to show up around here…?"

Dubious, Arbiter watched Cayna mumble and grumble and wondered if there really was a foe that could have kept her so held up.

Noticing his staring, Cayna waved her hand lightly and attempted to deflect with an "Oh, don't mind me."

Then, just as everyone decided to search the area for evidence of remaining ogres…

…they heard what sounded like an avalanche from far off, and shortly thereafter felt an earthquake-like tremor beneath their feet.

"…Oh?"

"The heck was that?"

The mercenaries turned their heads this way and that to pinpoint the direction of the noise and found it was coming from where they'd entered the forest. Every which way one thought about it, the sound could have only originated from the village. Arbiter halted their search and quickly gave orders to return home and aid their comrades.

"Go on ahead of us, miss! If anything happens, we're countin' on ya!"

"Right! I'm off, then."

Racing ahead, Cayna cast Flight and soared into the sky with gusto. She picked up speed and spotted the open village amid the spread of forest. However, Cayna racked her brains as soon as she spotted a fracture east of the main road extending from the village. It definitely hadn't been there the day before. This mark, which appeared to have felled several miles of forest, was no doubt related to the noise and tremor from before. Roxilius and Roxine could have accomplished such a feat, but they were assigned to protect the villagers and act as Luka's guardian. They wouldn't have any reason to travel outside.

Cayna had a bad feeling about this. She added Speed Up to her Flight spell and made her way home.

When Cayna descended into town, she found the adults scolding Lytt and Latem.

"Going outside when the village is already on edge about the monsters! What were you thinking?!"

"*Sniff... Hic...* I-I'm sorryyyy."

"C'mon, Mom. She's upset enough and obviously reflecting on her actions, so why not forgive her already...?"

Lytt was sniffing and sobbing in front of Marelle. Luine attempted to pacify their mother, but it was a drop in the ocean.

"You hush! There's no way we can show our faces in front of

CHAPTER 5

Cayna and Mr. Arbiter after they've done so much to protect us from the monsters without asking anything in return!"

Marelle's angry voice echoed through the village. She paid no heed to her husband's and Luine's attempts at arbitration, and her ogreish countenance made Lytt cry even harder.

Across from them, Latem was kneeling on the hard ground and receiving the lecture of his life from Sunya and her terrifying grin.

"Are you listening, Latem? What do you think *that* person would say if they heard you instigated the young ladies of other families into going outside?"

"U-um, M-Mom?"

"Oh, do you have some sort of excuse? How unmanly. You are a disgrace to Lux's proud dwarf lineage!"

"Y-yes, I'm very sorry…"

"Honestly, you've always been so…" *Yada, yada, yada, yada…*

Sunya started going on about her son's shortcomings, whether they were related to the incident or not. Latem trembled at his mother's prattling, and if one looked closely, it was clear there was no smile in his eyes. Having his past pranks aired in front of the entire village one after the other turned the boy pale.

"*Sniff… Hic…*"

"My lady, please do not worry. Lady Cayna will not be upset over something like this."

"A broken pendant is nothing in the hands of Lady Cayna. She will make it as good as new."

Roxilius and Roxine did their best to console the sobbing Luka.

"*Pheeeew.*"

Cayna had been expecting the worst, but the children were safe. That said, something bad must have happened.

Her shoulders relaxed at the harmless scene and she heaved a deep sigh of relief. Luka jolted in shock when she saw Cayna, who tottered toward her, head hung low. Marelle and Sunya noticed and stopped their lecturing. Cayna wrapped Luka's small body in a tight embrace from where she was seated on the ground. Even the villagers who had been expecting an explosion of anger gripped their chests in relief.

…The sobbing they heard in that next instant wasn't coming from Luka.

"*Sniff*… Urgh…I-I'm so glad you're safe, Lukaaaaa… UWAAAAAGH!"

"*Hgh?*" squeaked Luka.

"Huh? Ummm… Lady Cayna?"

Watching their master wail as she held Luka close threw Roxine— and everyone else present—for a loop. The villagers were equally dumbfounded at the sight of Cayna bawling in earnest.

"H-hey, Cayna! Your daughter's fine! Come now, don't go crying like a lost child!" Marelle insisted.

"Sh-she's right, Cayna! This was entirely my son's fault, so there's no need to spill tears for his sake!"

"I-I'm sorry! It really was all my fault," said Latem. "I forced Luka to come with us."

"I'm sorry, Miss Cayna," came Lytt's apology.

"L-Lady Cayna?! Please pull yourself together!" Roxilius urged.

The one most thrown by all this was Luka in Cayna's arms. Just when the girl was sure she'd be yelled at, she was wrapped in a safe, gentle hug. In the brief instant that she thought *Ah, I can still stay with these kind people*, her guardian had begun sobbing.

Cayna was also far stronger than Luka, so escaping her embrace was nigh impossible. The adults all consoled the older girl and looked at the younger with concern. Lytt and Latem had joined in on their hug and started crying out of sync with Cayna's own sobs. On top of that, Luka's clothes were already soaked. How could she be anything other than flustered?

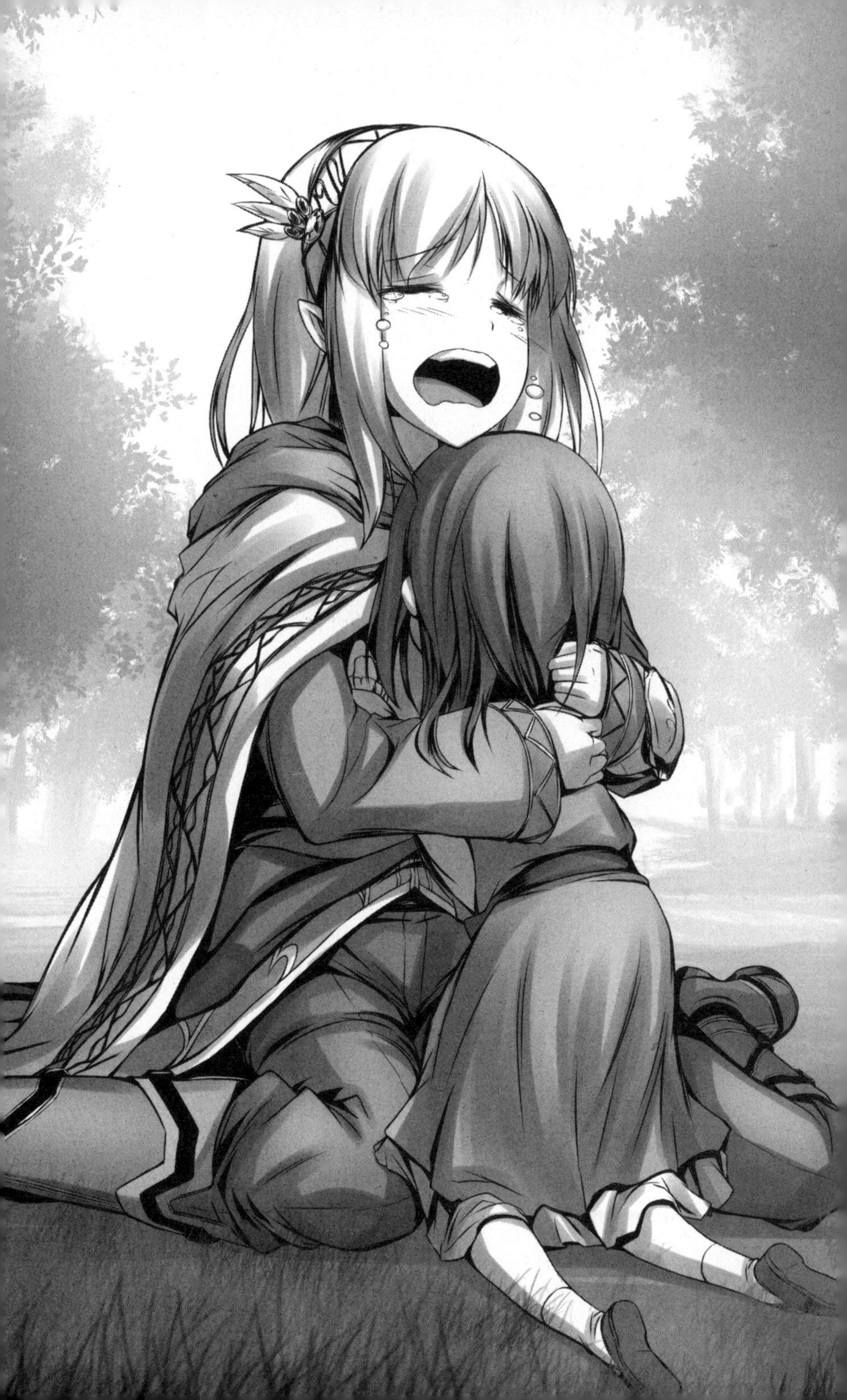

The clamor continued until Arbiter and the others returned, and the sun had long set by the time Cayna stopped crying and released Luka from her arms.

"I'm...tired."

Luka sank into an exhaustion so foreign to her that she wasn't even sure if she'd dream about her real parents cheering her on once night fell.

For several days following this incident, the villagers witnessed Cayna following Luka around like a little chick.

Take the mornings, for example.

"Hmm? Where are you going, Luka? Want me to come with you?"

"...I'm going to...the bathroom... I'll be okay."

Then during study time.

"You okay, Luka? Anything here you don't understand?"

"...I'm fine, but...he might—"

"Caynaaa, I don't get this at all!"

"Rox, please help Latem."

"Yes, ma'am."

Smile ← (Cayna grinning ear to ear at Luka, no intention of leaving her side.)

"........." ← (The collective sweat drop at Cayna's behavior.)

Then in the evenings...

"Okay, Luka. Come join me in bed!"

"...I think you'll be...okay...by yourself...Mommy Cayna."

"*Squeeee!* Cie! Cie! Luka called me Mommy! Did you hear? Did you hear that?"

"Lady Cayna, that was the twelfth time today."

Cayna watched over (?) Luka like this for days, leading Luka to swear never to worry her again.

CHAPTER 5

* * *

Cayna's helicopter parenting at last came to an end with the words "Mommy Cayna...you're annoying me."

This harsh statement from her daughter was apparently enough to make Cayna stand frozen in her room with a ghastly look on her face. The damage such an arrow caused when it pierced through her heart was beyond description.

That said, she recovered after just one night. Although a bit subdued the next day, she put on a cheerful face for the villagers.

Elineh and the others set off for Felskeilo the day after the incident. There were injuries among them, but Arbiter had told her, "It's a bunch of light scratches, so we don't need magic. Save that sorta thing for the people who really need it," and refused her healing abilities.

The real issue was the children's recklessness. Their intention had been to find a place to make flower crowns where Cayna couldn't hear the plants' voices, so she couldn't find the strength to be mad at them.

It seemed the adults were raking the children over the coals to make up for this. Sunya was furious with Latem, and Lux even more so when he returned from his deliveries. The boy's face swelled from the pummeling he received, and his parents ended up having to use one of Cayna's potions on him. Sunya felt that Lux had gone too far, making her even *more* furious.

"Lady Luka, if something like this ever happens again, you will never get another snack!"

"*Sniff...* I-I'm...sorry..."

Crestfallen, Luka hung her head at Roxine's chosen punishment.

"I dunno if this is considered peaceful or not..."

Cayna watched them uncomfortably, and Roxilius gave a wry smile as he explained.

"Snack time is quite important. She would be losing a luxury normally only nobles may enjoy."

233

In Cayna's household, they enjoyed the same routine she'd also had when she was alive in the real world: breakfast, lunch, snack, and dinner.

However, the villagers normally had only two meals a day and never ate sweets unless they had the time to make them. The confections they did make were limited to cookies kneaded together with nuts and berries. Since these consisted of only flour, goat's milk, nuts, and berries, the sweetness all depended on the final two ingredients. Thus, when Cayna had brought the villagers cake the other day, it was no exaggeration to say their appreciation of it was over the moon.

"Such sweetness exists in this world?!"

"So good. So, so gooooood!"

"Heaven is a place on earth…"

"Uwagh?! Hold on—you can't eat it that fast!"

Although they had gone a bit overboard, since the cake had been introduced as a way to entertain a party, the majority of villagers calmed down and realized it was something Cayna made for banquets and the like.

"Giving them cake so soon probably set the bar too high."

As Cayna pondered what to show from her repertoire next, Roxine put her on hold.

"It's fine to return to basics, Lady Cayna. You create out of the goodness of your heart, so there is no need to respond to their every request. If there are any complaints, I will be happy to be of service."

Roxine had an obvious arrogance in her eye, and she wore a strained smile. No matter what she said, her way of dealing with things would never change. Either her harsh tongue would grow even worse or she'd learn to say mean things more gently.

"You can just make normal cookies and have the stupid cat talk them up."

"By 'talk them up,' do you mean give a sales pitch?" asked Cayna.

CHAPTER 5

"Rhetorical flourishes will make your cookies seem like the only ones in the entire world. Squeeze him hard enough and he should be able to work something out, right? Of course, I'll have nothing to say if doing so sends him to the grave."

As usual, Cayna wanted to run from this palpable malice toward Roxine's fellow werecat. Was it because of Opus's influence as her original creator? Or maybe Opus actually hated himself deep down? When Cayna considered this, sadness and loneliness gripped her heart, and her shoulders suddenly slumped.

"Wha—? Lady Cayna?! Why are you curled up in a corner like that?"

"...Reasons."

"Is that a storm cloud I see hanging over your head?! If I have so foolishly offended you, I shall humbly commit *seppuku*!"

"Your big mouth is the entire problem!"

It was a never-ending slapstick comedy routine. They were the spitting image of a happy family—at least, in some way or another.

At any rate, one day a meeting was called to discuss the children's heartless act.

Although called a "meeting," it consisted only of the village elder, the hunter Lottor, and the innkeeper Marelle, as well as Lux and Cayna, both of whom had recently moved in from the outside world. They gathered in the quiet dining hall in the early afternoon. Again, despite being labeled as a "meeting," it was more like a gathering to discuss various matters within the village.

"For now, Sir Lottor is teaching Latem of the dangers that exist outside and how to deal with them effectively. This entire incident occurred because of my failure to educate him. I truly apologize!" Lux, who had a conflicted expression on his face the moment he walked in, bowed forcefully.

"N-now, now, Lux. The children are already being punished enough over this, so there's no need for anyone else to bow in apology."

"If Lux is going to speak up, then I will, too. This all happened because I took the kids on a flight tour."

Lottor tried to stop Lux from bowing, but Cayna quietly held up her hand in regret. It seemed like the meeting would spiral into a contest of lowered heads.

It was here that Marelle mercilessly dropped trays on Cayna and Lux.

"Gwagh?!"

"Fwah?!"

"There, now both of you have been punished. Bowing all day won't get this conversation anywhere, so just drop it."

Her rather violent methods caused Lux and Cayna to exchange glances and then nod in embarrassment. They turned to Marelle meekly.

"Sorry."

"I'm sorry."

Marelle waved the trays around, and with a sour look on her face, she said, "Don't do it again."

The village elder waited for them to finish before beginning to speak.

"I think it would be best if we fortify the fence as soon as possible."

Cayna was taken aback by the sudden introduction of the subject and the solutions that soon went flying. She glanced at everyone with a confused look of *Huh? We're starting on this already? Since when??* However, fellow village newcomer Lux didn't seem to question it. The village did things spur of the moment, and Cayna was forcefully swept along.

"Wait, Elder. Rather than blocking off the entrance, shouldn't we be reducing our need to venture outside?" Lottor asked.

CHAPTER 5

"Now that I've warned Lytt, I doubt she'll be up to those antics again," said Marelle.

"Wouldn't it be best, then, to teach everyone how to use the charm stones?" Lux offered.

Opinions burst forth like a broken dam, and Cayna listened in silence.

Aside from Lottor, Cayna was the only fighter in the village. However, from the viewpoint of one with excessive battle strength, even if she offered an opinion, it would likely be something outlandish that included prerequisite skills.

As she listened to opinions fly and converted them to manga speech bubbles within her mind, Lottor asked, "What do you think, Cayna?"

"...Even if you ask me, I can only provide manual labor."

""""Like feats of strength?"""""

Since everyone questioned her thus, Cayna explained her plan from the very beginning.

"First, I'd put a barrier over the entire town. However, only the people I know would be able to enter, and no one could leave. Any travelers who suddenly showed up would naturally be repelled. Next, I'd set up patrol golems disguised as soldiers. Since they can only obey basic orders, if instructed to protect the village from outside enemies, anyone who came across the golems would be their next victim. I'd also call out summonings that possess free thought and have them protect the village. A lot of high-level summonings don't look like people, so—"

"Wait, wait! Hold up!"

When Cayna started listing off her different defensive plans, everyone's faces paled. Lux rushed to interrupt her train of thought.

"I don't really get everything you're saying, but I do at least understand your suggestions are rather unsettling, Lady Cayna."

"Oh... They are?"

The fact that Cayna herself was unaware of this made the plans even more so.

First, there was the odorless, tasteless, and invisible magic barrier that would cover the village. Those known to the user could enter easily, but everyone else was repelled. Cayna had obtained this skill during a quest to protect a closed-off elven village from outside invaders. However, since the magic was a prerequisite for learning Isolation Barrier, it was used only once for that particular quest.

Second, there was the spell to create rock golems, which she'd used for Adventurers Guild requests in Felskeilo. Originally, it was developed so solo players could create traveling golems that would aid them and act as disposable battle units. Since they were built for fighting, the only commands the golems understood were "Protect" and "Attack." In this new world, golems were now capable of carrying out several more complex commands, but even so, this improvement pretty much amounted to "Protect the village from outside enemies" and "Capture invaders." Since there was a good possibility everyone who approached the village would be exclusively viewed as either an enemy or an invader, turning the golems into guards proved difficult.

Third, there was the option of calling upon summonings that possessed free thought. However, like the aforementioned examples, their appearance was problematic. Those obtained in the special Heaven and Underworld areas were commonly referred to as "angels" and "demons." The fact that they possessed free will and were able to think was fine, but their supreme confidence in themselves, which granted them the ability to shift their appearance, was not. If travelers along the main road were greeted by a demon at the entrance or saw a huge, multi-winged angel flying above them, they would fall into a panic.

As the village elder and the others listened to her explanation in detail, they were all in mute shock at this extreme power beyond any

CHAPTER 5

of their imaginations. Only Lux's eyes sparkled upon hearing about the golems.

In the end, no one was able agree on a single opinion, so it was decided that they would save the issue for next time. In the meantime, Cayna proposed that Roxilius freely patrol the village. The people could report anything they sensed was odd, no matter how big or small. Cayna and the werecat pair would also handle any fight too big for Lottor.

Since Cayna was often out of town, Roxine and Roxilius would also serve as the village's military force while she was away. Since the two appeared to be a young boy and girl, many villagers rejected the idea of recruiting them, but when told both could single-handedly crush a horned bear, they reluctantly agreed.

Despite the werecats' appearance, the two were powerful warriors who, at level 550, were only half as strong as Cayna. Even so, the question of getting the people to understand that power was an issue.

The horned bear brought out to help make the comparison was a poor soul indeed.

After the meeting, Cayna headed to the bathhouse. This time, her goal was to show appreciation to the one who had shared what she knew about the children.

"Thank you so much, Mimily."

"All right, enough of that. You've already thanked me a million times!"

Cayna sat next to Mimily in the warm water, and the mermaid waved her hand modestly as she lost track of how many times Cayna bowed her head.

Who could say what would have happened if Mimily hadn't heard the children scheming nearby and immediately informed Roxilius? Although the White Dragon had indeed manifested from the pendant, the children would have been left defenseless after it disappeared. The danger of being attacked by a second wave of monsters was very real. Thinking of it that way, one might say Roxilius and Roxine had indeed arrived in the nick of time.

If Cayna had discovered that Luka and the others had fallen to a monster, she would have most likely given in to her rage and burned down not only the forest but half the country as well. She would have become nothing more than a demon of destruction beyond anyone's reach.

When Mimily listened to this possibility blankly, she gave a heartfelt sigh of relief.

"…Thank goodness. I'm so glad I told someone!"

"Um, I was kidding about going crazy."

"It's no laughing matter! That was absolutely terrifying!"

Mimily cowered at the edge of the bath, and Cayna tilted her head, wondering if she'd done anything to scare the mermaid. When she asked, it turned out the dragon was the cause.

"You can summon such an enormous dragon out of nowhere—how is that *not* terrifying?!"

Mimily let out a sort of half yelp, and Cayna realized the dragons in Mimily's world were considerably different from how she remembered.

When *Leadale* was a game, dragons existed only with Summoning Magic; aside from a small number of wild dragons (those related to quests), they were nowhere to be seen. At most, some would make their way into stories and legends on occasion. And even then, they were almost always the mighty allies of the just.

It seemed that in Mimily's world, dragons were selfish, acted without any consideration for others, and constantly caused others massive amounts of trouble. It was a dragon that had spread the false rumor that eating the flesh of a mermaid would extend one's life. To

CHAPTER 5

a certain degree, they were the source of all evil. Although corrupt nobles and greedy merchants lacked the same power, they lived similar lives.

"Dragons aren't scary at all, really."

Cayna summoned a level-1 White Dragon in front of the frightened Mimily. The magic circle itself was the size of a washbasin, but the fluffy White Dragon that popped out of it was as small as a cat and could easily fit in one's hand. While its silvery-white horns and four wings marked it as a White Dragon, it was more like a cute, tottering, mini, plush version of its grown self.

The dragon gave a small cry of *"Myaagh."*

Mimily's eyes sparkled at the sight of the adorable creature, and she instantly jumped out from the rock she was hiding behind.

"Oh my goodness, it's so cute!"

"It is, isn't it?"

Soon enough, the White Dragon was in Mimily's arms, tilting its head with a *"Myagh?"* Hearts appeared in the mermaid's eyes, and she rubbed her cheek against the dragon.

Cayna nodded in satisfaction; Li'l Fairy popped out of her hair and clung to her. It looked like the fairy and the White Dragon were about to go toe-to-toe, but when their eyes met, the dragon lost its nerve and tried to flee.

"Huh? What? Wh-what's wrong?" said Mimily.

"Good question…"

The White Dragon was proud of its fine plumage and surely didn't appreciate having to slip out of others' hands like an eel. After struggling for a bit and realizing it would be difficult to escape Mimily's grasp, it undid the magic that kept it materialized and quickly disappeared.

"What?! Seriously?!"

Cayna was astonished to see the White Dragon going against its summoner's will and leaving of its own accord.

For some reason, she could now see why the fairy feared it.

Then several days later...

Although Cayna didn't understand why Li'l Fairy was afraid, after doing some comparisons with several other summonings, it was clear she reacted to those that possessed high levels of free will. She didn't know the cause and had no choice but to give up on asking Opus.

"Aghhh, I feel like I've gone down a huge rabbit hole. I guess I'll go see Caerick."

"Don't you think that's because you've been obsessed with Lady Luka?"

"........."

Cayna had been mumbling to herself and stretching when Roxine made a biting remark. Cayna froze mid-stretch, then twisted her neck with an audible *crack, crack, crack* until she was facing Roxine. The werecat pretended not to notice and bowed. "My apologies. I spoke out of line."

It was best to apologize while Cayna still viewed it as a joke. Everything would end fine that way, but if Roxine or anyone else ever seriously set Cayna off and made an enemy of her, there was no way they'd ever win.

As soon as Cayna looked at her reproachfully and said "Okay, then," Roxine gave a deep sigh. If her master began seeing her as an odious subordinate, that was the exact treatment she was going to get.

Accompanied by Roxilius, Luka followed Cayna out of the house. Cayna then patted her on the head. The girl planned on helping Lytt and Latem clean the bathhouse from then on.

The village elder had ruled it was Lytt and Latem who had been the truly reckless ones during the previous incident and handed down their punishment of cleaning the bathhouse. At present, there was no set time limit to this, and it looked like it might continue

CHAPTER 5

forever. However, since the women's bath doubled as Mimily's home, it was already perfectly clean. Thus, the three would primarily be cleaning the men's washroom and the area around it. Both sides of the bathhouse were cast with Purification, which affected only the water quality, so the spell included no actual cleaning.

Lytt and Latem were keenly aware that they would have lost their lives if Luka hadn't been with them, so they reflected deeply on their actions and worked with everything they had. Unsurprisingly, the task was impossible for just two children, so Roxilius was assigned to both give them a helping hand and act as supervisor.

Luka felt some responsibility for being unable to stop the two and volunteered to help. Cayna had fixed her pendant, and it once again hung around her neck.

A White Dragon with level-9 summoning power couldn't remain active for very long, so Cayna made a few tweaks: Now she'd downsized to a Brown Dragon with level-6 summoning power. A level-660 dragon was still a force to be reckoned with, however.

Although the White Dragon had healing and barrier-creation abilities, its battle strength was the bottom of the barrel among dragons. Nevertheless, it did have its Prism Buster attack, and the dragon's level only further added to that power.

If a Black Dragon, which specialized in range attacks, had appeared at the same level, the earth along the eastern main road would have likely turned into a crater.

The horned Brown Dragon, which looked like an ankylosaurus, had low attack power, but in terms of protection, it was the best among the dragons.

The all-powerful White Dragon that she'd set to be summoned without proper consideration had unfortunately been large enough to be seen clearly from the village. Cayna reflected on the disturbance it had caused, and this time, she made the dragon no bigger than a mobile crane. However, if the people ever saw its fiendish face, Cayna was almost certain they'd panic. That was the sort of mess people who knew no limits caused.

"Well then, I'll be off in Helshper for a bit…"

"I'll…be okay…Mommy Cayna. Don't…worry."

"The two of us will keep a proper eye on her this time, so please be at ease."

Luka nodded, and Roxilius gave a respectful bow. Hearing "Mommy" from her daughter threatened to overwhelm Cayna with emotion, and she gave Luka a big hug. Luka, who was well used to this by now, weathered her good-bye with a strained smile.

Raising children was never easy. Luka had a feeling she'd caused more trouble for herself and resigned herself to the fact that her efforts at easing her mother's worry had incited Cayna's maternal love.

A purple light rose up from Teleport's magic circle to envelop Cayna, and she disappeared. Luka let out a "*Phew*," and both Roxilius and Roxine, the latter of whom had seen Cayna off from the entranceway, laughed.

"Well done, my lady."

"I want…Mommy Cayna to trust me…"

"It cannot be helped. Not much time has passed since then, after all. Rather, she is pleased you have accepted her. Our master is quite attached to family."

"…She…is?"

Luka thought back to Skargo and Kartatz, whom she had met in the capital, and wondered if Cayna was lonely because her children, Luka's stepbrothers, had left the nest. In actuality, Cayna's attachments had existed back when she was living in the real world, so Luka's and Roxilius's line of thinking was entirely mistaken.

When Cayna flew off toward Helshper's western gate, the

CHAPTER 5

gatekeepers gave her a strange look. The combined subjugation army had only just returned, so travelers and merchants were wary of passing through the western trade route. A harmless-looking young girl appearing from that direction obviously made the guards wary.

Excited to be back in the hustle and bustle of the city, Cayna headed to the market before making her way to Sakaiya. She stocked up on the ingredients Roxine had requested and glanced around in the hopes of discovering a rarity.

There were fruits and vegetables of all colors. Preparations of large freshwater fish. Wives churning delicious-smelling pots. Packed crates of egg-like mushrooms the size of chickens. It was mostly food being sold, but there were also chairs and shelves, plates and other dishware, sari-like clothing, shoes, and much more. When she saw one stall selling rather warped Buddha-esque statues, she passed by quickly; they were undoubtedly influenced by the wooden Buddha statues Elineh had sold out of last time.

She then purchased soup at a stall and relished some baked sweets. When she bought over twenty skewers for Luka and the others as souvenirs, the nice older man threw in an extra for free.

Cayna finally headed to Sakaiya. As usual, the entrance was packed with the coming and going of workers and customers. As she tried to pass through the crowd with a meat skewer in her mouth, she spotted a face she hadn't seen in some time.

"Yoo-hoo, Cohral!" she called.

"Huh? Oh, Cayna. Funny meeting you here."

When Cayna crossed paths with the sword-wielding Cohral and his four friends, the group looked puzzled at first, but their expressions soon changed to relief as they greeted her.

"That's some fancy grub you're eatin' there. You get a good job?" said Cohral.

"Are these skewers famous or something?" Cayna asked.

"Hey now, don't tell me you bought 'em without a clue. You're somethin' else."

She heard from Cohral that they were made from the meat of a ballrat, a creature that commonly ravaged orchards. It stored nutrition in its tail rather than in its body and could live on this for up to a month. Since they were shockingly nimble, successive generations of trap specialists had passed on the task of capturing them. The tail had a spongelike quality, and when dried out, it could be made into a high-quality brush item. Since the creature's diet consisted mainly of fruit, its meat had a sweetness that made the ballrat considerably expensive gourmet fare.

"Huh, neat."

"That's all you've got to say?! Guess I wasted my breath."

"By the way, you got business with Sakaiya, too?"

"Yeah, kinda. There was a guard request at the guild, so we took it on…but with all these people runnin' around, we have no idea who the client is or how we're supposed to meet 'em."

"Oh-ho, guard work, huh?"

Taking on a request was fine, but it looked like the group had come across the problem of not knowing what their client looked like. Indeed, with various races going in and out, it was impossible to tell whether someone was a worker or a customer.

Cayna scanned the crowd and approached a werecat using an abacus.

"Excuse me."

"Ah, hello. How may I help you?"

"Is Idzik available? Could you tell him Cayna is here?"

"The young master…? Yes, please wait just a moment. This may take some time. Is that all right?"

"Not a problem. I figured as much, seeing how busy things are here."

CHAPTER 5

The werecat employee bowed, then withdrew into the shop. Although she'd been told it would take a while, Cayna doubted Idzik would keep her waiting very long. She'd been fully aware of that when she replied to the werecat.

Cohral and his party waited on the opposite side of the road by a row of storehouses. It seemed to be an area packed with merchandise that didn't need to be constantly rushed in and out, and they watched workers pass right by.

Cayna waved to the group as she approached and said, "Just asked to see the young master."

In that instant, the faces of Cohral's party simultaneously went from confused to aghast. Such expressions were clearly asking with concern how a mere adventurer could personally call upon the young master of Sakaiya, a company whose name and foothold were well-rooted across the continent.

The only ones who didn't seem especially struck by this were the adventurer Cayna herself and their fellow party member Cohral. The two continued talking amiably.

"Come here often, then?" he asked her.

"Every now and again, yeah. It's nice having connections."

"What? You damn elites got all the luck."

"You gotta get yourself some grandkids."

"No idea what you're on about... Anyway, I haven't seen you in Felskeilo at all lately. What've you been up to?"

"I've been thinking about setting up a bar around here. Beer, whiskey, that sort of thing."

"Ohhh, whiskey, huh? Gimme some of that."

"Don't order me around! If you want whiskey, just make it yourself."

"Huh? I obviously can't do that. Not without a brewery and a giant still, at least."

"I get it now. You've completely abandoned the opportunities that Craft Skills can bring."

"What?! There's a skill that makes whiskey?! Teach me!"

"No way."

"You're gonna turn me down just like that?!"

Their harmonious back and forth turned to the most delicious way to drink whiskey, and as Cohral told her what vintages tasted best, Canya listened diligently with murmurs of "Yes, yes, I see." She had Kee remember all the most vital information.

As this was going on, a young yet dignified elf approached Cayna from the other side of the street and bowed. The werecat employee behind him who had announced Cayna's arrival looked on in disbelief.

Unless they understood the circumstances, a simple employee had no way of knowing why their young master would immediately stop what he was doing just because Cayna had asked for him by name.

"My apologies for the wait, Great-Grandmother. What brings you to us today?"

"Long time no see, Idzik. Sorry for having you come out here to meet me. Is Caerick in?"

"Ah yes. Father is inside as usual…"

"My five adventurer friends here also have business with you. They said they took on a guild request."

"Oh? …Ah, I see. My deepest apologies for having you come all this way."

Idzik's disappointed look lasted for a merest moment before resuming the countenance of a serious merchant. He respectfully bowed his head to Cohral and his party, each of whom looked perplexed.

Cayna smirked, knowing full well he expected something of her. The requester's excessive courtesy made his response even more laughable.

CHAPTER 5

Idzik told the werecat employee standing at attention behind him to call for a kobold servant. It seemed this person was one rank below Idzik. He left Cayna with the servant and took Cohral and the others inside to discuss his request.

Cayna herself was led to Caerick's private room, where he always spent his leisure time, and her grandson greeted her with a look of surprise.

"How lovely to see you, Grandmother. How might I assist you?"

"I received the magic rhymestones and wheat you sent. I got the approval pretty quickly, but are you really okay with me making beer and whiskey?"

"Yes, it was some very fine alcohol. I tasted it together with several friends who thought highly of it. The flavor is quite rich."

"Yeah, someone mentioned to me once that you can, like, dilute it with ice or water. Apparently, whiskey gets more flavorful when you let it settle over long periods of time. One, five, and ten years, I think?"

"Mm, so that is the sort of drink we are dealing with. It seems this knowledge is rather new to you as well, Grandmother."

"Right, I just heard about it from my adventurer friend Cohral, who came here on a request for Idzik. You should ask him for the details."

Cayna was technically underage, so there was no way she could have known the finer points of alcohol. She had plenty of knowledgeable friends, but even they couldn't teach her if the subject never came up.

With a murmur of "I see, I see," Caerick scribbled notes on several sheets of paper.

Cayna had received a large amount of wheat from Lux when he returned to the village after delivering the two barrels to Helshper. Unsurprisingly, she put this in her Item Box, since there was no other place for it, and she ended up needing an additional storeroom. She was in no particular hurry, so it was decided the village carpenters would build one. Furthermore, the storehouse would include a cellar where the whiskey could be stored.

If the whiskey was going to be there for a long period of time, Cayna thought it would be best to have staff from Sakaiya who were well-versed in humidity and temperature manage the spirits. She could even produce endless beer right in the village as long as she had the proper ingredients, so she planned for the products to be made-to-order.

The problem was the magic rhymestones.

If infused with a basic technique, one could create a lethal weapon that any average person could handle just by supplying it with magic. Just like the Fireball Staff the mage who attacked them at the checkpoint had wielded.

"Still, though, to think you would gather so many magic rhymestones in such a short amount of time. I was really impressed."

"I used the same method I heard from you, Grandmother. I questioned the children selling rocks, and with enough compensation, they told me where I might find them. Once I gathered a number of skilled mages who could sense magic, finding a vein of such stones was simple."

"I only heard you used money and force tactics to buy your way out of the problem…"

"…That was supposed to be a secret."

Perhaps embarrassed that she'd hit the bull's-eye, Caerick looked away as he answered.

"Anyway, I came over to talk to you about putting these to work."

The topic now at hand was the main reason for her visit.

Several prototype balls about two and a half centimeters in diameter rolled across the table.

"…What are these?"

CHAPTER 5

"They're processed versions of the stones you sent. You use them like this."

Together with her concise explanation, Cayna snapped her fingers. An instant later, light released from the ball and shot straight above them. Caerick watched in amazement as the ceiling was dyed pure white and glowed like a floodlight. The steady direction of light was filled with the fixed spell Additional White Light Level 5: Light. It was a magic tool that, when inserted into a cylinder, worked just as well any flashlight. It was filled with ample MP, so it would run nonstop for several days, even when used as a light in this manner. Magic rhymestones themselves also absorbed magic from the surrounding space little by little, so even if the light shut off temporarily, it would be operational again in no time.

"I'd like you to use these in ceilings as a way to light up rooms… but perhaps you have other ideas in mind?"

"N-no, no, no, Grandmother, have you mistaken me for some sort of merchant of death?! I am perfectly satisfied with using them solely as a light source!"

Caerick trembled at the sight of his grandmother's pent-up anger, and he cleared up any misunderstandings with both words and gestures. Of course, it wasn't as if he *hadn't* considered the attack power of such a magic item. Given that he was calculating a way to sell them as a light source, he hoped to avoid her wrath here.

Cayna had threatened him to make sure he wouldn't try to pull anything funny, but by his frazzled reaction, she could tell there was no chance of that. She said, "I'm kidding," and dialed down her righteous indignation.

"P-p-p-please don't scare me like that… *Phew.*"

"Ha-ha, sorry. Well then, I'll use what I have on hand to process several more like these as light sources. Can I send them your way once I'm done?"

"Hmm, about that. If possible, do you think you could perhaps ship them along with a caravan? Although your methods of transporting goods in an instant greatly fascinates me, please allot a portion of goods to those who make their living along the trade routes."

"Ohhh, I see, I see. Even though my skills can complete the work of several in an instant, when you think about it, they also take away just as many jobs. Still, it'll be less expensive if I do it…"

"My apologies, but Sakaiya will not fall to ruin over such a minimal fee. I ask that you do not underestimate us."

"Ah, sure, you got it. Everyone knows their business best. Yup. Let's just leave it at that."

She continued negotiating the transport fee with Caerick. If she entrusted the merchandise to Elineh's familiar caravan, Sakaiya would pay upon delivery and handle the shipping costs.

There was also the matter of recent circumstances.

"Huh, so Helshper is reinforcing the eastern checkpoint?"

"We've finally crushed the bandits flowing in from the west for the time being. Even if it straddles the border, the village you currently reside in is still close by, Grandmother. Our nation's upper echelons are naturally aware of your presence, but it is necessary for us to prepare in ways that cannot be made public. Our company has been providing you raw material, and it seems one of our representatives, along with the country's leaders, will meet with an emissary of Felskeilo at the checkpoint."

"Ah, that must be what Cohral and the others are here for. Why not leave protection to the knights who are always sticking by the nation's leaders, though?"

"As I mentioned before, Grandmother, money leaves a trail."

"Indeed it does… If we're being thorough, I guess I've got no choice but to make things that can be shipped out."

Keeping her response noncommittal, Cayna looked out at the

CHAPTER 5

garden and noticed the sun was starting to tinge with orange. She had flown to Helshper before noon, walked around the market, bought lunch from a food stall, and made her way here. Cayna never said she'd be back before evening, but she was worried about Luka and decided to finish up the conversation so she could return home. She also realized her deep love and longing for Luka outweighed her concern, and she grinned at how much she was wrapped around her daughter's little finger.

"Let's end here for today. Thank you for your warm welcome despite me dropping in like this, Caerick."

"Come to think of it, you've recently adopted a little girl, correct? You undoubtedly must be worried. Please hurry home. If there is anything else we can help with, please do not hesitate to ask."

"Ah-ha-ha..."

Caerick was completely mixed up over who was worried about whom in this situation. As Cayna gave a stiff smile and went to leave, she remembered a request she wanted to ask back when she was building her house.

"Oh, Caerick..."

"What is it, Grandmother?"

"When you send the caravan, could you add in some goats and chickens?"

"Very well. I'll ask you to pay for them upon delivery."

"Sure. Sorry for the trouble. See you later."

Since live creatures couldn't be added to the Item Box or included in a party, she wouldn't be able to use Teleport with them on her.

Speaking of which, she still wasn't sure how party members were added. In the game, players would send a request, and if the other person accepted, they would be added to the sender's party. Currently, the difference between a known player and the average person depended on whether one received a notification.

The system was a mass of mystery that seemed like it could be improved upon with some earnest wishful thinking. It was this very mass of mystery that recognized players, but what exactly unified the system and where its core was located were unknown. The players' dilemma was they couldn't do anything without depending on such vagueness.

Exiting the garden, Cayna waved good-bye to her grandson and disappeared in a flash of purple lightning.

Fascinated, Caerick waved back and stared at the place where his grandmother had vanished. The magic circle dimly lit by purple light turned to a fine powder and disappeared without a trace.

"Appearing and disappearing as always. What a busy person she is. Well then, shall I start with the correct method of enjoying that delicious drink? As for the light, Grandmother asked that I first recommend it to my noble acquaintances and gather their opinions about this streetlight."

He would hear more about the adventurers from his son and ask for more details on the information he'd gleaned from Cayna. He would also ready the caravan and purchase livestock. Wondering to himself how much would be needed to provide for one family, among other thoughts, he harkened back to when he had first founded Sakaiya.

Now that his son was managing the shop, all Caerick had to do was review his business. There was a pleasantness to the memories his grandmother's requests rekindled.

Caerick stopped by his son's room, taking care to quell his restless mind.

Epilogue

She went from standing in front of her grandson to standing in front of her home in an instant. It didn't quite yet feel like "home," though, so there was a lingering strangeness that still remained in the new house.

The village sky had turned half orange, and the smoke rising up here and there from the houses signaled that dinner was well underway. Cayna picked up the delicious aroma of a familiar soup that wafted by.

"I've sure grown used to the cooking at Marelle's inn."

The inn's fare was a staple of the village, and her stomach growled at the very thought as if to say *Feed me!*

"Lady Cayna, it troubles me that you do not seem to share such an affinity to our own home cooking."

As Cayna stared out over the roofs and let her empty stomach sniff the spicy aroma, Roxine opened the front door to greet her. Roxine and Roxilius had learned how to cook the standard meals of this village after asking the local wives. Fundamentally, most food made with Cooking Skills required expensive ingredients. Collecting ingredients not already found in the village and using Teleport to go shopping in Felskeilo and Helshper also took time. If they were going to be extravagant with each and every meal, there were some limits even money couldn't overcome.

"Welcome back, Lady Cayna. Did your discussion go well?" Roxine asked.

"Ah, yeah. For the most part. I asked Caerick to send goats and chickens, so if I'm not here when they arrive, accept them for me."

"Yes, understood. Thank you for your hard work."

Cayna handed over the ingredients she'd bought, and when she peeked inside the house, she thought it was too quiet.

On top of not smelling any dinner cooking, she didn't sense Luka coming to greet her. When Cayna tilted her head, Roxine gestured toward the inn with her hand and provided an explanation.

"Lady Luka went to the inn. That fool also went with her, so there is no need to worry."

"The inn?"

"Yes, it seems someone important has arrived from Felskeilo."

"An important person? But that has nothing to do with Luka—"

Just as she was about to finish her sentence, Cayna remembered what she'd heard from Caerick earlier. Felskeilo, along with its neighbor, had decided to station an emissary at the checkpoint. As for who might be assigned this duty and also wish to meet Luka, Mai-Mai, who hadn't seen the girl yet, was a prime candidate. However, as the headmistress of the Academy, would she really abandon her work to come to the remote village?

When Cayna headed to the inn to at least meet her and find out what was going on, something peculiar was parked near Lux Contracting.

It was a magnificent, standout carriage ornamented in griffins and dragons of gold and silver. Along with it were the six horses she'd seen during the expedition. The animals were poking their heads into a nearby pile of fodder. The Game Era had stables to take care of the horses, but this place was rife with vacant plots of land filled with weeds that harshly asserted themselves.

EPILOGUE

"...Something that gaudy can't belong to Mai-Mai. No way."

"No, if one is the representative of a nation, such a display may be necessary."

She could see where Kee was coming from. Thinking she still didn't want some noble clashing with the village, Cayna hurried over to the inn. However, even if the checkpoint was only a day away from the village, it was about nine days from Helshper. Cayna thought with amazement that the envoys must have had a lot of free time on their hands if they could take off eight days.

...However, in that next instant, she grimaced as she saw someone leaving the inn.

It was a male elf dressed in the blue robes of a high-ranking priest, which were stitched in gold with the symbol of their main deity, the God of Light. His long golden hair was silky and well-maintained, and he had handsome features that would captivate any woman. For some reason, he saved his bewitching smile mostly for family.

He was Cayna's eldest son and biggest problem child, Skargo. Behind him was an accompaniment of armored knight bodyguards who were better-looking than average but not quite in the realm of *hot*.

Luka and Roxilius followed Skargo outside, and his eyes (literally) sparkled the moment he laid eyes on Cayna. As a Pointillism background appeared and he exploded into Waterworks, he approached her with oddly large steps that went *whoosh, whoosh!* and got down on both knees before her with a *whishhh!*

"Mother Deaaar! I'va 'ome to shee youuuu!"

He held out his arms in happy, drunken appeal. On top of the Blue Roses in Full Bloom background that shot forth all around him, *"The Language of Flowers Is Eternal Love"* flowed on endlessly in (terribly misspelled) subtitles.

He took the back of Cayna's left hand and planted a big kiss on it. The mother had paled at her son's approach, but this got her moving again. As Luka watched in mute amazement and Roxilius's expression remained unchanged, they thought they heard a *snap!* come from somewhere.

"W-welcome...back...Mommy Cayna."

"Thanks. I'm home, Luka."

For some reason, Cayna felt a wave of relief when she held the timid girl in her arms again. She took something out of her pocket and placed it in her daughter's palm. When Luka saw the three small fragments of red, blue, and green crystals, her face lit up with joy.

"There are three, so be sure to share with Lytt and Latem."

"...I will. Thank you...Mommy Cayna."

In the evening twilight, the charming family held hands as they headed home.

When the tactless outsiders incapable of reading the air tried to call out to them with an "U-um...?" Roxilius quickly staved the group off. The smartly dressed werecat butler emitted an intense aura that caused both Skargo, whose mouth was partly open, and his entourage of knights to go "*Ggh*" and freeze.

"My master is quite busy. I shall listen to any business you may have."

One of them mustered up their pride as an imperial knight and asked a question.

"Wh-what should we do about the High Priest?"

Everyone turned their attention to the *Zhu Bajie* pig who was moved to the point of tears—more specifically, Skargo in his blue robes from the neck down, but with a pig's face that looked more like an orc's.

"You may leave him be," Roxilius replied curtly with a shrug before turning on his heel to follow after his master.

The remaining six guards could only look at one another in bewilderment.

BONUS SHORT STORY
The Day He Became a Knight

"Huh...?"

He looked at the scene before him and rubbed his eyes. He thought his sight was deceiving him, but the scenery remained unchanged. The man filled his lungs with the scent of nature and glanced around.

A road continued in front and behind him. It was wide enough for ten adults to stand shoulder to shoulder across, but it was unpaved. The hard earth was completely bare. Furthermore, the areas to the left and right of him were covered in thick trees and brush that were impossible to see through. It was clear these were the source of the half-wet plant life he'd been smelling.

He instinctively wondered if his neighborhood had always looked like this, then nodded.

"Right, this must be a dream. Ha-ha-ha-ha-ha."

About a minute later...

Without someone to cut him off with a sharp comment, even his vague laughter couldn't continue.

He calmed himself, took another look around, and after checking his outfit, murmured, "What the heck?" There was a slightly hoarse tremble in his voice. If broken down into a composition, it would be

40 percent shock and 30 percent concern. Sixteen percent of him no doubt wanted to cry, and 14 percent wanted to scream.

Long story short, he was standing in the middle of a forest-enclosed road dressed as his avatar. The avatar known as Shining Saber murmured, "Seriously?" and fell to the ground in helplessness.

Looking back, he'd been enjoying his final game session just before everything changed.

December 31. The VRMMORPG *Leadale*'s last day of service.

There was wailing, bemoaning, laughing, mourning, et cetera… All throughout *Leadale*, players let their emotions fly free.

Notice that service was ending had come out of nowhere only a month prior. It was all so sudden. Even enterprising players who had trillions in assets couldn't make the words go away. These players tried to throw their weight around on the official forums by asking for donations to "build our own *Leadale II*!" The sight of his wealthy friends involving themselves out of concern only to be stopped by a full force of guild members was nothing short of sad.

Thus, he went to the capital of the Red Kingdom as always, joined open parties, and went hunting here and there. In his heart, he held the feeling that he'd do the same thing the next day, too.

Just around twelve AM in real time, the quickly formed party spoke casually as they went to part.

"Later, then."

"Let's meet up again somewhere."

"Hey, Shiny. Let's duke it out with bigger weapons next time."

"No way—that's crass."

"C'mon, quit bein' so damn fussy. Why're you like this but still crazy good?"

"One's usual behavior and personality probably have nothing to do with gaming skills."

"I at least wanted to square off with the Silver Ring Witch in the end…"

"Don't wish for a dangerous comedy act at the finish line!"

"That would surely spell the end for *Leadale*…"

"Scary!!"

He went to log out after their rowdy conversation…but although he'd been satisfied with how things ended, before he knew it, he was not in his own bedroom but in the middle of a nature road. Furthermore, he was not his normal human self but rather his avatar, Shining Saber.

He had no idea what was happening and tried cutting his arm with his sword as a test. The burning pain and iron taste of the blood that poured forth was all too real. He vowed he'd never try this again. Despite the great pain, he took a potion out of his Item Box, and it was as if nothing had ever happened.

Turning into one's own game avatar felt like something out of an anime.

Mercifully, sliding to the ground allowed him to hear the rumbling echo from afar.

Pressing his ear (?) to the earth, he tried to sense where it was coming from. A blue sky spread out before him, but it wasn't as if someone normally immersed in modern civilization could pinpoint their direction without the sun.

Since he'd only get in the way if anything approached while he was sitting, he got up. At the moment, he didn't at all consider whether it might be a foe or a monster come to do him harm.

That alone as enough proof of how massively overwhelmed he was by his current situation.

Soon enough, a group of about twenty people appeared. They were dressed as knights and rode atop horses. Naturally, a cavalry of this number wouldn't miss sight of him, either, when they galloped by. There were some women among the majority of men, and they all wore gleaming white armor. A man at the forefront noticed Shining Saber, and the group came to a halt.

They all stared at him with concern. Among them, the leader of the group alighted from his horse and stepped forward while gripping the sword at his waist. He was apparently their representative. Behind him, the man's comrades unsheathed their swords and readied their spears. Tension filled the air.

As for Shining Saber, he got the impression that involving himself with this group would be a major hassle. He'd be happy enough to just get out of the situation.

However, it looked like things weren't going to be so simple. The man who stopped about twenty meters from him while keeping a battle stance seemed to be in his thirties. He spoke with a grim expression on his face.

"Who are you?! Did you take this path knowing full well that doing so without the king's permission is forbidden?"

"...Huh? What?"

While Shining Saber struggled to comprehend what he'd just heard, a sharp *shing!* came from the man's waist as he unsheathed his sword. Along with this came an intensity that warned he would attack at any second. Anyone would cower if they were not only clueless to their situation but also unsure of how to react when met with hostility by the first villager they came across.

No sound came from Shining Saber's dry mouth. His arms trembled, and the thought of drawing his sword to protect himself never once crossed his mind.

He was a carp on a cutting board.

Just as Shining Saber was about to be helplessly cut down, he noticed not his attacker's face but his own two feet. He had apparently been struck by paralyzing fear. Later on, he would wish he had at least not wet his pants.

A voice went "*Pfft*" over his head.

"Looks like you're not a bandit or an assassin."

A voice that sounded a degree gentler than moments before hit Shining Saber. Shivers ran across his body, and when he looked up, he saw the man grinning.

"A coward like you isn't the type to go after His Majesty's life, but rules are rules."

The man turned toward his comrades, who had suddenly closed in, and told them, "Take him away and put him in a cell."

Shining Saber's weapons and equipment were confiscated, and then he was bound with a rope, blindfolded, and taken away. Before he knew it, he was a prisoner. Less than two hours had passed since he found himself in the middle of the road.

"…Ain't this goin' off the deep end…?"

What else could he even say?

Looking at the iron jail bars before him made him extremely weary, as if his entire body was bound in heavy chains. Pessimism took hold, and the feeling that *It's no good. Everything is over* stuck with him as he prayed to be buried in the depths of the earth. Strangely enough, as soon as he mumbled "I know all about how people in jails feel," he felt like he might as well just keep saying whatever he wanted.

"…Anyway, my underclothes can come off, huh?"

Whether willingly or not, Shining Saber looked down at his body to find ripped muscles he had no memory of building. It was the exact opposite of his usual gangly body, and even he couldn't believe this was really him. His arms were covered in visibly rough scales, while the sections beneath this were covered in thin, almost imperceptible scales as smooth as human skin.

In the game, all players wore a minimum amount of underclothes regardless of gender. Private areas were depicted by only the faintest outline, and careful consideration was made to remove any detailed shapes.

He had just taken everything off and was now wearing a single pair of underpants. He couldn't have done so in the game even if he tried, and it further hit him how real this world really was.

"Still, it looks like I've got some time to kill," he murmured.

He laid on the hard bed in his cell and glanced around the sour-smelling room. His tail got in the way when he laid flat on his back, so he turned on his side. The horns on the back of his head kept him from sleeping in a sprawled-out position like he did as a human, but he was thankful that this dragoid body kept the hard bed from being too uncomfortable.

Shining Saber thought all the more that his own room was much like a jail cell. After all, it had been nothing more than a place for him to sleep and play games. Although his mood was now dark, he felt a sense of ease.

Saying "This is all we've got," the guard passed Shining Saber a blanket. He wrapped himself in it and told himself he would answer the following day's interrogation honestly.

The next day.

He was woken up early, and several knights questioned him with watchful eyes. It seemed they were members of this nation.

At first, the captain of the knights, named Arbiter, questioned him directly, but the gentle-natured young man who served as his co-captain said, "You already have enough work to do," and chased him out.

After starting with the basics by asking Shining Saber's name, they continued with "Where did you come from?" "What were you doing there?" "What is your occupation?" "Where do you live?" and so forth. They asked everything from his personal information to his career history.

BONUS SHORT STORY

He would undoubtedly confuse even himself if he gave his real-life circumstances, so he provided the facts about his avatar.

Nevertheless, there wasn't all that much to talk about.

His name was Shining Saber. He was an adventurer. He didn't really have much of a personal background, and he increasingly felt like his existence was as thin as a piece of paper. However, as they delved into his story, he asked his own numerous questions that disturbed the guards.

His homeland, for example. When he answered "The Blue Kingdom of Aulzelie," they replied, "That country was destroyed two hundred years ago." And when he asked what happened to the others, he was left dumbfounded when they said, "There's only three now. Doesn't everyone know that?"

The knights reckoned he was a country bumpkin ignorant of the modern world, and they returned Shining Saber to his cell before even two hours had passed.

"You've gotta be kidding me…"

He wasn't sure how many times he'd said this already, but murmuring the phrase would likely become a habit while he was here.

"Here" was now the capital of a nation in the center of the continent known as Felskeilo. He was in a jail within the castle. He was being charged for the crime of trespassing upon a road that directly connected each capital. The details weren't fully explained to him, but it was likely the same as stowing away on a government plane.

From what he'd already heard, the seven nations of the game no longer existed. Instead, there were three unified nations: Helshper to the north, Otaloquess to the south, and Felskeilo in the center. Moreover, the original seven had already been gone for over two hundred years. In that moment of darkness when he went to log out, he had apparently surpassed space and time like a dimensional traveler.

"As if the game becoming reality wasn't enough, I also jumped eras? It's like some kind of Urashima effect…"

While he wasn't entirely sure of this, his heart could find no ideal noun that applied to this phenomenon.

The questioning continued for several more days. And then one day soon after that…

Shining Saber, equipped in leather armor tailored to fit him, stood in a corner of a parade ground with a wooden sword.

"I have no clue what's goin' on…"

The captain of the knights had suddenly visited him, and as soon as he let Shining Saber out of jail, he handed him clothes, armor, and a sword.

Not left with much choice, Shining Saber got changed. In the game, you could easily go into your Item Box, tap, and change outfits in an instant, so having to physically dress was naturally tiring. However, since Shining Saber hadn't checked his stats, he was unaware he could have used his Item Box as normal.

The captain of the knights brought him not to his usual cell but instead outside. Like him, the knights were dressed in light armor and carrying either wooden swords or spears. As he stood there unable to process what was going on, the captain explained their intent.

"Listen up. This is the punishment for your crime."

"…My punishment?"

From what he could tell, this scenario could only mean the knights were about to give him a full beatdown. He thought to himself, *Ain't this more vigilantism than due punishment?*

"It looks like you're misunderstandin' something. You've got it all wrong."

"Aren't you about to beat me to your heart's content?"

Probably unable to bear looking at Shining Saber's dead fish eyes any longer, the captain and co-captain refuted his assertion.

"From today forward, you will join our ranks and learn to become a knight."

"Huh? ...WHAAAAAAT?!"

"You'll be more of a servant at first, but you'll show us just how well you can fight. Your adventuring taught you how to handle a sword pretty well, right?"

A hysterical voice had released from the pit of Shining Saber's stomach. Among the lineup of knights, there were those who had questioned him in the past several days. The nodding of their heads said *His shock makes total sense*.

He was apparently going to work for the country as punishment. He asked, "Isn't it more common to make people slave away in the mines?" but it seemed that the continent had no slave system. He also heard that if the High Priest had found out he'd been treated in such a way, the knights would be reprimanded. A bolt of lightning might literally come crashing down on them.

Besides, mines were more the territory of dwarves and other similar races. Neither Helshper nor Felskeilo had that sort of environment.

"First, we'll get a good taste of what you can do by actually facing off in battle. Let's go one by one."

"I-I'm going to fight this many people...?"

"Correct. Isn't that how we'll learn your habits and fix problem areas?"

At the co-captain's command, the knights formed a neat row. A quick glance would suggest there were about fifty people total, which would be a slightly large number for a martial arts kata.

Even so, considering he was level 427, Shining Saber was confident the fight would be tiring but not insufferable. He readied his wooden sword and faced a knight who had stepped forward from the end of the line.

With the co-captain's sharp cry of "Begin!" the two exchanged blows.

Shining Saber suffered an overwhelming defeat.

His level was high, and as a dragoid, he had incredible power and defense. However, those three points were all he had for beating an average knight.

In other words, he had absolutely no technique or finesse.

In *Leadale*, each race had default attack movements, and it was commonplace to download free sword techniques via software. There was a plethora of different ones available. Although data provided by renowned schools of swordsmanship and those who actually knew how to wield a sword were preferred, there were also combinations of original, messy motions that any specialist in the field would call highly unorthodox. For amateurs, the problem was identifying what was a true sword technique or not. Shining Saber was one such person under this strange influence, which was why he was unable to move properly or wield his sword with any skill.

His battle opponents, the captain, and the co-captain watched on in pity, while others displayed shock by covering their faces and facing the sky.

And thus, his ranked dropped from *"Let's see your sword skills"* to *"Keep running around the outside of the parade ground."*

"...Yet you somehow managed to become captain of the knights three years later, right?"

In a bar flooded with the sound of food orders, laughter, and rage, Cayna fully appreciated Shining Saber's efforts despite his ill fate.

"Well, this guy was nothin' but brute force. If he'd had even an ounce of skill, he would've torn through the ranks in no time."

With a tankard in one hand and several meat skewers in the others, Arbiter put his arm around Shining Saber's shoulders.

Although Shining Saber was wearing casual clothing, Cayna frowned as the meat sauce sat moments away from dripping on him.

"Yes, he was a worthy student. Quite worthy indeed…"

The co-captain of the knights at the time and current co-leader of the mercenary group the Flame Spears narrowed his eyes nostalgically and tilted his glass. Shining Saber sat between him and Arbiter with a beer in one hand. He looked at Cayna with half-lidded eyes and an expression that said he had a bone to pick.

"Hey, Cayna. Why are we sittin' with these guys like it's no big deal…?"

"Huh? What do you mean, why? They called out to us, right?"

Just past noon, Cayna happened to come across Shining Saber in the capital while he was off duty. She was about to go shopping, and he decided to join her, since he had some free time. As thanks, Cayna invited him out for a few drinks.

After seeing how well the two got along, it was only natural that rumors among the current knights that Cayna was "*Captain Shining Saber's fiancée*" sprouted not only fins but legs and horns as well.

When the pair went to a popular bar a friend had told her about and grabbed a seat in the crowded space, Arbiter and his co-captain had appeared to the left and right of Shining Saber. Completely ignoring the dragoid and his surly look, Arbiter had begun divulging how they first met. The co-leader corrected the occasional exaggerated scene and explained to Cayna how Shining Saber had come to join the knights.

As for Shining Saber himself, their retelling resurfaced his feelings from that time, and the added embellishments made him feel indignant.

After the story finally came to a good stopping point, Shining Saber asked Cayna why the two were even there.

"Hey now, Shiny. What're you being all grumpy for, hmm? Who do you think told the miss about this place anyway?" said Arbiter.

"I KNEW ITTTTT!!" Shining Saber shouted, falling onto the table.

Cayna was technically a minor and unlikely to have a deep knowledge of taverns and the sort. Furthermore, when one considered the friends who did join her, the list didn't stretch much farther than Cohral in the capital. Her own children were more or less candidates as well, but if asked how she felt about the high-class restaurant catering to nobles that the three, particularly Skargo, often frequented, Cayna didn't see it as an option.

When asked "Do you go to taverns with your kids, Cayna?" she replied, "Kartatz and I often eat meat skewers from the stalls. I've had tea with Skargo in his office, but I don't remember doing much with Mai-Mai." Since she was based in the remote village now, it was rare for Cayna to do this sort of thing in the capital.

As Shining Saber's former boss acted drunk and tried to put the moves on Cayna, the co-leader mildly put a stop to his antics as she completely iced him out.

When the dragoid looked upon this scene, his three years of asceticism flashed before his eyes, and he let out a great sigh.

Noticing his gaze, the co-leader looked at Shining Saber with unusual seriousness.

"Do you regret your time with us?"

He had spent those days learning sword fighting, etiquette, and basic knowledge before finally becoming captain of the knights. Objectively speaking, these were pretty simple accomplishments, but those three years were well drilled into his body. Although the time had been fulfilling, he also had more than a few regrets. It was the very reason he was able to become not "himself" but "Shining Saber."

"Nope, none at all."

Answering honestly, Shining Saber knocked glasses with the co-leader.

Character Data

Character Data

Exis

A gray dragoid.

His account is registered as Xxxxxxxxxxxx, which, when shortened to Xs, led to his name, Exis. His main account was Tartarus, and he was a member of the Cream Cheese guild. He occasionally played as his close-range attacker, Exis, to relieve stress. When Leadale became reality, he did grunt work at a tavern without realizing that his in-game money was now real money, too. That's also where he met Quolkeh.

Character Data

Quolkeh

A lightly armored female human warrior.

This user lied about their gender and played as a female character, so her physical body clashes starkly with her demeanor. There are suspicions that she used an illegal program to slip past the physique-based character creation system, but what's done is done. She met Exis at a tavern where she was forced to work after a dine-and-dash attempt. They hit it off, and she became an adventurer. Still acts a bit manly.

Afterword

Good morning, good afternoon, and good night. I'm Ceez, the author. Thank you very much for buying the third volume of *In the Land of Leadale*.

Now that I think about it, I'm surprised at everything that has happened between volumes two and three. Before I debuted ten years ago, my life wasn't nearly as hectic as it is now (*sob*). *Leadale* got a manga adaptation, the novel series made it to the top ten on Bookwalker's 2019 New Light Novel Series Poll and was introduced in a live broadcast, and Melonbooks gave out Tenmaso's illustrations as freebies. I don't know how many times I've seen Cayna these past few months whenever I go outside! I must say, the reality of it all has me positively trembling…

I once again made edits to what I originally wrote seven years ago and relived many memories of "*This part was like this, and then that part was like…*" My fingers tapped across the keyboard as I continued to add more and more. The story is a lot different from what

AFTERWORD

I uploaded to Shousetsuka ni Narou. I regret not including the character I referenced in the previous volume—that was a mistake on my part. My timing was off (*sulk*).

This volume was rough, since the revision deadline and my qualification exam for work happened to overlap. I can't multitask the way characters do when they play double boards in Go manga. I'm not that talented! The lateness is definitely my fault, though.

Finally, my thanks and apologies.

I'm so sorry for always taking so long and dragging things out. To my illustrator, Tenmaso, thank you for going along with the extended schedule. To Dashio Tsukimi, the artist behind the *Leadale* manga adaptation, thank you for always bringing such charm to the characters. And to everyone who made this release possible, thank you so much again!

Ceez

Our last meeting was in Volume 2. I'm Tenmaso, the illustrator.

The cover illustration is blue this time. I worried I was at risk of copying the Volume 1 cover, but this one takes place in the ocean, and I felt like it'd be better to do a repeat than force myself to vary things, so blue it was. I think it'd be fun to make the next volume's cover either yellow, bright red, or green so that the books will be colorful when you line them up.

Until next time.

Tenmaso

THE Eminence IN Shadow

ONE BIG FAT LIE
AND A FEW TWISTED TRUTHS

Even in his past life, Cid's dream wasn't to become a protagonist or a final boss. He'd rather lie low as a minor character until it's prime time to reveal he's a mastermind...or at least, do the next best thing—pretend to be one! And now that he's been reborn into another world, he's ready to set the perfect conditions to live out his dreams to the fullest. Cid jokingly recruits members to his organization and makes up a whole backstory about an evil cult that they need to take down. Well, as luck would have it, these imaginary adversaries turn out to be the real deal—and everyone knows the truth but him!

YEN ON For more information visit www.yenpress.com

IN STORES NOW!

KAGE NO JITSURYOKUSHA NI NARITAKUTE !
©Daisuke Aizawa 2018 Illustration: Touzai / KADOKAWA CORPORATION